# Berried
## Secrets

A CRANBERRY COVE Mystery

"Cozy fans and foodies rejoice—
there's a place just for you and
it's called Cranberry Cove."
—Ellery Adams, *New York
Times* bestselling author

## FIRST IN A
## NEW SERIES!

# eg Cochran

tional Bestselling Author
of *Iced to Death*

BERKLEY
PRIME
CRIME

**$7.99 U.S.**
$10.49 CAN

S > EAN

ISBN 978-0-425-27450-7

9 780425 274507

5 0 7 9 9

*continued . . .*

"Once I started reading *Iced to Death*, my eyes stayed right on those pages. I had to keep reading to find out whodunit. There are plenty of plot twists to keep you guessing. The author has thoughtfully included some yummy and healthy recipes. So if you like your mystery filled with mouthwatering and juicy details, then you should be reading *Iced to Death*."

—MyShelf.com

## Steamed to Death

"The damp and dreary Connecticut setting adds nicely to the suspense as Gigi investigates a house full of suspects. This is a very entertaining and fluid mystery. Savvy entrepreneur Gigi's personal life blends nicely with the elements of the mystery, making this a solid cozy."          —*RT Book Reviews*

"This is such a fun series—I love the main character and her friends. As with the first book in the series, *Allergic to Death*, I read this book in one sitting. It is an extremely appetizing read—a well-crafted cozy."          —MyShelf.com

"This is a frothy and tasty mystery treat sure to please fans of foodie mysteries."          —*Kings River Life Magazine*

## Allergic to Death

"The meals that Gigi Fitzgerald makes may be low in calories, but author Peg Cochran serves up a full meal in her debut book."

—Sheila Connolly, *New York Times* bestselling author of the Orchard Mysteries

"Mouthwatering gourmet meals and a scrumptious mystery—a de-liteful combination!"

—Krista Davis, *New York Times* bestselling author of the Domestic Diva Mysteries

# Berried Secrets

## Peg Cochran

BERKLEY PRIME CRIME, NEW YORK

**BERKLEY
PRIME
CRIME**

**An imprint of Penguin Random House LLC
375 Hudson Street, New York, New York 10014**

BERRIED SECRETS

A Berkley Prime Crime Book / published by arrangement with the author

ISBN: 978-0-425-27450-7

PUBLISHING HISTORY
Berkley Prime Crime mass-market edition / August 2015

PRINTED IN THE UNITED STATES OF AMERICA

10  9  8  7  6  5  4  3  2  1

Cover illustration by Dave Seeley; *vintage label with a cranberry fruit*
© by amorfati.art/shutterstock.
Cover design by George Long.
Interior art: *Cranberries ornaments* © by Kate Vogel/Shutterstock.
Interior text design by Laura K. Corless.

**Penguin
Random
House**

*To Faith Black Ross,*
*who took a chance on me as a writer*
*and helped make my dream come true.*

# Acknowledgments

I would like to thank the good people of DeGrandchamps Farm in South Haven, Michigan, for answering my many questions about cranberry harvesting. Thanks also go to my fellow writers and plot spinners Krista Davis, Daryl Wood Gerber, Kaye George, Marilyn Levinson, Janet Bolin and Laurie Cass.

My husband deserves a nod for being a good sport about the fact that almost all my spare time goes toward writing. And many thanks to editor Julie Mianecki, who helped me plug my many plot holes.

# Chapter 1

Monica Albertson coaxed her ancient Ford Focus up the last hill, past the boarded-up vegetable stand, the abandoned barn and the Shell station. As usual, she paused at the crest. Cranberry Cove was spread out before her—a view that still thrilled her, even though it had been five weeks since she'd fled Chicago for this idyllic retreat on the eastern shore of Lake Michigan.

From her vantage point, Monica could see the sparkling blue waters of the lake and the horseshoe-shaped harbor, where several white sails bobbed in the wind. The Cranberry Cove Yacht Club, where wealthy summer visitors sat on the deck sipping cold drinks, was a speck on the horizon, and the pastel-colored shops that lined Beach Hollow Road were bathed in a soft light by the early morning sun.

Monica took her foot off the brake and rolled down the hill toward town, relishing the cool breeze from her open window and the warmth of the sun on her arms.

She drove down Beach Hollow Road, where all the shop fronts were painted in sherbet hues of pink, lemon yellow and melon. The streets were quiet and the sidewalks nearly empty—it was late September, so the summer crowd had gone back home to their everyday lives and the carloads of tourists on autumn foliage color tours hadn't arrived yet. Cranberry Cove wasn't Chicago, but Monica found it very charming with its old-fashioned gaslights, planters overflowing with the remains of the summer's flowers and the white gingerbread gazebo that graced the middle of the small vest-pocket park.

Monica pulled the Focus into a space in front of Gumdrops, a candy shop that was housed in a narrow building painted the palest pink. Fancy lace curtains hung in the window, and a ceramic Dutch couple kissing sat out on the doorstep, which had been swept clean of any sand borne by the winds of the most recent storm.

Miss Gerda VanVelsen came rushing forward almost before the bell over the door finished sounding Monica's arrival. Or was she Miss Hennie VanVelsen? Monica could never be sure—the VanVelsens were identical twins, spinsters sharing the home that had belonged to their parents. Their grandparents had been part of the wave of immigration from Holland to western Michigan in the 1800s, and the sisters had retained many of the traits of their ancestors— thriftiness, cleanliness and efficiency.

Monica stole a glance at the name tag pinned to the woman's top—this was Hennie, dressed in a pastel pink sweater and skirt that almost matched the color of the front of the candy shop. Her gray hair was set in elaborate curls and waves, and her pink lipstick matched her sweater.

"Hello, dear," Hennie said warmly. "How are you settling

in? It's been a couple of weeks, hasn't it? Have you got your little cottage fixed up yet?"

Monica nodded. "Yes, I'm almost done. It's turned out very well." Actually Monica adored her cottage, but from the time she was little, her parents had discouraged hyperbole.

"Terrible shame about your brother. We were all horrified when we heard," Hennie said, leaning her elbows on the counter. "So many young men lost over there. I suppose he can count himself lucky he came home at all."

Monica's half brother, Jeff, had been deployed to Afghanistan for a year, where he had been injured in a surprise raid. The nerves in his left arm had been damaged, leaving it paralyzed. She had been nearly beside herself with worry the entire year he was gone for fear of losing him.

"So good of you to come and help him with the farm." Hennie smiled at Monica. "And just in time, too, with the cranberry harvest coming up any day now."

Guilt washed over Monica like a wave. If she'd been able to make a go of it in Chicago, would she have been so keen to rush to Jeff's rescue? The small sliver of a café she'd rather unimaginatively named Monica's—three tiny round tables and a glass case full of her homemade goodies—had been put out of business when a national chain coffee bar opened directly across the street. Monica might have tried again in a different location but the death of her fiancé in a swimming accident shortly afterwards took all the steam out of her, and she was glad to escape to Cranberry Cove.

The curtain to the stockroom was pushed aside and Gerda VanVelsen entered the shop. She was wearing an identical pink skirt and sweater, had her hair set the very same way and sported the exact same shade of pink lipstick as her twin.

Monica was tempted to rub her eyes. It was like seeing double.

"You haven't seen Midnight, have you?" Gerda asked with a slight tremor in her voice.

Midnight was the sisters' much beloved cat. She was black from the tip of her nose to the tip of her tail, and a lot of people in town considered her bad luck, which Monica found silly. She herself was neither superstitious nor given to flights of fancy.

"No, I'm afraid I didn't. Is she missing?"

Gerda fiddled with the strand of pearls at her neck. "Not missing exactly, but we let her out an hour ago, and she would normally be back by now for her breakfast. I always worry you know." She knitted her gnarled hands together. "There are people who would wish her harm because of her coloring. But she's a sweet, gentle old thing and wouldn't hurt a soul."

"I'm sure she'll be back any minute now," Hennie said consolingly, putting an arm around her sister and giving her a squeeze. "Now, dear." She turned her attention to Monica. "What can we get for you?"

"I've developed a real taste for your Wilhelmina peppermints," Monica said, pointing to the white box with the red and blue ribbon and the silhouette of Queen Wilhelmina's profile.

While Gerda fussed about selecting the appropriately sized white bag with *Gumdrops* printed on it in varicolored letters, Monica looked around the shop. It was as tidy and spic-and-span as the VanVelsen sisters themselves. A large case held a dazzling assortment of sweets—from root beer barrels to Mary Janes. The sisters also carried an array of uniquely Dutch treats, and while Monica had developed a taste for the peppermints, she had yet to succumb to the appeal of the sweet and salty black licorice so beloved by the Dutch.

Gerda rang up the purchase, and Monica handed her the money.

Gerda gave Monica the bag. "You have a good day, dear." She paused. "And would you mind keeping an eye out for Midnight?"

"I'd be glad to," Monica reassured her as she left the shop.

Monica strolled down Beach Hollow Road, checking in alleys and doorways for the missing Midnight. She passed Danielle's Boutique, a pricey store that catered to the summer tourists with its stock of bathing suits, cover-ups, gauzy caftans and expensive costume jewelry. Next to it was Twilight, a New Age shop where you could have your palm read or your fortune told with Tarot cards.

The door to the Cranberry Cove Diner was propped open, and the seductive smell of bacon frying drifted out to the sidewalk. It was a gathering spot for the locals, who gave the evil eye to any tourists who dared to darken its interior—which Monica suspected hadn't changed in the last forty years.

Book 'Em, a bookstore specializing in mysteries, was tucked in next door. Monica was in need of a new book, having finished the one she'd brought with her from Chicago. She hadn't liked it very much, which had made for rather rough sledding, but she never allowed herself to put a book down without finishing it. To her, that smacked of being a quitter.

This was Monica's first visit to the small, untidy and rather dark shop. She stood on the threshold and took a deep sniff. She loved the scent of books. The store itself was quite a mess, with volumes spilling off the shelves and piled haphazardly in every nook and cranny, and a narrow spiral staircase leading to an upper balcony. Monica's fingers itched to bring some order to the place.

She noticed a man with his back to her—he had dark hair, was slightly taller than Monica and was humming softly under his breath. He had a stack of books in his arms that he appeared to be shelving, although there was hardly any room on the already overcrowded stands.

Monica strolled over to the paperback section and began browsing. Books were six deep in the racks, and the book in front was not necessarily the same as the one behind it or the ones in the middle. It was like a treasure hunt—Monica had no idea what she would find tucked away in the chaos.

She found a classic Agatha Christie and picked it up. It was one of the mysteries she remembered reading in high school—*The Murder of Roger Ackroyd*. She scanned the back blurb, trying to remember the plot. Perhaps she'd buy it and read it again.

"Ah, the famous, or should I say infamous, unreliable narrator." The fellow who was stocking books came up behind Monica and pointed at the paperback in her hand.

The lines around his eyes suggested he might be a few years older than her, but his rather shaggy hair and worn corduroys and crewneck sweater made him look appealingly boyish.

Monica smiled. "I was trying to remember this particular book—it's been ages since I read it, but now it's coming back to me."

"One of Dame Agatha's best, don't you think?" He ran a hand through his hair, leaving it even more disheveled. "Everyone knows *Murder on the Orient Express* or *And Then There Were None*—at least that's what it was titled here in

America—but *Roger Ackroyd* is far more clever if you ask me." He looked at Monica, his head tilted to one side. "Are you a Hercule Poirot fan or a Miss Marple fan?"

Monica thought for a moment. "Both, actually. And a Miss Silver fan as well," she threw out to see if he was really as up as all that on his English mysteries.

"Ah, Patricia Wentworth's redoubtable heroine."

Monica smiled, feeling absurdly pleased that he'd understood the reference.

He extended his hand. "I'm Greg Harper, Book 'Em's owner, manager and general dogsbody."

He had a firm handshake, which Monica returned. "Monica Albertson." She hated to admit it, but she was almost disappointed when he let go of her hand.

"How are you liking Cranberry Cove? I heard you've come to help your brother with his farm."

Monica was startled, and seeing the expression on her face made Greg laugh. "This is a small town. Everyone knows everyone else's business."

Monica wasn't sure how she felt about that. She was used to the anonymity of the big city.

She ended up buying the Christie book—she wanted to see if she agreed with Greg about its being one of Dame Agatha's best works. She'd also picked up the newest Peter Robinson—a current favorite author—but then put it back down. It would give her an excuse to come back again later in the month to purchase it.

Monica rather reluctantly left Book 'Em and headed next door to Bart's Butcher—the type of old-fashioned place where they had sawdust on the floor and tied your package in paper fastened with string.

She planned to pick up a steak. She'd invited Jeff to have dinner with her—he was looking entirely too thin for Monica's tastes. She suspected he subsisted on takeout and microwave dinners, neither of which was particularly high in nutritional value. That, combined with his worry about the farm, had turned him from lean and muscular to almost scrawny.

Monica selected a prime looking T-bone, and Bart Dykema, a round barrel of a man, pulled a sheet of paper from the roll on the counter and placed the steak on it. He gestured toward Monica's package with his chin.

"See you bought something in that shop next door."

Monica nodded.

"Nice guy, Greg Harper." He measured out a piece of string from the roller attached to the counter and cut it. "Ran for mayor last year but was defeated by Sam Culbert, who's holding the office now. Harper's widowed, you know." He wrapped the string around the neat bundle he'd created. "Not seeing anyone so far as I can tell."

Monica felt her face getting red. Was Bart insinuating that she and Greg . . .

"How's your brother doing?" Bart said, suddenly changing the subject. "Got a good crop of cranberries going? I imagine he'll be harvesting any day now."

"He's managing," Monica said, although in reality, the farm was bleeding money, and Monica hoped she'd be able to help Jeff staunch the flow. Sam Culbert, who was the farm's former owner in addition to being the mayor, had managed the farm for Jeff while he was overseas, and Jeff had returned to find the place in near financial ruin.

Monica took her package, bid Bart a good day and headed toward the farmer's market at the end of Beach Hollow

Road. She picked up salad fixings—tender lettuce, a cucumber and tomatoes still warm from the sun. Her shopping completed, Monica headed back toward the farm.

On her return trip to Sassamanash Farm—so named because it was the word for cranberry in the Algonquin Indian language—Monica stopped at the crest of the hill again. This time she could see the farm in the distance. It looked like a carpet of green dotted with the brilliant fire engine red of the ripe cranberries. The berries had been pale pink when Monica had arrived at Sassamanash Farm, but as the weather had become cooler, they had turned their characteristic ruby color.

If she squinted, she could see the dollhouse sized cottage she was in the process of renovating, the stretch of black macadam where tourists parked when they came to watch the harvest, and the dot of white that was the clapboard building that housed the small store where they sold baked goods made with cranberries, and kitchen items decorated with the fruit, such as tea towels, napkins and pot holders.

Monica continued down the hill toward the farm. She parked in front of the little cottage she now called home. She had seen its inherent potential the minute she arrived from Chicago. It had dormer windows, a gabled roof and a trellis with the remains of summer's climbing roses. It had taken a month of painting, scrubbing and sheer elbow grease to make it habitable, but Monica was pleased with how it had turned out.

She stowed the steak she'd purchased at Bart's in the refrigerator along with the salad fixings. The cottage still smelled of sugar and spice from the goodies she'd baked early that morning—cranberry muffins, cranberry scones dusted with sugar and a cranberry salsa she was still experimenting with to get the right balance of flavors—both sweet and hot—with accents of lime, cilantro and jalapeno. Monica packed everything in a basket and headed back out the door.

Darlene Polk was behind the counter of the Sassamanash Farm store when Monica arrived. She was taller than Monica's five foot eight—almost six feet—with a lot more meat on her bones. Her nondescript light brown hair was gathered into a ponytail, and her bangs were curling in the humidity.

She glanced up when she heard Monica enter. Her face bore its usual resentful expression, her lower lip stuck out as if she was continually pouting. Monica had tried to become friends with her, but Darlene preferred to keep to herself.

Monica put down her basket and turned to Darlene, who was leaning against the counter reading one of those magazines that grocery stores sell by the checkout lane.

"Can you help me put these out?"

Darlene stared at her blankly for a moment before shuffling over, the sulky expression on her face intensifying with each step.

"I don't see what was wrong with the stuff we carried before," Darlene whined. "It sold, didn't it?" She glared at Monica challengingly.

When Monica had arrived at Sassamanash Farm, she'd discovered that the shop was selling mass-produced cranberry products—muffins preserved in plastic wrap, scones filled with trans fats to keep them fresh, and preserves that Darlene had slapped a Sassamanash Farm label on. Having made all the baked goods for her own little café, Monica got to work creating fresh products for the store.

"I'm sure it was all very fine," Monica said soothingly.

"But customers today want fresh, homemade-tasting goodies. They can get mass-produced products anywhere. We need to sell something that's special."

Monica carried the containers of salsa over to the cooler where they kept bottled water and pop for the tourists. "What happened to the salsa I brought over yesterday?"

"Sold it." Darlene cracked her gum and stared at Monica from under her bangs, the ends of which were caught under her smudged glasses.

"You sold all of it?" Monica couldn't believe it. Although locals occasionally frequented the shop, most of their sales were from tourists stopping by the farm to get a firsthand look at the cranberry bogs. The store didn't exactly do a brisk business, except during the harvest.

Darlene was already back at the counter, flipping through the pages of her magazine. "Some guy came in and bought them all. Said he was from the Cranberry Cove Inn. Said it was the best salsa he'd ever tasted, and he wanted to put it on the menu."

Monica's heart skipped a beat. Perhaps she'd found the perfect balance for the salsa after all. And if the Cranberry Cove Inn wanted to buy it, there might be others as well. She chewed on a ragged cuticle. Goodness knows, they needed as much cash as they could get to keep the farm running. Jeff had sunk his life's savings into it, and she wasn't going to let him lose it if she could help it.

Monica arranged the fresh muffins in a basket lined with a red-and-white gingham napkin and placed the scones in an orderly row on an antique silver platter she had found at an estate sale.

She felt Darlene's beady eyes on her as she went about

tidying the shop—dusting the jars of preserves she'd made herself and creating a display with the cranberry decorated tea towels and napkins a local woman sewed for them.

There was a noise outside, and Darlene looked up. She made her ponderous way to the window and peered out. She turned around, her scowl deepening.

"It's that Sam Culbert. I thought we'd seen the last of him around here. He sold the farm to your brother, didn't he?"

"Yes, but I imagine there may still be some things they need to discuss."

Monica watched as Jeff and Culbert said good-bye.

Culbert was broad shouldered with thick gray hair and slightly bowed legs. Monica was surprised to see him get into a dark, late-model Lexus.

"That's quite the car," she said to Darlene. "I didn't realize there was so much money in cranberries."

Darlene snorted. "About a penny a berry—and only the unblemished ones. The rest are worthless. The Culberts own a lot more than Sassamanash Farm. They have real estate all over the county, own half the buildings in town and have a huge house with a view of the lake. You should see the place. I clean it for Mrs. Culbert once a week." Darlene scowled again. "Must be nice. I grew up in a double-wide with secondhand furniture and hand-me-down clothes. Of course my mother, bless her soul, did the best she could seeing as how I didn't have no daddy."

Monica made comforting noises to the best of her ability. Darlene would complain about the deprivation of her upbringing out of one side of her mouth while out the other side she would insist that despite their lack of means, her childhood had been nearly idyllic.

Monica brushed some dust off her sweatshirt. "I guess I'll be going now."

Darlene gave her a sour look.

Jeff only kept Darlene on because it was hard to get anyone to work in the store when they could make more money waitressing or clerking at one of the shops in town.

Monica walked back to her cottage, where she planned to spend the afternoon reviewing the farm's accounts. Jeff had just borrowed a considerable sum from the bank to keep things afloat. Monica had learned a little something about business while running her café, and she hoped that she would be able to straighten things out for Jeff. She set up her laptop on the kitchen table and plugged in the flash drive that held the data from Jeff's computer.

Going over the accounts for Sassamanash Farm was a long and tedious process, but Monica had plenty of patience. By the time she finished examining the pages and pages of Excel spreadsheets, and all the statements from the bank, she had the answer to why Sassamanash Farm was failing to produce a profit.

But how was she going to break the news to Jeff?

# Chapter 2

Monica thought about what the farm's accounts had revealed while she cleaned lettuce and sliced tomatoes for a salad. Probably the best way to break the news to Jeff was to do it quickly—like pulling off a bandage in one swift motion. She grimaced at the thought.

Jeff arrived exactly at six o'clock, just as Monica was preheating the broiler for the steak. He and Monica had both gotten their father's height and auburn hair that had a slight curl to it, although Jeff's blue eyes and cleft chin came from his mother. He was wearing jeans and a plaid flannel shirt with the sleeves rolled up, revealing his forearms—the strong right one, and the left, which looked wasted in comparison. It hurt Monica to see it, and she glanced away quickly.

"You look tired."

Jeff ran a hand across the back of his neck. "I am. The temperature really dropped last night and I was worried about a frost. I had to go out and check the temperature sensors in the bogs. It'd be just my luck to lose the crop the day before we plan to harvest."

Monica looked at him curiously. "It didn't seem that cold to me."

"The cranberry bogs are lower than the surrounding land. They can run ten to twenty degrees cooler, especially at night."

Monica absorbed that fact. There was still so much to learn. "But what would you do if there was a frost?" She couldn't imagine how they could blanket the acres and acres of cranberries that made up Sassamanash Farm in order to keep the fruit warm.

"It sounds crazy," Jeff said with a grin, "but we run the irrigation system and spray the berries with water. The water turns to ice, releasing heat, and the heat warms the berries. It's a law of physics known as the heat of fusion."

"Oh," was all Monica could say. While Jeff had excelled at science in school, she had been more inclined to have her head buried in a book—preferably a mystery. She'd started with Nancy Drew and had worked her way up to P. D. James before she was out of middle school.

"I have some cold beer in the fridge," she said as Jeff plopped down at the kitchen table, making the small space suddenly seem even smaller.

Jeff scrubbed a hand across his face. "Sounds great." He reached out his good arm, pulled open the refrigerator door which was right behind him and yanked a bottle from the cardboard six-pack Monica had stashed there. He twisted off the top and took a long pull before putting the beer down on the table and tilting his chair back on two legs.

"How's Gina?" Monica turned toward Jeff and leaned on the counter. "Have you heard from her lately?"

Gina was Jeff's mother and technically, Monica supposed, her stepmother, although she wasn't even ten years older than Monica and looked even younger than that, since she visited the best hair salons, had a personal trainer and had had enough Botox injections to paralyze an elephant. Monica couldn't help but think of her as *the woman who stole her father away from his family*. Although strictly speaking, her parents' marriage had been on the proverbial rocks even before Gina had dug her well-manicured nails into John Albertson's arm.

Monica had been besotted, however, with the younger brother who had arrived a year after their marriage, and she had gradually come to realize that Gina wasn't as bad as all that—vapid, for sure, but in a harmless sort of way.

"She's okay, I guess," Jeff said in answer to Monica's question. He took another long draft of his beer. "She's coming to visit."

Monica stopped with her hand halfway to the oven door. "When?"

Jeff glanced at his watch. "In about an hour."

"What?" Monica squeaked.

Jeff shrugged. "She called last night and said she was at loose ends and could she come and stay for a bit. The timing couldn't be worse, but what could I say?" He shrugged.

Monica was flabbergasted. She didn't go anywhere without making plans. Even a trip to the grocery store would be on her to-do list at least twenty-four hours in advance.

"Where is she going to stay?"

"She's got a room at the Cranberry Cove Inn." Jeff grinned.

"The presidential suite probably. If there is such a thing. She's getting in late so she said she won't be by until sometime tomorrow. Knowing Mother, that won't be before noon."

Monica pulled the broiler pan from the oven and put it on the top of the stove. "What is she going to do while we're harvesting the berries?"

Jeff shrugged. "Dunno. Shop, I guess."

Monica tried to picture Gina, with her salon processed blond hair and long, manicured nails, strolling around Cranberry Cove in her Louboutin pumps. Even the wealthier tourists, the ones who disembarked from the biggest yachts in the harbor, rarely wore anything fancier than boat shoes. Cranberry Cove was the sort of laid-back place where people walked around barefoot, in faded cutoffs and an old T-shirt.

They ate their meal in near silence. Jeff was obviously hungry, and soon he'd polished off three-fourths of the steak, a huge helping of salad and a baked potato heaped with butter and sour cream. Monica was gratified as she watched him devour the meal.

Jeff chased the last bit of lettuce around his plate and looked up with a smile.

"That was delicious. Thanks." He swiped his napkin across his mouth.

*Time to rip off the bandage*, Monica thought.

She pushed her chair back and began to gather their plates and silverware. "I've been going over the farm's books," she said, with her back to Jeff.

"Oh." His tone was flat.

Monica turned around and leaned against the counter, her hands braced against the edge. *Just get hold of the corner and rip*, she told herself.

17

"There's a reason you haven't been making the profit you expected."

Jeff's brows rose, wrinkling his broad forehead. Monica could see a trace of pale skin at his hairline where his hat usually rested. "What's that?"

"Sam Culbert was cheating you. He embezzled thousands of dollars from the farm's accounts."

Jeff jumped up, nearly overturning the kitchen table in the process. The dirty cutlery, which Monica hadn't yet collected, slid to the floor.

"If you're right," Jeff began, "if you're right, I'm going to kill the bastard."

Monica was up and out of bed before her alarm went off the next morning. Today was the big day—the beginning of the cranberry harvest.

Her clothes had been laid out the night before—jeans, an old turtleneck she used to wear around the apartment to stay warm during the fierce Chicago winters and a plain gray sweatshirt that was slightly frayed around the edges.

She dressed quickly. It was cold, and she started to shiver. She pulled on her sweatshirt gratefully.

It was still dark, and Monica flipped on the overhead light in the kitchen. She pulled a box of instant oatmeal from the cupboard, tore open a packet and emptied it into a bowl along with half a cup of water. While it was in the microwave, she leaned her elbows on the counter and looked out the window. The sky was overcast with a few streaks of light to the east. Monica shrugged. She had learned the old Michigan saying that if you didn't like the weather, all you had to do was wait five minutes.

The microwave pinged and Monica retrieved her bowl, poured some milk on top and added a handful of fresh blueberries—the remains of Sassamanash Farm's summer crop. She ate the oatmeal and was putting the bowl in the dishwasher when there was a knock on the door. She opened it to find Jeff standing there. He was dressed similarly in jeans and a sweatshirt, and he had a baseball cap pulled low over his forehead.

"Ready?" he said economically.

Monica nodded and followed him down the path toward the open field that led to the cranberry bogs. Walking slightly behind him, she could see the stiff set of his shoulders and head.

Jeff whirled around suddenly. "I can't believe Sam Culbert would cheat me like that. There must be some mistake." His jaw clenched tightly. "He's a well-respected businessman for Pete's sake."

Monica hung her head. They'd been over all this the evening before. "I doubt there's any mistake, but we should have a professional come in and audit the books."

Jeff slammed his clenched fist into the open palm of his other hand. "How could he do that to me? I trusted him. While I was over in Afghanistan dodging bombs and bullets, he was lining his pockets at my expense." He kicked savagely at a bare branch that was blocking their path. "And just yesterday he came around to see how I was doing." Jeff gave a bitter laugh. "Here he was offering me help with one hand while stealing from me with the other."

And he strode ahead, leaving Monica to break into a slow trot in an attempt to catch up.

The leaves on the trees ringing the bog were just beginning to change color, tinged with the barest hint of red and gold. Soon they would be in their full glory. Monica took a deep breath. She loved this time of year.

The bog had been flooded the previous evening and was now under more than a foot of water. A large truck was pulled up close to the side, and there was a chute running from it to the water.

Jeff gestured toward it. "A pump will suck the berries out of the water, up the chute and into the cleaner, where they'll be separated from any twigs, leaves, pieces of vine or other debris. Once that's done, the berries will be pumped into the truck."

Monica noticed that Jeff's crew had already gathered at the edge of the bog. They, too, were dressed in jeans and warm sweatshirts, most with scruffy beards and knitted caps pulled down over their foreheads. They were nursing Styrofoam cups of coffee, and a nearly empty box of dough- nuts sat open on the remains of a tree stump.

Jeff introduced the five men who would be helping him with the harvest. They nodded at Monica briefly, their hands shoved in their pockets, obviously impatient to get going.

Jeff gestured toward the bog. "That's a year's worth of work right there. Watering and tackling weeds in the sum- mer, sanding the bog and keeping it protected from frost in the winter, fertilizing in the spring and finally harvesting. There's a lot riding on this crop."

One of the men turned toward Jeff. "Should we get going, boss?" He had blond curls sticking out from under his cap, and crinkles around his blue eyes.

"Let's go."

The men took off at a trot toward a pile of waders—they looked like waterproof overalls with feet—and donned them swiftly, thanks to years of practice. Two of them headed toward a pair of machines that looked like a cross between a jet ski and a lawn mower.

"What are those?" Monica asked, pulling her sweatshirt down over her hands. It was still cold—the sun was low on the horizon, and the sky to the west was barely lit.

"Those are water reels, although we jokingly call them eggbeaters," Jeff explained. "They agitate the water and remove the berries from the vines."

Just then one of the reels started up with a roar. Two startled loons rose from the bog and streaked across the sky. The reels moved up and down the bog, churning the water and shattering the silence. Slowly the cranberries were freed from the vines. They floated to the surface like bright red bubbles.

Two of the men plunged into the bog, wading through the thigh-high water. The one in the red cap turned toward the bank where Jeff was standing. "Just my luck," he yelled. "These waders have a hole in them."

"Blame Sam Culbert," one of the other men shouted back. "He wouldn't spend a dime if he didn't have to."

Jeff put his hands to his mouth and yelled above the noise of the reels. "I'll replace them as soon as I can."

Monica noticed the look of worry that crossed his face. She knew he didn't want to spend any more money than he had to.

He turned toward Monica. "Ready?"

"As ready as I'll ever be," she said, as Jeff handed her a pair of the special socks they would wear inside the waders.

She picked up a pair and tried to put her right leg into them. That caused her to nearly lose her balance, and she realized the safest way for a novice to don them was sitting down. She lowered herself to the ground. It was damp, and she felt moisture soaking into her jeans. Monica was quickly developing a newfound respect for people who worked the land.

She managed to get her feet and legs into the waders, but Jeff had to help her stand up—the waders were awkward, and she felt as graceful as the abominable snowman in them. Jeff's crew had made walking in them look so effortless, but it was far from it.

A small group of early bird tourists had gathered on the opposite bank of the bog. Lauren, an attractive blonde who had been hired as a part-time tour guide, was explaining the harvesting process to them.

There was a lull as the water reels were briefly turned off, and Lauren's voice carried clearly across the water to where Monica was standing. "Cranberries are one of three fruits native to North America," she heard her say.

She saw Jeff glance in Lauren's direction and wave, his entire face brightening for a brief moment. Monica knew they'd been to the movies a couple of times, and the way Jeff talked about Lauren led Monica to believe that this might become serious.

She watched, biting her lip, as Jeff struggled with his shoulder strap. He didn't like to feel as if he was being coddled because of his injury, and in the five weeks she'd been living at the farm, Monica had learned to let him do things on his own. She gave a sigh of relief when he adjusted it to his satisfaction.

He smiled at Monica. "Let's go."

Monica shivered at the thought of getting into the water but gamely moved toward the bog, which by now was crimson with floating berries. The brisk breeze was blowing them to the side farthest from the truck.

"Just our luck," one of the men called out. "The wind is going in the wrong direction."

"Yeah. More work for us." The fellow who had complained about his waders shouted back.

Monica sat on the edge of the bog, as she had seen the men do, and swiveled until she was standing thigh deep in the water. The bottom of the bog was sandy and uneven, and she stumbled and nearly lost her footing.

"Careful, there." Jeff put a hand on her elbow to steady her. He handed her a wooden rake. "We need to head over there." He pointed toward the pump.

The cranberries were at least six inches deep and swirled around Monica's legs in a kaleidoscope of colors—from nearly black to crimson to a pale pink. She trailed her hands through the cold water and watched the berries bob and spin.

Jeff plucked a cranberry from the water and handed it to Monica. "Bite it in half."

Monica did, and the tart taste flooded her mouth.

Jeff pointed at the half in her hand. "See. Each berry has four air pockets. That's what makes them float."

Monica looked out across the bog. The sun had risen a little higher in the sky, the early clouds had scattered, and the light was glancing off the berries. It was magical.

"Come on," Jeff said. "The guys are going to need our help."

Monica made her way through the water as best she could. The rest of the crew was busy attempting to corral the berries. Monica pointed at them. "What is that they're using?"

"That's a boom," Jeff said. "There's a chain on the bottom and foam rubber on the top. It's similar to what they use to contain an oil spill. They'll sweep the berries together with it. Our job," he held out his rake, "is to push the berries toward the pump."

Slowly the cranberries were pulled toward the center of the bog, creating a growing carpet of brilliant red. A chorus of "ahs" rose from the small crowd that was watching the early morning harvest.

The sea of crimson grew as they corralled more and more of the harvest and slowly tightened the boom, like a noose tightening around someone's neck. Monica and Jeff stood in the middle along with two of the other crew members, sweeping the berries toward the pump with their rakes.

The berries floated easily enough, and raking them wasn't difficult, but keeping her balance on the sandy bottom of the bog was challenging Monica's leg muscles.

"You okay?" Jeff looked over at her.

"Fine." Monica smiled. If Jeff could do the job with only one good arm, she ought to be able to tough it out.

Monica reached out her wooden rake to capture a small group of berries that had drifted away when it caught on something. She pulled but it didn't want to budge.

"What's wrong?" Jeff looked at her in concern.

"The rake is caught on something." Monica pulled again, even harder this time.

"Could be tangled in one of the vines," one of the men said, holding out his hand for the rake.

Monica shook her head. She could do this. She pulled one more time. The rake finally came free and she nearly fell, stumbling backward several feet before regaining her footing. Water splashed onto the back of her sweatshirt, and she shivered. She finally steadied herself and was reaching for the small pocket of errant berries when something began to rise from the depths of the flooded bog.

"What the . . ." Jeff said.

They all stopped working and watched in grim fascination as a body, its clothes completely sodden and its face bloated with water, slowly rose to the surface.

Monica screamed and dropped her rake, and a gasp rose from the group of tourists on the bank. Jeff stifled an oath, and the other workers turned off the water reels and waded over to Monica and Jeff as quickly as possible, their brisk movements sending up splashes of water.

"Querido Deus," one of them muttered.

The fellow in the red cap turned toward Jeff. "Who is it?"

Jeff looked stricken, his face as white as a sheet of paper. It took him a moment to answer. "It's Sam. Sam Culbert," he said finally.

# Chapter 3

Everyone was momentarily frozen. The thought crossed Monica's mind that they must form an utterly bizarre tableau, standing stock-still, thigh deep in cranberries and clad in chest waders. The cry of a loon flying overhead broke the spell, and they all began talking at once.

Jeff raised his voice to be heard above the excited babble. "We need to get the police."

"Maybe he's not dead? Does anyone know CPR?" The worker with the curly hair and the red cap looked around at the rest of them.

Jeff shook his head. "I've seen enough death to know it's too late for that." But he reached out and felt Culbert's neck for a pulse. Culbert was wearing the red-and-white checked shirt and jeans Monica had seen him in the day before.

Jeff removed his hand, shook his head again and turned toward Monica.

"I left my cell phone up on that tree stump." He gestured over his shoulder. "Where the box of doughnuts is sitting. Can you go call nine-one-one?"

For a moment Monica couldn't move. Her feet were rooted to the soft, sandy bottom of the bog, and the scene before her looked hazy as if she was about to faint. She shook her head to clear it and began making her slow and laborious way to the side of the bog, pushing the massed cranberries out of the way as she walked.

The men had dropped the boom, and all the berries that had previously been corralled were now drifting free, blown by the wind to the opposite bank.

Getting out wasn't as easy as getting in, Monica discovered, and by the time she managed it, her sweatshirt was wet and muddy. She stripped off the waders as fast as she could and ran toward the tree stump Jeff had indicated. Her hands were shaking as she dialed 911, and she nearly dropped the phone. She tightened her grip and waited for a voice to come over the line.

The operator answered almost immediately. Monica explained what had happened and then had to repeat the farm's address twice. Her teeth were chattering so hard by now that the woman couldn't understand her.

The dispatcher promised a patrol car would be around immediately and advised them not to do anything or touch anything until the officers arrived. Monica clicked off the call and put the phone back on the stump.

"Someone is coming," she called to Jeff as soon as she was within earshot of the bog.

"I'll stay with the body. You all get out and get warm," Jeff said to the crew.

Now that they were no longer working, and with shock setting in, the men had started to shiver.

Jeff was shivering, too, but Monica knew better than to try to persuade him to let someone else stay with Culbert's body. There were plenty of things Jeff couldn't do because of his arm, but if something needed to be done that he could manage, Monica knew he wouldn't let anyone else take over.

"Shouldn't we get him out of there?" the fellow in the red cap asked.

"No!" Monica said hastily. "The woman said not to move him and not to touch anything unless absolutely necessary."

By now Lauren had wisely moved her small group of tourists away from the scene, although some had obviously been reluctant to leave the excitement. She had had to herd them together like a sheepdog, all but nipping at their heels.

The crew climbed out of the bog and stood around, stamping their feet and wrapping their arms around themselves to get warm. One fellow picked up his abandoned Styrofoam cup of coffee and took a sip of the dregs. He made a face, shuddered, and poured the rest of it onto the ground.

Monica wondered if she ought to run back to the cottage to put on a fresh pot of coffee, but just then they heard sirens in the distance.

Monica couldn't help but notice the look of panic that came over the face of one of the men. He had thick, chestnut hair and hazel eyes and was very good-looking. He had caught Monica's eye almost immediately, although he was probably ten years younger than her.

He hesitated for a moment, plucking at the hem of his sweatshirt, then took off at a run, across the field, away from the road where the sound of sirens had become louder.

"Mauricio," Jeff called after him. "Come back. Mauricio! What's wrong?"

Mauricio continued running, and by the time the police cars came barreling down the dusty, rutted road, he was gone from view.

Monica looked at Jeff, but he just shook his head.

The patrol cars swerved to a halt, and their doors flew open. Monica heard garbled voices overlaid with static blaring from the radios. Two uniformed officers exited the vehicles and began walking toward the bog. One was young, with cropped blond hair and a pair of dark, wraparound sunglasses. The other was older, his white face shining with perspiration. He kept hitching his pants up as he walked, as if his holster, gun and nightstick were weighing them down.

Jeff shimmied out of the bog and joined the rest of the crew.

The younger officer chomped down on a piece of gum, snapping and popping it before he spoke. "What have we got here?"

His partner had finally caught up with him, his breath whistling audibly in the still air. "Drowning?" He looked around, his gaze settling on Jeff, as if he could tell Jeff was in charge.

Jeff shrugged his shoulders, his left arm hanging limply by his side. "Doubt it. Water's barely more than a foot deep."

"Got any idea who he is?" The blond peered over the edge of the bog at Culbert's body, which was now floating freely, a long strand of cranberry vine trailing across his chest.

"Sam Culbert." Jeff looked down at his feet.

The heavier officer whistled. "Thought he looked familiar." He glanced at his watch. "Detective Stevens should be on the way."

At first Monica thought he'd said *Steven,* so she was

surprised when a car pulled up and a woman got out. She was heavily pregnant and wearing an unbuttoned trench coat over a navy jumper and white blouse. She went around to the trunk of her car, opened it and fished out a pair of rubber boots. She perched on the edge of the backseat and pulled them on.

Monica noticed that the officers' posture straightened ever so slightly, and the one in the sunglasses momentarily stopped snapping his gum. Detective Stevens made her way across the muddy ground to where they were all standing. She had blond hair cut slightly shorter than chin length and tucked behind her ears.

She, too, picked Jeff out of the crowd, sticking out her hand briskly. "Detective Tammy Stevens."

Several of the crew looked startled, and Monica thought she could read the look on their faces. *A female detective? What gives?*

"The coroner will be along shortly. Meanwhile, I'd like to ask you some questions."

Monica looked her over. They were around the same age. This must be a late in life pregnancy for Stevens. She was pretty, but her blue eyes, only lightly touched by wrinkles, were sharp.

The men shuffled their feet and looked down at the ground. Monica pulled her hands up inside her sleeves. Shock was making her shiver. Stevens put a hand on Monica's arm.

"You okay?"

Monica nodded briskly and lifted her chin. She could handle this. She glanced at Jeff out of the corner of her eye. He looked worried, as was to be expected, but not particularly shaken.

Stevens turned toward the officers. "Do we have an ID on the body?" She said the word *body* almost apologetically, glancing at Monica to see if she was okay.

"Sam Culbert," the heavier officer hastened to say, like an eager student showing off in class. The blond gave him a dirty look.

"Sam Culbert, huh?" Stevens edged closer to the bog and peered over the edge, both hands on her back. "Any idea how he got in there?" She gestured toward the water and turned around.

"No," Jeff said. He looked around at the crew, as if for confirmation. They hung their heads, suddenly becoming fascinated with their shoes.

"Seems unlikely he drowned." Stevens seemed to be speaking to herself. She turned around to look at the body again. "He knows this farm well. It's been in his family for years."

"I bought the farm from Sam just over a year ago," Jeff said quietly. "He managed it for me while I was over in Afghanistan."

Stevens scratched idly at her swollen stomach. "Any idea what he was doing here then? You two have an appointment or something?"

"No."

"He just dropped by?"

Jeff shrugged. "Yeah. To see if I needed any help with anything."

Monica noticed Jeff couldn't keep the sneering tone out of his voice. She hoped Stevens wouldn't pick up on it.

Jeff took off his hat and scratched his forehead. "But he was alive when he left."

Monica cleared her throat, and Stevens turned toward her. "I saw Sam leave yesterday. I saw him get into his car. He was wearing the same clothes. I remember the shirt."

"Really?" Stevens's eyebrows rose nearly to her hairline. "Could he have come back?"

"He must have," Jeff said. "And someone killed him. Because like I told you, he was alive when he left the farm."

They heard the rumble of a car in the distance.

"Probably the coroner." Stevens turned to the two officers. "Get everyone's name and number." She swiveled around toward Monica and the crew. "As soon as my men here have your information, you can go. But no one leave town, because I'll have more questions for you."

The crew rattled off their names and addresses, then scattered like marbles tossed onto the floor. Monica gave her contact information but lingered, waiting for Jeff to be ready to leave.

Stevens had pulled a camera from the pocket of her trench coat and was taking pictures of the body in the bog.

A car came along the road and pulled up close, edging onto the grass. But it wasn't what they'd all been expecting. This was a late-model Mercedes, as clean and shiny as if it had just come from the car wash. It was highly unlikely it belonged to the coroner, for whom this was only a part-time job.

Jeff put his head in his hands and gave a loud moan. Monica looked at him curiously.

The driver's side door opened, and a pair of legs emerged. Good ones with a very artful looking spray tan. They ended in a pair of sky-high designer pumps. The owner of the legs wriggled her way out of the car, pulling down her short, tight skirt as she emerged from the confines of its interior.

"Gina," Jeff groaned.

The woman stood still for a moment, surveying the scene in front of her. Her professionally streaked blond hair was arranged in a loose twist in the back and with bangs that brushed her eyebrows. Her nails were long and as red as the cranberries, and she had a very expensive handbag hanging from the crook of her arm.

"Jeffie," she called when she spotted her son.

Stevens was brought up short. She swiveled around as fast as her vast stomach would allow. "Who the heck is that?"

Gina began picking her way across the muddy field, the heels of her hideously expensive shoes sinking into the soft turf with every step. Stevens started toward her, one hand on the small of her back, the other held out in front of her, gesturing for Gina to stop.

"Please, ma'am, if you'll just stop where you are."

Gina paused with one foot raised in the air, her glossy pink mouth forming a startled *O*.

Stevens continued toward where Gina was standing. "This is a crime scene. I'm afraid I'm going to have to ask you to leave."

"A crime scene?" Gina shrieked, already backing up. "Jeffie, honey, are you in trouble? Should I call Arthur Sullivan?" She caught sight of Monica and waved.

"I don't need a lawyer. I'm fine, Mom. Why don't you go back to the Inn, and I'll call you when I'm done here, okay?"

Gina was already headed toward the Mercedes. She slid behind the wheel quickly, started the car and pulled away, spitting dust and gravel in her wake.

Stevens looked at her watch. "The coroner should be along any minute now. Why don't you two go home? You may not want to see this. I'll catch up with you later."

Monica was more than ready to go. She was chilled to the bone and still feeling the effects of shock.

"I'll stay if you don't mind." Jeff raised his chin.

"Your call."

The patrolmen had started to string up strands of yellow police tape. It fluttered in the breeze, making a sharp snapping sound.

Monica turned and began to walk back toward her cottage. She gave one last backward glance at Jeff, who was pacing up and down, his good arm clasped across his chest. She hated leaving him, but she desperately needed to get warm and dry.

Monica thought about what had happened as she made her way home. Jeff hadn't said a word about Mauricio and how he had taken off so suddenly. Monica felt guilty that she hadn't mentioned it herself.

She let herself into her cottage, stripped off her wet clothes and wrapped herself up in her terry cloth robe. It had seen better days—the fabric was matted down and rubbed nearly bare in spots—but she couldn't bring herself to part with it.

Monica filled the teakettle, and when it began to whistle, she grabbed it off the stove. She filled her mug with the hot water and dunked a tea bag in it mindlessly. Her head had started to ache, and she thought she might go lie down for a few minutes.

Monica carried her tea into the cottage's small living room and curled up on the sofa. There was a soft, woven throw in muted shades of blue and gray tossed over the arm. She pulled it up and snuggled underneath it. She could have gotten in bed for a nap, but she was afraid she might sleep too deeply.

Besides, she wasn't comfortable with the whole concept of taking naps—they seemed like a waste of time.

Monica's eyes closed, and she was drifting off when someone began banging on the front door. Her eyes flew open, and she tossed back the throw. Before she could reach the foyer, the knocking started again, even harder this time. Monica couldn't imagine who it was or what was so urgent, but the frantic pummeling of fists against the door sent a shiver of unease down her spine.

"I'm coming," Monica called to whoever was out there.

# Chapter 4

Monica flung open the door, and Gina stumbled into the tiny foyer. Her hair was coming down on one side, and her Louboutin pumps were caked with mud. She had a leopard-print trench coat cinched tightly around her waist, and two-carat diamond studs winked in her ears.

"I don't know why Jeffie decided to buy this place," she grumbled as she wiped her feet on the mat outside Monica's door. "I'd never have let him spend all those summers on my parents' farm if I'd have known it was going to turn him into a farmer."

She followed Monica into the living room and tossed her coat on a chair, but instead of sitting down, she flitted about the room—lifting the curtain to peer outside, examining the photographs on Monica's mantel and fingering the books stacked on the coffee table.

"I just don't know what we're going to do." She wrung her hands distractedly.

Monica jumped up from her perch on the sofa. "Why don't I get you some tea? That will make you feel better."

"Honey, the only way tea's going to make me feel better is if you put a big old glug of Jack Daniel's in it."

Monica looked at her watch. "It's barely noon."

"Monica, you've got to unbend a bit, you know? Loosen up. Throw out the rule book once in a while. You've had a shock. We all have. I think it calls for something a little more fortifying than a cup of tea."

"Will a shot of Dewar's do?" Monica had a dusty bottle of Scotch in the cabinet—a relic of her days of entertaining in Chicago.

"Make it a double, and you've got a deal." Gina finally lit on the end of an armchair, one leg crossed over the other, her skirt inching even farther up her thigh, her foot jiggling furiously.

Monica refilled the kettle and unearthed the bottle of liquor from the back of one of the kitchen cabinets. It was still three-quarters full. She brewed a cup of tea and added a splash of Scotch. She hesitated, then added another splash. She carried it out to the living room, where Gina was once again prowling around the room.

The cup rattled slightly in its saucer as Monica set it down on the coffee table. Gina plopped into the armchair opposite. Monica noticed Gina's hand was shaking, too, as she lifted the cup to her mouth.

Gina sighed with satisfaction and replaced the cup in its saucer. She leaned back in her chair, tucking an errant clump of hair back into her French twist. "I hope you don't mind me barging in on you like this."

Actually Monica minded quite a bit. Her head was throbbing and every fiber in her body ached to lie down for an hour or two. But obviously she would never say that. She'd been raised to be polite, accommodating, and to be seen and not heard.

"I imagine you're wondering what I'm doing here." Gina twirled her five-carat diamond engagement ring around and around her finger. "It's like this. Your father and I have decided to go our separate ways." Gina traced a pattern on the coffee table with her finger. "Actually, your father decided to go *his* separate way." She went back to twirling the enormous diamond. "And he's not exactly going alone."

Her brows drew together, her lips clenched in a thin line and her nostrils flared. Her expression made Monica think of an approaching thunderstorm.

"He took off with some floozy who cuts his hair. Who ever heard of a female barber? Barbers are supposed to be old, bald and smoke cigars." Gina frowned and tossed back a huge gulp of her tea.

Monica was sorely tempted to mention to Gina that if taking off with someone else's husband was the criteria for being considered a floozy, the term could be applied to her as well. Gina had been behind the counter in the cosmetics department of one of the stores at the mall when John Albertson had walked in to buy Monica's mother her annual bottle of Valentine's Day perfume. Gina had latched onto him like a terrier with a bone, and the next thing Monica knew, her parents were getting divorced and they were moving out of their house in Lake Forest to a smaller home just far enough away to mean changing schools.

"It's just that it's left me at loose ends. I didn't want to mill around while John cleaned his things out of the condo. I hope you don't mind me hanging around for a bit."

Monica shook her head. "No, not at all, I'm sure . . ." She searched for something positive to say. "Jeff will be glad to spend some time with you."

Gina polished off her cup of tea and leaned back in the chair, her arms crossed over her chest.

"Just what was that all about this morning?"

Monica explained about finding Sam Culbert's body in the cranberry bog.

Gina leaned forward. "Is Jeffie in trouble?"

"No . . ."

"There's something you're not telling me." Gina tapped a long, manicured nail on the table.

"Culbert was cheating Jeff. He'd embezzled thousands of dollars from the farm while Jeff was overseas. Jeff claims he didn't know, but I'm not so sure. How could he not?"

Gina's eyes widened, and her hand flew to her mouth. "But Jeff would never . . ." She narrowed her eyes and looked at Monica. "Did you tell the police—"

Monica was already shaking her head. "No, I didn't say a thing. But that detective, Stevens, is smart. I don't think it will take her long to put two and two together." Monica was quiet for a moment. "And Jeff threatened to kill Culbert."

Gina's indrawn breath was audible across the room. "He did?"

Monica nodded. "But I'm sure it was just letting off steam. People say things like that when they're mad. They don't mean it. Jeff wouldn't do something like that."

*But he'd probably killed people in Afghanistan*, Monica thought.

"There was something else I didn't mention to the police, and neither did Jeff. There's this fellow who works for Jeff—Mauricio—who acted very oddly. He took off shortly after the body was discovered."

"Before the police arrived?" Gina's foot had started jiggling again.

"Yes. As soon as he heard the sirens approaching, he began to run. Jeff called to him, but he didn't listen—didn't even turn around."

Gina snapped her fingers. "He's our murderer then. Why else would he bolt like that?"

Monica couldn't think of an immediate answer but she suspected there were other reasons why Mauricio might have been leery of talking to the police.

"What do you know about this Mauricio?" Gina was sitting up straight in her chair now, her expression more animated than it had been since her arrival.

"Nothing, really. Nothing at all."

Gina sprang to her feet and began to pace Monica's small living room. The room wasn't particularly conducive to pacing—it didn't take more than a handful of steps to get from one wall to the other.

Monica stopped beside the armchair suddenly. "Let's call Jeff and see what he knows." She retrieved her purse from the floor and began to ferret through the contents, muttering softly under her breath. "Here it is," she declared triumphantly as she pulled her iPhone out of the depths of her bag.

She tapped out the number with the tips of her nails.

"He's coming," Gina said after a brief conversation. She clicked her phone off and tossed it back into her purse. "Meanwhile, why don't you show me around?"

"The place is small. You've already seen most of it." Monica gestured around the tiny living room, with its redbrick fireplace and bay window. It was her favorite room, although it was probably more shabby than chic. The furniture was softly worn but overstuffed and inviting. Gina poked her head into the kitchen but didn't seem to be particularly interested in that room.

Monica led her up the stairs to the tiny second floor. She used the front room as a bedroom and at the moment the back one was half guest bedroom and half dumping ground for miscellaneous items—paint cans and brushes, a folded tarp and a chair that didn't fit anywhere. They just had time to peek into the two rooms before they heard knocking on the front door.

"Hello?" Jeff's voice drifted up the stairs toward them.

"Coming, Jeffie." Gina made her way down the steep stairs, nearly tripping in her high-heeled pumps.

She threw her arms around her son and hugged him, then stood back to examine him.

Monica noticed the intense weariness on Jeff's face. That morning he had seemed so eager—excited for the harvest. Now his shoulders sagged and there were dark shadows in his eyes.

Gina took Monica's spot on the sofa and patted the seat next to her. Jeff sat down, stretched his long legs out under the coffee table, and leaned his head back against the cushions.

"You look like you could use a cup of tea or coffee," said Monica, having been forced reluctantly into the role of hostess.

"Make him a cup of your special tea," Gina said and winked at Monica. She reached over and patted Jeff's knee.

As Monica ran water into the kettle and heated it, she could hear the murmur of voices from the other room. She filled a cup and added a tea bag. Her hand hesitated briefly over the bottle of Scotch and then she resolutely twisted off the cap and added a modest amount to Jeff's tea. He looked like he needed it.

Monica placed the cup and saucer in front of Jeff and took a seat in the armchair recently vacated by Gina. The faint scent of her perfume still clung to it.

Jeff took a sip of his tea and made a face but then immediately took another large gulp. He put the cup down and it clattered in the saucer.

Gina leaned forward eagerly. "So what can you tell us about this Mauricio character?"

Jeff raised his shoulders and let them drop again. "Not much, I'm afraid."

Gina made an impatient tsk-tsk sound. "Where does he live? Is he married? Any kids?"

Jeff scowled. "I don't know."

"Well then, what on earth do you guys talk about while you're out there all day working?" Gina demanded.

Jeff shrugged again. "I don't know—the chances of the Detroit Lions making the playoffs, where's the best place to take a truck for a tune-up, who does a better burger—the Cranberry Cove Diner or the Cranberry Cove Inn. Stuff like that."

Gina gave a gusty sigh. "Men have such uninteresting discussions." Her left foot began its customary jiggling. "We need to find out more about him."

Jeff held up a cautionary hand. "Whoa, you don't think Mauricio had anything to do with this, do you?"

"Why did he take off running like that then?"

Jeff shrugged. "My guess is he's overstayed his visa or

doesn't have any papers in the first place. Although he gave me a social security number, and as far as I'm concerned, that's all I need to know."

"That might be true, but I'd still like to know more about this Mauricio. Maybe he had a grudge against Culbert for some reason. After all, who else could have done it?" Gina's foot picked up its tempo and began to move faster. "We know you didn't, but if we don't convince the police of that . . ." She let the sentence trail off. To emphasize her point, she made a slashing motion across her throat with her index finger.

"Why would the police think I had anything to do with Culbert's murder?"

"I don't know," Monica admitted. "Detective Stevens asked so many questions. And she sounded as if she didn't believe you. Besides, you knew Culbert and did business with him. And he was found dead on your land. . . ."

"And you think that makes me a prime suspect?" Jeff scrubbed his hands over his face. "Frankly, I'm more worried that they'll discover Mauricio didn't have a work visa. Sure, he gave me a social security number, but I didn't ask to see any papers. He was a hard worker and reliable. . . ." Jeff shrugged.

"Could you get in trouble for that, Jeffie?" Gina asked.

Jeff gave a weak smile. "I don't think they'd throw me in jail, but there would be a hefty fine, and right now I couldn't afford that."

"So we need to find Mauricio before the police do." Gina pointed a finger at Jeff. "If he is the murderer, I doubt the police are going to bother you over a little matter like some missing paperwork."

"Someone in town is bound to have some information

about Mauricio," Monica said. "That fellow who owns the bookstore knew who I was and where I lived before I even entered his shop."

"News travels fast in a small place like Cranberry Cove." Jeff smiled.

"What are we waiting for then?" Gina jumped to her feet. "Let's go into town and start asking questions."

Monica turned to Jeff. "Are you going to come with us?"

Jeff shook his head. "I have work to do. Besides, I suspect you ladies will manage just fine without me."

# Chapter 5

Monica followed Gina out of the driveway, keeping Gina's car in sight until it crested the hill on the road into town and her Mercedes disappeared from view. Monica had fallen behind while attempting to coax her reluctant Focus up to thirty miles per hour. It was making an unusual noise—a groaning sound—that couldn't possibly be good. She decided she didn't want to think about it at the moment.

Gina was headed toward the Cranberry Cove Inn, where apparently the fellow behind the desk had been trying to catch her eye since her arrival. She planned to use that to her advantage to get him talking. Monica had tried to dissuade her from coming along into town—the locals clammed up faster than a Venus flytrap when out-of-towners were around—but she didn't think Gina would do much harm as long as she stuck to talking to the clerk at the Inn.

Monica was tackling Gumdrops first. Despite being very

circumspect, the VanVelsen sisters loved to talk. And Monica was hardly looking for salacious gossip. All she was after was some information that would help them track Mauricio down. She didn't think they would see any harm in that. Jeff had tried the phone number Mauricio had given him numerous times already, but the calls went straight to voicemail. Jeff didn't even have an address for the man—just his name and social security number.

Beach Hollow Road was quiet when Monica got there. The sun was low in the western sky, putting Cranberry Cove's main street in shadow. Monica found a parking space two doors down from Gumdrops and pulled in.

"Hello," she called out as she pushed open their door.

Hennie was fussing over a display of Droste chocolate pastilles, creating a tower of the blue, red, orange, purple and yellow hexagonally shaped boxes. Monica waited as Hennie balanced the final box on top and stood back to admire the effect. The tower swayed, steadied and then swayed again, sending the boxes tumbling to the floor.

"Here, let me help you," Monica said, striding over to the counter.

"Gerda is the one with the steady hands," Hennie said. She was red-faced from bending over, but Monica noticed her hair had not moved a millimeter out of place.

"Is Gerda okay?" Monica looked around the shop, but they were the only ones there.

Hennie gave a sigh and picked at an imaginary piece of lint on her spotless lavender sweater. "She's quite . . . distraught." She fingered the gold locket around her neck. "Midnight still hasn't come back, and she fears the worst." She took a deep breath as if to brace herself. "We both do."

A tear escaped and trickled down Hennie's cheek, leaving a trail of moisture in her pink-tinted face powder. "It's just that we're afraid she might be trapped somewhere with no water or food. We can hardly bear to think about it."

Monica knew less than nothing about cats other than that they were independent creatures given to wandering off on a whim.

"I'm sure Midnight will be back soon," Monica said, knowing that the platitude was unlikely to soothe Hennie but unable to think of anything else to say.

Hennie swiped at her cheek and threw back her shoulders. "I'm sure you're right," she said, every bit as insincerely.

Hennie leaned on the counter, her blue eyes brightening slightly.

"Now you must tell me all about what's happened out at the farm. I ran into Tempest Storm—you know—she runs Twilight, that New Age place." Hennie turned her nose up a little, indicating her disapproval. "She said she saw a police car head down the drive to the farm, going a mile a minute and with the flashers on. I hope there hasn't been an accident." She looked at Monica with concern shadowing her eyes.

Monica hesitated. How much should she tell Hennie? She shrugged. Everyone would know soon enough. It was impossible to keep anything a secret in Cranberry Cove.

Monica was tempted to sugarcoat things, but Hennie's sharp eyes belied her innocence. "Jeff and his crew and I had just begun the harvest when a body floated to the surface along with the berries." Monica still found it hard to believe, although she could picture the scene in her mind with complete clarity. She felt a frisson of delayed shock, and shivered.

Hennie gave a sharp intake of breath. "Oh, my goodness

me." She shook her head and her silver curls quivered. "What on earth is the world coming to?" She put her hand on Monica's. "Was it some vagrant who was trespassing and fell into the flooded bog?"

The beaded curtain to the stockroom rattled, and both Monica and Hennie turned in that direction. They watched as Gerda approached the counter. Her shoulders were slumped, and there were circles under her eyes. Monica could tell she had been crying. She held a balled-up tissue in her right hand.

"What is this about a body in the bog?" Her eyes lit up, and her shoulders lifted.

"Monica said a body floated to the surface of the bog during the harvest. Can you imagine?"

Gerda shuddered and leaned on the counter. Monica was pleased to see that her entire demeanor had brightened considerably. At least some good was coming of the tragedy— even if it only took Gerda's mind off the missing Midnight for a few moments.

"Who was it? Do you know?" Gerda repeated Hennie's earlier question.

Monica looked from one woman to the other. "Sam Culbert."

The sisters gasped, and Gerda's hand flew to her mouth.

"You can't mean that," Hennie said. "Sam Culbert? Are you sure?"

"Yes."

"What was he doing out at the farm?" Gerda asked.

*That's exactly what I'd like to know,* Monica thought. She'd seen him leave earlier that day—why had he come back?

Gerda came out from behind the counter and began stack-

48

ing the Droste chocolate boxes that Hennie had left in a heap on the display table.

"It must have been an accident?" Hennie said with a question in her voice. "Perhaps he had a stroke or a heart attack and fell in?"

Monica hesitated. "I'm afraid not," she said finally.

Gerda paused with one of the pastel-colored boxes in her hand. "Well, it was an accident of some sort, wasn't it?" She carefully placed the box on the second row of her pyramid.

"No. I'm afraid the police think it was murder."

This time the sisters were too stunned to gasp and instead stared at Monica openmouthed. Hennie recovered first.

"Murder! In Cranberry Cove?"

"And one of our own," Gerda said, "although I'm sure there are a lot of people who won't be sad to hear the news."

Monica looked at her questioningly.

"Let's just say Sam Culbert wasn't much liked around here, even though he was a local boy. At first people were proud of him for making good, living in that big house high above the lake, driving fancy cars. But when he began throwing his weight around . . ."

Hennie nodded agreement. "Sam didn't mind whose toes he stepped on to get what he wanted."

"Anyone in particular?" Monica asked, trying to sound as innocent as possible.

But the sisters had clammed up. Monica might be living in Cranberry Cove full time, but she'd have to be there a lot longer before being considered a local.

"I'm sorry. You must have come in for something," Hennie said, pulling the edges of her cardigan closer together and adroitly changing the subject.

"Actually I came in to ask you a question," Monica said. "And to get some chocolates," she said hurriedly, grabbing a box of the Droste pastilles and nearly upsetting Gerda's intricate display.

Hennie gave Monica a look that said *I don't believe you for a minute,* but curiosity obviously got the best of her because she folded her hands on the counter and looked at Monica, her head cocked expectantly to one side. Gerda joined her sister, echoing her pose, and for a moment Monica was struck by how eerily alike they looked.

"I'm after some information to tell the truth." Monica lowered her voice conspiratorially.

Hennie and Gerda leaned forward. They were suddenly as alert as bloodhounds after a scent.

"You and Gerda know just about everything that goes on in Cranberry Cove."

The twins preened and patted their identical silver curls.

Monica felt slightly overwhelmed by their sudden and complete attention. She fussed with the sleeve of her sweatshirt— the cuff had turned up slightly—before answering.

"There's a young man who was on Jeff's crew. We'd like to ask him a few questions, but he's not answering his phone. We . . . I . . . wondered if you ladies might know something about him."

"Do you think he's the murderer?" Hennie gave an exaggerated shiver.

Monica shook her head emphatically. "No, no. Jeff simply wants to contact him."

The sisters' faces assumed identical disappointed looks.

"His name is Mauricio. He speaks with an accent. Jeff

says he's from Portugal. Youngish—maybe early twenties—dark hair, good-looking."

The sisters stared at Monica blankly.

Monica racked her brain for some more descriptive qualities. "Medium height." She held her hand level with the top of her own head. "About my height. Slim. Tanned."

The sisters turned toward each other and shrugged their shoulders.

"If he was local, we would probably know him, but if not . . ."

Gerda nodded agreement. "Cranberry Cove is overrun with tourists in the summer." She sighed. "People come from all over."

"They come by land and by sea . . . well, not sea, maybe, but by boat for sure." Hennie chuckled.

"The streets were so jam-packed this year, you could hardly get down them. Now if it had been winter, he would have stuck out like the proverbial sore thumb. But during tourist season . . ."

Monica was disappointed.

"Now wait a minute." Gerda held up a hand and turned toward her twin. "Do you remember that young man—dark-haired—who we saw hanging around the diner late in the summer?"

Hennie pursed her lips. "Yes. But didn't that turn out to be Gus's grandson?"

"Oh, you're right." Gerda turned toward Monica. "Gus Amentas is the cook at the Cranberry Cove Diner. His grandson came for a visit this summer."

"All the way from Greece."

"He had dark hair and was about your height." Gerda held a hand up much as Monica had done earlier.

"I'm sure he's never seen a lake as big as ours," Hennie chimed in.

Both sisters laughed.

Monica paid for her chocolates and left Gumdrops. At least the visit wasn't a total waste of time—she had some delicious sweets to enjoy later.

The sun was lower in the sky now, and the air had turned colder. Monica glanced at her watch—almost five o'clock. The shops would be shutting soon. They kept longer hours in the summer, but once the bulk of the tourists left, it didn't pay to stay open late.

The lights were still on at Book 'Em, but when Monica tried the door it was already locked. She felt strangely disappointed. She didn't want to admit to herself how much she'd been looking forward to seeing Greg Harper again.

She was about to turn away when the door suddenly opened and Greg stuck his head around the edge. He saw Monica and smiled. His hair was ruffled—as if he'd been running his hands through it—and a piece of dust clung to the front of his red V-neck sweater.

"How are you enjoying the Agatha Christie?" he asked as he pulled the door wider and beckoned for Monica to enter.

"I don't want to keep you. . . ." Monica hesitated on the threshold.

"Not at all. I was just going to make a cup of tea and do some tidying up. You can tell me about the Christie," he called over his shoulder as he led the way through the shop and into the stockroom.

"To be perfectly honest, I haven't had a chance to start

it yet. We began the harvest today, and . . . and something unexpected happened." Monica hesitated for a moment, but she was quite certain the VanVelsen sisters were already telegraphing the news all over Cranberry Cove. She explained to Greg about finding Culbert's body in the bog.

A strange look crossed Greg's face but disappeared so rapidly that Monica didn't have the time to analyze it. He gave a long, low whistle.

"So Sam Culbert finally got his comeuppance." He ran water into two mugs and put them in the microwave.

"What do you mean?"

Greg ran a hand through his hair, leaving it even messier than before. "Let's just say Sam Culbert wasn't the most popular guy in town."

"So I've heard."

They were both silent until the microwave pinged, and Greg removed the two mugs of steaming water. He added tea bags and handed one to Monica.

"Milk or sugar?"

"This is fine." Monica wrapped her hands around the mug. The warmth felt good. She blew on the tea, sending a small tidal wave of liquid swelling across the cup.

Greg opened a cupboard, grabbed a shaker of sugar and poured a liberal amount into his tea. He stirred the mixture with his finger.

"What did Sam Culbert do to make himself so unpopular in Cranberry Cove?"

Greg hesitated. "Basically just threw his weight around— a veritable *master of the universe* to borrow a phrase from Tom Wolfe—at least in Cranberry Cove. He owns a couple of buildings here along Beach Hollow Road, and I heard he regularly raised the rent. Several of the stores closed—they couldn't afford it anymore. But I doubt Culbert lost any sleep over it."

Monica filed that bit of information away. She'd ask Greg more about it later. For the moment, she was focused on finding Mauricio.

"There is a fellow on Jeff's crew we're trying to track down." Monica told Greg much the same thing she'd told the VanVelsens.

"Dark hair, medium height, foreign accent?" Greg scrunched his face up in concentration. "Plenty of men around this summer who would fit the dark hair and medium height part, but we don't get too many foreigners visiting Cranberry Cove. It's a well-kept secret, and we like to keep it that way. The amount of tourists we get now is about all we can handle." He tapped his chin with his index finger. "I seem to remember someone though . . ." He snapped his fingers. "He was a relative of the short-order cook at the diner. I don't suppose that's who you mean?"

Monica shook her head. "Thanks anyway." She put her mug in the sink. As much as she was enjoying spending time with Greg, the events of the day had suddenly made her weak in the knees. All she could think about was home, a hot bath in the cottage's old claw-foot tub and some cheese toast for dinner.

Greg walked her to the front door. He gave her a slightly shy grin. "Stop in again."

"I will," Monica said as he closed the door.

The sun was setting behind her as Monica drove back to Sassamanash Farm. She glanced in her rearview mirror and could see it hovering over the surface of the lake like a hesitant swimmer putting a toe in the water before taking the plunge. Pinpricks of light sparkled on the tips of the waves, and the sky was awash with pinks, reds and oranges.

Monica kept peeking into her rearview mirror to admire the scene until she had a near-collision with a truck. She then focused all of her attention on the road ahead. She had no doubt that in a head-on with a semi, she and the Focus would come out on the losing end.

Monica was relieved to find her driveway empty when she got there. She wasn't up to dealing with Gina at the moment. Hopefully she had decided to stay at the Inn and have an early night.

It was dark inside the cottage, and Monica switched on some lights as soon as she opened the door. She then dragged herself up the stairs and into the bathroom, where she turned the hot water tap on as far as it would go. Her mother had sent her some Crabtree and Evelyn bath oil for Christmas that she hadn't opened yet. She ripped the plastic wrapping off now and poured a sizeable amount into the tub. Perfumed, fragrant steam soon filled the bathroom.

Monica was retrieving her robe from the bedroom when there was a knock on the door. She pushed aside the curtains and peered out her bedroom window. She could see the top of a dark-colored car pulled up in front of her door.

Who on earth . . . ?

Monica dropped her bathrobe on the bed, quickly turned off the taps in the bathroom and headed down the stairs toward the foyer. She yanked open the door, ready to tell whatever salesman was standing there that she was decidedly not interested in his or her wares. The words died on her lips.

Standing on the front step, one hand supporting her back, was Detective Stevens. The breeze, damp from their proximity to the lake, had curled the ends of her hair and sent a lock blowing across her eyes. She brushed it away impatiently.

"Mind if I come in for a moment?"

"No. No, of course not." Monica stepped aside.

Stevens grunted slightly as she mounted the single step to Monica's tiny foyer. They stood facing each other in the small space.

"Please come in," Monica said gesturing toward the living room.

Stevens eyed Monica's overstuffed sofa warily and dropped into one of the armchairs instead. She stuck her feet out in front of her and rotated her ankles, briefly leaning her head against the back of the chair.

"I've got a month to go," Stevens said, rubbing her stomach, "and I was hoping for a nice, uneventful couple of weeks. Maybe some idiot trying to rob an ATM or a radio stolen from someone's car. Not murder." She blew out a breath of air and her bangs flopped up and down.

"You're sure it was murder?" Monica perched on the edge of the sofa, her hands folded in her lap. All she could think about was the rapidly cooling water in her bathtub upstairs.

Stevens grunted and struggled to sit upright. "The autopsy hasn't been performed yet, but there's a sizeable dent in Culbert's skull that suggests he was hit with the proverbial blunt instrument before being dumped in the bog." Stevens leveled her gaze at Monica. "The pathologist estimates time of death to be between nine o'clock and midnight. Of course he won't swear to it." Stevens sighed. "Pathologists won't swear to much of anything unless maybe it's that the corpse is definitely dead. Even then . . ." Stevens rolled her eyes. She smiled and leaned as far forward as her stomach would allow. "You wouldn't happen to be able to give your brother an alibi for that time period would you?"

# Chapter 6

Monica stared at Stevens. She suspected her mouth was hanging open, and she hastened to shut it. An alibi? For Jeff? Monica had to clear her throat several times before finding her voice.

"Jeff came over for dinner. He's not been eating well so I made him a steak and . . ." Monica's voice trailed off. She suspected Stevens wasn't interested in hearing all the details. She desperately wished she could tell the detective that Jeff had been with her the whole time, but she couldn't lie. Not to the police. Not to anyone. She'd been brought up to tell the truth.

Stevens massaged the small of her back, her head cocked, waiting for the rest of Monica's reply.

Monica wet her lips and cleared her throat, attempting to delay the moment when she would land Jeff in the soup. She couldn't imagine Jeff killing anyone, but she'd read about soldiers who had come back from the war with post-traumatic stress disorder snapping and behaving in unlikely ways.

"Jeff left here about nine thirty." It had been closer to nine fifteen, but Monica figured there was no harm in rounding off the time.

Stevens grunted. "Culbert's wife said he left home on some undisclosed errand around nine thirty. I'm afraid that doesn't eliminate your brother. I don't suppose there is anyone who can vouch for you during that time?"

"Me?" Monica was aghast. It had never occurred to her that she might be considered a suspect. "But I didn't know Culbert . . . I only got here a couple of weeks ago . . . why would I—"

Stevens waved her to a stop. "It's just routine. I have to ask."

Maybe it was also routine that she'd asked about Jeff? Somehow Monica didn't think so.

Monica spread out her hands. "I was alone, I'm afraid. I went to bed early because we were getting up early to start the harvest the next morning."

"You didn't happen to hear anything, did you?"

"Hear anything?"

"Like maybe the sound of a car? Voices? Something like that? I know your place is pretty far from the bog, but we're quite sure Culbert was killed somewhere else and then moved to the bog in the wheelbarrow that was found near the site. Your brother has identified it as belonging to the farm." Stevens looked around Monica's living room. "Nice place, by the way."

"Thank you," Monica said, a little less stiffly. "No, I'm afraid I didn't hear anything. I was tired. I imagine I was asleep as soon as my head hit the pillow."

Stevens gave a tight smile. "It was a long shot." She put her hands on either arm of the chair and pushed herself to a standing position. "I was going to start decorating the nursery tonight, but . . ." She shrugged. "That's police work for you."

Monica followed her to the front door where she bid Stevens good-bye.

Monica closed the door and leaned against it briefly. It was too bad she and Stevens were on opposite sides of the law. Well, not opposite sides actually. Monica was all for getting at the truth and seeing justice served. It was just a shame she and Stevens had had to meet this way. Monica suspected that under different circumstances, she and the detective could have become friends.

She sighed as she headed back up the stairs to the bathroom. As she suspected, the bathwater was barely lukewarm. She let some of the water out and then turned the hot tap on full. Fragrant steam once again rose from the tub, and Monica sat on the edge for a moment letting it swirl around her face before heading into the bedroom to change into her robe.

Monica was tying the belt when the phone rang. She knew she was a bit of a dinosaur for insisting on a landline, but she often forgot to charge her cell, no matter how many sticky notes she left around the house to remind herself.

The phone shrilled again. Was it a robocall? A salesman? Someone taking a survey? The number didn't look familiar, and she almost didn't answer it, but grabbed the receiver at the last minute.

"Hello?" Monica said brusquely.

"Hello?" The voice was soft, a mere whisper. "Is this Miss Albertson? Jeff's sister?"

"Yes. Who is this?" Monica felt a tingling in her stomach. The man had a foreign accent . . . could it be?

"This is Mauricio. I work for Jeff this morning. Maybe you remember me?"

Monica gripped the receiver tighter. "Yes, I remember you," she said as gently as possible, terrified that Mauricio would get scared and hang up before she had the chance to talk to him.

"I need to ask you a favor, miss, please. I can't go to the police. I am afraid they will think I killed Mr. Culbert."

"Why would they think that?"

There was a long silence. "Because I am not from your country."

"I don't think that would—"

"Please, miss. You must tell them I didn't do it."

"They'll want to know where you were that night." Monica thought back to her conversation with Stevens. Culbert had been murdered sometime between nine o'clock and midnight.

"That will help?" Mauricio asked.

"Yes. If you can tell me where you were between nine and midnight."

"Yes, yes," Mauricio said eagerly. "I was down at Flynn's."

"Flynn's?" Monica asked, wondering if that was a person or a place.

"It is a bar down by the harbor. A little rough. Not the kind of place a lady like you would enjoy."

That was fine with Monica. She had no intention of frequenting Flynn's. Except to find out whether or not Mauricio was telling the truth.

On the one hand, she had instinctively liked Mauricio. On the other hand, she wanted the murderer to be anyone but her brother Jeff.

Monica was up early the next morning, although given the option she would have huddled under her down comforter for another couple of hours. She was stiff and achy not only from working in the bog the previous day, but from the tension caused by finding Culbert's body and everything that had happened since.

Jeff said he could manage the day's harvest without her. They still had several weeks of work ahead of them. Sassamanash Farm was forty-two acres, and each of the bogs was approximately an acre in size. Most cranberries were grown in five states—Massachusetts, Wisconsin, New Jersey, Oregon and Washington—and Sassamanash Farm was one of the few farms in Michigan. The majority of the berries went to a cooperative owned by the farmers themselves. Jeff was very proud to be one of their growers.

Jeff had been able to replace the missing Mauricio easily enough. He had been convinced that Mauricio would reappear, but Monica hadn't felt as positive. Fortunately, there were always people looking for work when the summer tourist season ended.

Monica brewed some coffee, microwaved a bowl of oatmeal and, while she ate, began measuring out flour, sugar and butter for another batch of muffins and scones. By the time they were ready for the oven, the sky had lightened, and it was nearly eight o'clock.

With the baked goods in the oven, she set to work on the

salsa—chopping the cranberries in the food processor and seeding and mincing the jalapenos. Some of the oil from the peppers got on her fingers, and when she touched her eye, it stung mightily. Tears rushed to her eyes, and for a moment Monica felt like crying in earnest. She had come to Sassamanash Farm to flee her abysmal failure as a small businesswoman, as well as her heartbreak over her fiancé's death. And now everything seemed to be in jeopardy again.

Monica squared her shoulders. No use in thinking about that now. She had a job to do. She had to help Jeff save Sassamanash Farm. Only then would she feel able to think about her own future.

Monica left the scones and muffins out to cool while she took a shower, ran a comb through her tangle of curls and threw on a pair of clean jeans and a sweatshirt. By the time she'd wrapped up the baked goods and packaged the salsa, it was nearly nine o'clock. Fortunately the store was rarely busy before lunchtime.

With her woven basket slung over her arm, Monica made her way toward the Sassamanash Farm store. It was turning into a beautiful morning, with the early clouds blown away by a brisk breeze, revealing crystal clear blue skies. Monica breathed deeply as she walked the well-worn path to the store. The air smelled of autumn leaves and damp earth with faint but tantalizing notes of wood smoke.

The police had roped off an area around the bog where Culbert's body had been found, but it was business as usual everywhere else. Monica expected the visitor's parking lot to be empty at this hour but was astonished to find it full. Some, not finding a parking space, had even driven up onto the grass alongside the macadam.

Lauren was leading a group of sightseers toward the wagons that would take them to the bog where Jeff and his crew were working that day. Monica could hear them asking about the body as they passed.

*Ghouls*, she thought, as she pushed open the door to the store. Still, there was very little real excitement to be had in Cranberry Cove, save for the odd boat running out of gas outside the harbor and needing a tow by the coast guard, or Tempest Storm scandalizing the town by holding a yoga class on the village green. She could hardly blame them for wanting to get in on as much of the action as they could.

Monica was even more astonished to find the store packed with people. They were standing three deep at the counter. Yesterday's supply of baked goods was completely depleted and a number of people were clutching tea towels, oven mitts and place mats. It seemed as if everyone wanted a little piece of Sassamanash Farm.

Darlene was behind the counter working a piece of gum with more intensity than she put toward anything else. Monica could hear it snapping and popping all the way over to the door. She could sense the impatience of the customers as they waited for Darlene to ring them up. She pressed each key on the cash register so tentatively it was as if she had never worked one before.

Monica plastered a smile on her face and slid behind the counter with Darlene.

"Next?" she called, holding out a hand for the products a middle-aged woman in a tracksuit clutched to her chest.

The woman handed over a set of matching place mats and napkins. She smiled tentatively at Monica.

"Were you here when . . ." she began.

Monica hesitated. She didn't want to encourage gossip so she shook her head.

"No. And I'm afraid it wasn't much of anything. Just an unfortunate accident."

The woman's face fell and her glance drifted over to where Darlene was in an animated conversation with a woman. Monica could tell her customer was disappointed that Monica wasn't as willing to chat.

The crowds continued all morning and into the afternoon. All of the muffins and scones Monica had baked were gone, as well as the cranberry salsa, and their stock of cranberry-decorated items was considerably lower. Monica would have to place an order as soon as possible.

She was rearranging the remaining items when the door opened, and Gina walked in, tottering, as usual, on a pair of stiletto-heeled black suede boots. She obviously hadn't slept well, and her hair looked as if she'd barely run a comb through it.

She grabbed Monica by the arm. "Is there any news?" She tightened her grip, making Monica wince. "I didn't get a wink of sleep last night from worrying. Poor Jeffie. What is this going to do to him?"

Monica glanced around the store. Darlene was staring at Gina with such intensity that Monica was surprised her stepmother didn't burst into flames.

"Let's go outside." Monica jerked her head in Darlene's direction.

She pulled open the door and shivered at the blast of cold air. The wind ruffled her sweatshirt and blew bits of hair around her face.

"What is it?" Gina asked, her eyes nearly popping. "Is it good news?"

Monica made a face. "Not really, but it is a lead. I talked to Mauricio last night—he claims he has an alibi for the time of Culbert's death. He said he was down at Flynn's, drinking."

Gina snorted. "That's easy enough for him to say, but can he prove it?"

"I don't know. But I think I need to tell Detective Stevens about this because if I don't I'm sure it would be considered withholding evidence."

Gina grabbed Monica's arm. "But if they find out Mauricio doesn't have work papers, Jeffie will get in trouble. You heard what he said."

Monica hesitated. "I suppose there's no reason we can't go down to Flynn's and check with the bartender and the waitresses ourselves. If Mauricio was there, someone may remember. Anyone out of the ordinary sticks out like a sore thumb around here."

Gina's eyes lit up. "Let's go tonight. I'll come by around seven o'clock and pick you up."

Monica wished she could share Gina's excitement about the evening's activity. She ate a quick dinner and changed into a pair of dark slacks and a turtleneck sweater. She hoped Jeff wouldn't stop by—she didn't want to tell him where they were going. He wouldn't like it.

The front doorbell rang at ten minutes after seven. Monica pulled it open and gasped. Gina was wearing a skintight miniskirt, a fitted angora sweater cut down to *there* and thigh-high faun-colored suede boots. Her hair was piled on top of her head with a studied casualness that probably took three hours to achieve, and her eyelashes were thick, dark and an inch long.

"You're not going to wear that!" they both said at the same time.

Gina sniffed. "What's wrong with my outfit? We want to get these men talking, don't we? There's nothing like a big dose of sex appeal to loosen a man's tongue."

"But Flynn's is more tavern than nightclub."

Gina pursed her glossy lips. "And what do you think you're going to get out of them dressed like a . . . a," she swept a hand toward Monica, "a nun."

"What?" Monica looked down at herself. She was perfectly presentable—pants nicely ironed with a sharp crease, clean sweater, polished brown loafers. She'd even put in a pair of gold earring studs Jeff had given her for Christmas back when he was in high school.

"We're going to Flynn's to get information, not a date," Monica protested.

Gina put a hand on her cocked hip. "It wouldn't hurt you to have a date once in a while, would it? Not that you're going to find one at Flynn's, but don't you think Ted has been gone long enough? Time for you to get on with your life."

"I don't know. . . ."

"Look, Monica. You and Ted weren't exactly a match made in heaven, you know. You like to read, and the only thing he ever read was the sports page. Your idea of a good time is an evening in watching an old movie on television, and he was a party animal. He was a daredevil and you're . . . not."

That last part was true, Monica thought. Ted liked taking chances. They were on vacation when he ignored the red warning signs on the beach and insisted on going swimming. He was caught in a riptide and never made it back to shore.

"You're a beautiful woman. I can't understand why you don't make more use of it."

Monica ducked her head. "I was never any good at flirting. Besides, I was taller than all the boys in middle school, and by the time they were at least my height, they were used to ignoring me."

"We're going to change that and make sure no one ignores you tonight." Gina put down her purse, slipped out of her black leather jacket and pushed up her sleeves. "Let's go see what's in that closet of yours."

Monica meekly followed Gina as they climbed the steep stairs to the second floor. Gina glanced around the bedroom, and Monica was glad she'd taken the time to pull up the comforter and fluff the pillows.

Gina made a beeline for the closet and pulled open the door. "Oh," she cried in dismay when she saw the contents.

"I didn't need a lot of clothes when I was running Monica's," Monica said defensively. "I wore an apron all day long."

"Still," Gina hissed. "You should have at least one *wow* outfit. You never know when you'll need it."

Gina clicked through the hangers in Monica's closet and heaved a giant sigh. She ruffled through the garments on the shelves and finally pulled out a V-neck sweater. She shook it out and regarded it thoughtfully.

"I guess this will have to do."

"I have the blouse that I wear with it—"

"No, no." Gina shook her head vigorously. "Just the sweater."

"But it's rather low-cut." Monica pointed to a spot on her chest.

"That's the point. You need to show a little skin."

"I don't think I'm comfortable—"

"Do you want to get this information or not?"

Monica wordlessly took the sweater, turned her back and pulled off her turtleneck. She slipped the V-neck over her head and turned around to show Gina.

"Much better. Now how about something to fill in the neckline a little?"

"A scarf?" Monica asked hopefully.

"No, absolutely not. I'm thinking a necklace of some sort. Something to catch the eye."

Monica dug through the drawer where she kept her jewelry—the bits and pieces Ted had given her and some costume stuff she'd bought at a jewelry party hosted by a good friend.

"What's this?" Gina pounced and pulled out a multi-strand necklace of iridescent crystal beads.

Monica wrinkled her nose. "That was my grandmother's. You don't think—"

"I do. Turn around and let me put it on you."

Gina fastened the clasp, spun Monica around and stood back to admire the effect.

"It's perfect. Now to do something with your hair and makeup."

Monica groaned. She didn't wear much makeup—a bit of powder, some lipstick and a touch of mascara, and she was done. If it weren't for Jeff . . .

Gina whipped a number of cosmetics from her Coach bag and set to work. Fifteen minutes later she stood back to admire the effect.

"Amazing."

"Amazing in a good way?" Monica asked. Her face felt stiff from the powder and foundation.

"A very good way. Go look."

Monica stood in front of the mirror over the dresser and slowly opened her eyes. She stifled the gasp that was her first reaction.

She actually looked . . . good. Her green eyes really stood out, and the smattering of freckles across her nose were gone. Her cheeks looked almost as hollow as a supermodel's. Her hair was piled on top of her head with some artfully arranged strands framing her face. Gina had truly worked magic. She felt like Cinderella ready for the ball. She had to remind herself they weren't headed to the ball, they were going to Flynn's— from what she'd been told, it was a rather seedy bar down by the harbor that was frequented by hardcore drinkers.

Gina glanced at her watch. "Come on, let's get going. Flynn's should be in full swing by now."

In something of a trance, Monica followed Gina out to her Mercedes and slid into the passenger seat.

The drive through town seemed shorter than usual, although it could have been because of Gina's complete and total disregard for the posted speed limits. Monica clung to her seat as they rounded corners on two wheels and shot down hills with the velocity of a roller coaster. They crested the drawbridge that spanned the inlet into the harbor, turned down a street that was little more than an alley and just as dark, and pulled up in front of the bar.

Flynn's gave the term *dive* new meaning, Monica thought as she got out. The only window was a small one set in the door, but the glass was so yellowed by decades of grime and cigarette smoke that it was impossible to see through it.

Monica closed her eyes and held her breath as Gina pulled open the door.

The room was dimly lit, but Monica could easily see that every single head in the place had swiveled in their direction. The customers stared openmouthed as Monica and Gina walked inside and made their way to the bar.

# Chapter 7

Flynn's smelled of stale beer, decades-old cigarette smoke that had seeped into the walls, and industrial strength cleaner. A handful of men lounged at the bar while others were scattered among the battered and scarred wooden tables and chairs. A dartboard hung on one wall and a Playboy calendar and an old poster for Marlboro cigarettes on the other. There was no other decor.

Monica and Gina were the only women in the place. The men were nursing either beers or shot glasses of whiskey or, in some cases, both. The bartender was a big guy with a belly that nearly obscured his belt. He was leaning on the bar and watched as Monica and Gina approached.

Several men began drifting in Gina's direction, and a few even looked Monica over, as if she were a prize piece of livestock at the county fair. It wasn't something she was accustomed to, and she wasn't sure she liked it. She signaled for the bartender. The sooner they got out of here the better.

By now men were clustered around Gina, offering to buy her a drink and vying for her attention. The bartender ambled over to where Monica was waiting impatiently.

"Help you?" he said economically, taking a swipe at the counter with a dingy gray rag.

Monica shuddered at the thought of touching anything in this place let alone actually having a drink. Besides, she doubted chardonnay was on the menu.

"I wanted to ask you about someone who says he was in here drinking all night last night. His name is Mauricio. Dark hair, about so tall." Monica held her hand slightly above her head.

The bartender sensed excitement and his eyes lit up. "You gals undercover cops or something?" He leaned his elbows on the counter, the edge of the bar pressing into his ample abdomen.

Monica shook her head, desperately trying to think of a good reason why she was asking these questions. "I'm his Alcoholics Anonymous sponsor," she said finally, blushing at the implication.

The bartender whistled. "I didn't know he had a drinking problem. Comes in here pretty regularly and rarely has more than one beer. Although last night he was really knocking them back. Three shots of whiskey followed by a couple of Buds."

He swished the gray rag around in front of Monica again, and she got a whiff of disinfectant mixed with alcohol.

"He seemed . . . I don't know . . . kind of upset I guess you'd say."

"Upset?"

"Yeah. Spooked almost. Of course he was always looking over his shoulder, expecting to see immigration hot on his heels."

"Immigration? Why?"

"I suspect it was because of his papers . . . or lack of papers. He worked for Sam Culbert. Culbert paid him under the table, and whenever Mauricio complained about the pay, the hours, the conditions . . . I don't know, whatever . . . Culbert would threaten to turn him in to the authorities. Kept him running scared, that's for sure."

Someone at the other end of the bar called for a refill, and the bartender ambled over to where the man was sitting.

Had Culbert, unlike Jeff, used Mauricio's illegal alien status against him? Maybe Culbert had threatened to turn Mauricio in one time too many and Mauricio had killed him. Thoughts were swirling around and around in Monica's head. But if Mauricio had been at the bar all night . . . She glanced over at Gina, but Gina was engrossed in a conversation with a man who barely looked older than Jeff.

Monica called out to the bartender as he passed her. "Was Mauricio here all night?"

The bartender shrugged. "Good part of it. Left around ten o'clock. Not quite steady on his pins, if you know what I mean."

"Do you know where he went after leaving here?"

"Probably to see his girlfriend. That was his usual routine." He jerked a thumb in the direction of the door. "She runs the bed-and-breakfast on the other side of the inlet. Primrose Cottage."

"Primrose Cottage."

"Yeah." He leaned his elbows on the bar again. "Sure I can't get you anything?"

Monica noticed his gaze drop to her chest, and she had to will herself not to tug her sweater up higher. Instead she shook her head and signaled to Gina that she was ready to go.

Gina disengaged herself from the group of men surrounding her and headed toward the entrance where Monica was now waiting.

They were about to leave when the door swung open and a man stumbled in. He looked to be in his late thirties. His thinning hair was slicked back with gel, and one too many buttons were open on his rumpled shirt.

He whistled when he saw Monica and Gina.

"I hope you lovely ladies aren't going? I'd like to buy you a drink." He pulled a wad of bills from his back pocket and signaled for the bartender.

"Actually, we are leaving," Monica said.

"Come on. Just one drink." He swayed slightly and grabbed for the back of a chair to steady himself.

"I really don't think so." Monica backed away.

"Hey, I bet I can guess how old you are," he said with a flourish of his right hand, like a magician conjuring a rabbit out of a hat.

He lurched toward Monica, and she took another step backward.

"And," he paused dramatically, glancing from Monica to Gina, "I bet I can guess how much you weigh." He ended the sentence with a burp.

"And I bet," Gina said, sticking her face inches from his, "I can guess why you're here alone." She grabbed Monica's arm. "Come on, let's go."

Monica needed no further encouragement. She pushed open the door and they burst outside.

"Scumbag," Gina called over her shoulder as the door swung shut.

Monica took a deep gulping breath of fresh air as they dashed toward Gina's car. "I feel like I need a shower now."

"I know what you mean. And I'm willing to bet Lothario there has a wife and kids waiting for him at home," Gina said.

They got into the car, and Gina put the key in the ignition.

"Did you find out anything?" Gina asked as she turned the key. "Any luck with the bartender? He was obviously quite taken with you."

"No, he wasn't," Monica insisted.

"Honey, if there's one thing I know, it's when a man's interested," Gina said as she put her key in the ignition. "And he was interested."

Monica shuddered. "Well, I wasn't."

"No, but it does go to show that you can get a man's attention if you try."

Monica's mind flashed to Greg Harper at the bookstore. Had he been interested in her and not merely polite because she was a potential customer? It was certainly food for thought.

"So is this Mauricio still our prime suspect or does he have an alibi?"

"Both," Monica said and Gina looked at her curiously. "The bartender says he was at Flynn's until ten o'clock, when he left for his girlfriend's."

"Any idea who that is?" Gina hesitated with her hand on the gearshift.

"She runs Primrose Cottage. It's a bed-and-breakfast on the other side of the inlet."

"Well, let's go then," Gina said as she peeled away from the curb with a roar.

• • •

Primrose Cottage was white with mauve trim that was only slightly weathered on the west side, where the sun hit it. It was dark when they pulled up in front except for a light spilling out one of the side windows.

Gina's heels made a clacking sound against the slate walk as they approached the large, screened, wraparound porch that enveloped the front of the Victorian cottage.

"Do you think anyone is here?" Monica asked doubtfully. "It's awfully dark."

"There's only one way to find out." Gina stepped up to the porch door and knocked on the frame. She frowned. "I don't think anyone is going to hear that. Maybe we should go around back?"

"Wait. There's a bell." Monica reached out and pushed it. They heard it peal inside the house.

Monica shivered and wrapped her arms around herself. She should have brought a jacket. September nights in Michigan could be quite chilly, especially near the lake.

A light came on just beyond the screened porch and a door opened. A woman stuck her head out and looked around.

"Yoo-hoo," Gina called from where they were standing.

The woman approached the screen door and opened it.

"I'm sorry, but we're closed." She swept an arm behind her, indicating the shrouded porch furniture. "We're only open on weekends in the fall."

Monica stepped forward. "We don't want to stay. We were hoping to talk to you."

A wary look came over the woman's face. She had faded

blond hair pulled back in a messy ponytail and looked to be a few years younger than Monica.

"What about?"

"Mauricio."

The woman's right hand jerked. "What about Mauricio?"

"Listen, can we come in?" Gina asked, putting a hand on the screen door. "It's getting cold out here."

"Sure." The woman reluctantly opened the door wider. "I'm Charlotte Decker by the way, but everyone calls me Charlie."

Monica and Gina introduced themselves as they followed her through the darkened porch and into the main part of the house.

"Why don't we go into the front parlor?"

Charlie led them into a room that looked as if it had been lifted straight from the nineteenth century.

Monica stopped and looked around. "How old is the house?"

Charlie smiled. "It's Victorian era. My great-great grandfather built it in 1863. Cranberry Cove barely existed at the time. But then Joshua Taylor built the first sawmill here, and the area began to boom. It was easy to ship lumber across Lake Michigan to bigger cities like Chicago and Milwaukee." She motioned to a tufted, velvet-covered settee. "Please, have a seat. Can I get you something to drink? Tea or coffee?"

"I'd love a cup of tea," Monica said as she perched on the edge of the sofa.

Charlie looked at Gina and raised her eyebrows. Monica devoutly prayed that Gina wouldn't ask to have hers spiked.

"Tea would be lovely," she said, and Monica breathed a sigh of relief.

They were quiet as they waited for Charlie to return. An

ornate clock on the marble mantelpiece ticked loudly in the silence.

Suddenly Gina poked Monica. "I have the feeling she has something to hide," she whispered.

"Really? I didn't think so," Monica whispered back.

"Honey, everyone has something to hide. Even you."

She leveled a glance at Monica, and Monica could feel her face getting warm. She didn't have anything to hide, did she? Then she remembered that time she had walked out of the grocery store with a package of steaks she hadn't paid for. They had been on the bottom of her cart, under her purse, and she hadn't noticed them as she went through the checkout line. She had vowed to go back and pay for the meat but never had.

Charlie came back at that moment with a tray holding a silver teapot and delicate china cups.

"You didn't have to go to so much trouble," Monica said, feeling guilty that their real agenda was to quiz Charlie about the whereabouts of her boyfriend the night Sam Culbert's murder took place.

"It's no bother. I'm used to it. People who stay here want the whole Victorian experience—tea in bone china cups, period furniture, plenty of porcelain figurines that have to be dusted almost daily, but a comfortable bed and a modern bathroom."

Charlie put the tray down on a small, marble-topped table.

"Is the furniture authentic?" Monica accepted the cup Charlie handed her.

"Most of it." Charlie pointed to the sofa Monica and Gina were sitting on. "That's a rosewood recamier that my great-great grandfather probably bought when he finished the house." She indicated two filigree-carved armchairs upholstered in red damask. "He probably bought those around the same time." She sat down and poured herself a cup of tea in a large mug with *I Love Cats* written on it.

She must have noticed Monica looking at it. "I'm something of a klutz, I'm afraid, so I leave the good china for the tourists to break." She took a sip of her tea. "Some of the furniture was my great-grandfather's. A couple of the pieces are from Baker and Kindle. They had factories in Grand Rapids, which is only about an hour from here." She smiled. "Well, an hour in one of today's cars. It must have taken them considerably longer in those days." She held out a plate toward Monica and Gina. "Would you like some?"

Monica helped herself to a piece of the pastry. "Mmmm, this is delicious," she said. The crust was flaky and the filling tasted of almonds. "What is it?"

"It's called banket." Charlie cradled her mug in her hands. "It's a traditional Dutch pastry. It's a must on any Dutch table at Christmastime, but the tourists enjoy it all year long."

They were quiet for a moment, then Charlie broke the silence. "So what was it that you wanted to ask me?"

Monica cleared her throat. She felt awkward probing into people's private lives. But if Jeff was to be freed from suspicion in Culbert's murder . . . She cleared her throat. "It isn't easy to explain."

"I usually find the beginning a good place to start," Charlie said, a smile hovering around her lips.

"Okay." Monica cleared her throat again. "You probably know that a body was found in one of the bogs at Sassamanash Farm."

Charlie nodded. "Mauricio told me."

Monica spread out her hands. "It's like this. Just before

the police arrived, Mauricio took off running. He obviously didn't want to have anything to do with them."

"For good reason." Charlie put her mug down and folded her arms across her chest.

"But you must see how guilty it makes him look."

"I thought we were supposed to be innocent until proven guilty in this country? Besides, why would the police jump to the conclusion that Mauricio had something to do with the murder?"

"Because the murdered man was Sam Culbert."

Charlie tilted her head to one side. "Who?" she asked with a puzzled look on her face.

Monica didn't doubt for a moment that she knew perfectly well who Sam Culbert was. "Sam Culbert ran my brother's farm while Jeff was overseas. Mauricio was working for him at the time. Supposedly he knew that Mauricio didn't have the proper papers."

"I'm surprised Mauricio didn't mention that to you," Gina said.

"Does your boyfriend tell you everything?" Charlie shot back.

"But if he has an alibi . . ." Monica looked at Charlie encouragingly.

"The bartender at Flynn's told us he was there a good part of the evening drowning his sorrows, and didn't leave until ten o'clock," Gina prompted. "Then he said Mauricio probably hightailed it down here to spend the rest of the evening with you."

"They think the murder was committed sometime between nine o'clock and midnight. So if he was with you after leaving the bar, that puts him in the clear."

A strange look crossed Charlie's face. It was so fleeting that afterward Monica thought she must have imagined it.

"He *was* with me. We had a bit of an argument, as a matter of fact. He was three sheets to the wind, and I was mad at him. It wasn't like him. I didn't need him charging around the place like a bull in a china shop." She pointed at a table full of fragile, porcelain figurines.

"But you didn't throw him out?" Gina jiggled her left foot restlessly.

"No. I made him drink a glass of water and take a couple of aspirin and then I sent him up to bed where he couldn't do any harm. When I checked on him an hour later, he was sleeping soundly."

"If he tells that to the police, he'll be in the clear." Monica put down her empty teacup carefully.

"If he goes to the police, he'll be deported," Charlie said, her lips set in a firm line. "He doesn't have a work visa and he's already overstayed his welcome."

"Isn't there some way . . ."

Charlie shook her head briskly. "No. We'll just have to ride it out until the police figure out who really did it."

*Not my brother*, Monica thought. She was almost positive that Jeff was innocent. There was just that one tiny kernel of doubt, but it nagged at her, and she knew it was going to keep her up at night.

# Chapter 8

As Monica had suspected would be the case, she didn't sleep well that night. She was worried about Jeff. The conversation she and Gina had had with Charlie kept running through her mind. She had the distinct feeling that Charlie had been lying to her about Mauricio. If they were a couple it would be natural for her to want to protect him. But how to prove it?

She rolled out of bed and took a hot shower—a short one; the boiler in the old cottage was obviously not very big—and headed down to the kitchen to begin her baking for the day. She planned to double the quantity she normally made in hopes that they would have as many customers as they'd had the day before. She was also making a special cranberry coffee cake that was proving to be a best seller.

The coffee cake came out of the oven looking perfect— golden brown on top with a liberal dusting of sugar mixed with chopped pecans and coconut. Monica inhaled the delicious scent as she set it on the counter.

By the time she had finished baking the cranberry scones, the coffee cake had cooled. She cut it into individual slices and arranged them on a platter. On impulse she grabbed a piece and put it on a plate to have with her mug of coffee.

Monica drank her coffee and ate her breakfast while she packed all the new stock she'd made into baskets. She peered out the window. The day was overcast and looked like rain. She tucked her folding umbrella into her purse and headed out.

Monica felt drops of moisture on her face as she walked the path from her cottage to the store. The cranberries in the bog nearest the path had already been harvested and the bog had been drained. Monica was able to see the tangle of cranberry vines that formed a canopy, as Jeff said it was called, on the sandy bottom.

The store wasn't open yet, and Darlene wasn't due for another fifteen minutes, so Monica enjoyed the peace and quiet as she went about setting up her baked goods.

Double swinging doors separated the store from the screening room behind it. Jeff pushed open one of the doors and stuck his head into the shop.

"Good morning."

Monica jumped. "You startled me. I didn't hear you." She followed Jeff into the large room, where machines whirred and hummed and cardboard boxes of cranberries with *Sassamanash Farm* printed on them were stacked against one wall. "I thought you'd be out at the bogs."

Jeff shook his head. "The crew can handle it. I've got to start getting the trucks emptied and the berries processed so we'll have room for today's harvest."

Monica frowned. "I imagine you must have a lot less than usual since the berries from that one bog are useless. Having a dead body floating in there . . ." She shivered.

Jeff nodded curtly and turned away abruptly.

"I mean, I imagine you had to discard that part of the harvest?"

"Sure. Of course. Of course we did. We'll have to absorb the loss of an acre of fruit."

Something in his voice struck a false chord with Monica, but she didn't pursue it. He looked as tired as she felt. The sanitary white coat he wore over his clothes was already speckled red from the berries. He went over to one of the machines and made an adjustment.

"What is that?" Monica watched as the berries made their way down a conveyor belt.

Jeff pointed toward the door that led to the outside. "The trucks pull up there. The berries are dumped into vats, where they're sprayed with water to clean them. Then they make their way along the conveyor to this machine." He rapped it with a knuckle. "This is known as a Bailey separator. It puts the berries to the bounce test. The berries are dropped through a compartment. The good ones will bounce over the four-inch partition. The bad ones will fall to the bottom to be discarded."

"That's amazing."

Jeff nodded. "Cranberries are fascinating. It's the air pocket inside that causes them to float that also makes them bounce. They say the method was devised by a grower from New Jersey called Peg-Leg John. He stored his berries in the loft in his barn but because of his wooden leg, he couldn't carry them down the ladder. So instead he poured them down. He noticed that the good berries bounced to the bottom while the damaged fruit stayed on the rungs. I don't know if it's true or not, but it makes a good story."

"It does." Monica was quiet for a moment. "Are you and Lauren doing anything tonight? I thought I might have you and Gina for dinner."

Jeff made a face. "I'm afraid it's over between me and Lauren." He turned away abruptly so that his back was to Monica.

"What happened? I thought you liked each other."

"We did. We do." Jeff turned and Monica could see him swipe at a tear. "But I liked her too much to let her get involved with a guy with a useless arm." He lifted his paralyzed arm with his good one. "And I have no idea if I'm going to be able to make a go of this farm." He scowled. "And now the police suspect me of murder." He shook his head. "It wouldn't be fair to her."

"But you don't know that—"

"Oh, she might not mind right away. Maybe not the first year or even the second. But five years down the road, when Sassamanash Farm has gone belly-up, and I can't get a job because I'm a cripple? How would she feel then? No, she's better off without me."

Monica didn't think so, but she held her tongue. This wasn't the time to talk to Jeff about it. After things settled down, she'd try to get him to see a counselor for a couple of sessions. There seemed to be a lot of things he needed to get off his chest.

She just hoped murder wasn't one of them.

Monica was halfway into town when the rain started up again. At first it was just a few fat drops, but it quickly intensified until she had to flick on her windshield wipers and turn on the window defogger. Her hand hovered over the button for heat. She pushed it and was grateful for the sudden rush of warm air. She wondered if Jeff and his crew would continue to harvest the berries in this rain. She suspected they would. The season for harvesting was short, and they had to take advantage of every minute of it.

She was heading to the drugstore to pick up a prescription for Jeff. He had a nasty cut on his hand, and the doctor had prescribed a course of antibiotics to ward off an infection.

By the time Monica pulled into a space in front of the Cranberry Cove Diner, it was raining heavily and the wind had picked up, sending the drops slanting sideways. Fortunately Monica still had her small folding umbrella in her purse. She pulled it out but then decided she hardly needed it to dash across the street. She wasn't like her mother, who always worried about getting her hair wet and ruining her set. Monica's hair was rarely ever more than a tangle of curls that she occasionally attempted to control by pulling them back into a ponytail.

The Cranberry Cove Drugstore was more general store than anything—like the old-time five-and-dimes. It sold greeting cards, small gift items and housewares alongside headache remedies and pills for acid indigestion.

Monica pushed open the door. On one of the end caps was a display of merchandise left over from the summer— brightly striped towels, a handful of colorful beach umbrellas, sand toys and beach balls—all reduced to half price. It was at odds with the rest of the store, which was already done up for Halloween with plastic pumpkins, creepy dangling skeletons and fake cobwebs. Along the far right wall was a counter where you could still get ice cream sundaes, banana splits and milkshakes in the summer and hot chocolate topped with whipped cream in the winter.

Monica made her way down a narrow aisle to the back of the store. Two women were standing by the prescription counter. Monica recognized them as locals although she didn't know their names.

The one woman had a rather loud voice, and Monica caught the tail end of her sentence. "Maybe he has post-traumatic stress disorder."

Monica stopped in her tracks and pretended to study a display of acne preparations. Were they talking about Jeff?

The other woman spoke. Her voice was softer, but Monica could still hear the words. "I'm sure he must have killed people in Afghanistan. Besides, Sam Culbert wasn't much liked by anyone."

"Not even his wife from what I've heard," the other one added.

"No doubt he did something to set the young man off like that. Or maybe he was having some kind of flashback. I've read that that's very common with these soldiers returning from overseas."

They *were* talking about Jeff! Monica wanted to plug her ears and run out of the store, but she stayed where she was.

The druggist handed the woman with the loud voice a small, white bag, and the two ladies moved away. Monica's heart was hammering fiercely as she approached the counter. She half expected the clerk to say something when she gave Jeff's name—he must have heard the women's conversation— but he merely turned away and went in search of her prescription.

Monica fled the drugstore as quickly as possible, stuffing the pills in their little white bag into the pocket of her coat. She had been planning to stop in at the Cranberry Cove Diner for a bowl of their famous chili, but she had lost her appetite. Did everyone in town think Jeff was a murderer?

She was crossing the street toward her car when she heard someone call her name. She looked up to see Greg Harper standing outside of Book 'Em, waving to her.

Monica wasn't sure she wanted to face him. Was he thinking what everyone else seemed to be thinking? But he waved her over, and she dashed under the awning that shaded the front of Book 'Em.

"Lovely day we're having, isn't it?" He smiled at Monica.

She felt her spirits lift a little. "Truly lovely." She laughed. "But fall is my favorite season, even with the rain."

Greg nodded. "It will be snowing soon enough, and then we'll all be complaining about that." He bent down and plucked a dead flower off the plant that stood in a terra-cotta pot by the front door. "Are you going to the fundraiser tomorrow night?"

"Fundraiser? I'm afraid I don't know anything about it."

"Hang on just a minute." Greg disappeared inside the shop and reappeared moments later with a slightly crumpled piece of paper in his hand. "Here's the flyer." He handed it to Monica. "It's a spaghetti supper in the Cranberry Cove High School gym to raise money for Charlie Decker's mother's medical bills. Probably not the sort of thing you were used to in Chicago."

Monica smiled. "You're right, but it sounds charmingly small town to me. Coincidentally, I just met Charlie yesterday. But only briefly. She didn't mention anything about her mother's illness."

"It's one of her mother's friends who's organized the whole event. Charlie is too proud to ask for help. She was taking care of her mother all by herself until some of the ladies from their church got together and pitched in to help her out. Charlie was run off her feet as it was keeping Primrose Cottage going." Greg pulled another dead flower off the batch of mums. "It was rough while Debbie—that's Charlie's mother—was going through chemo, but I gather this round is almost over for the moment, so there'll be some respite."

"That's too bad." Monica didn't know what to say. She felt sorry for Charlie and her mother, but she hardly knew them.

"Anyway." Greg tapped the paper Monica held in her hand. "All the details are there. It starts at six o'clock."

"It sounds like fun."

"Maybe I'll see you there?"

"Sure."

Monica waved as she turned to go back to her car. She didn't exactly have a date, but that was certainly as close as she'd come to one since Ted had died.

# Chapter 9

By the time Monica was on her way back to Sassamanash Farm, the rain had stopped, the sky to the west was brightening and puddles gleamed in the rays of sun peeking through the scattering clouds.

She pulled into the parking lot by the farm store, pleased to see that it was quite full. She hoped Darlene was coping okay—she seemed to get flustered if there were more than two people in the shop at a time.

A dark car was pulled up almost onto the grass bordering the building. It looked vaguely familiar to Monica, but she couldn't place it, and she couldn't imagine why the driver didn't park in one of the spaces like everyone else.

She opened the door to the shop to find the small space crowded with people, and a line forming in front of the cash register. Despite the cool temperatures, Darlene's face glowed red and shone with perspiration. Monica could sense the impatience of the customers waiting as Darlene care-fully punched in each number on the cash register, her lower lip caught between her teeth, her brows clenched in concen-tration.

It looked as if Monica had arrived just in time. If the store was going to continue to be this busy, she would either have to spend more time there helping out or they'd have to hire someone part time. She just hoped that the sales would jus-tify the extra expense.

"I'm sorry you've had to cope with this all by yourself," Monica said, taking a place behind the counter and reaching for the purchases of the next person in line.

Darlene pushed a strand of hair off her damp face and nodded. Her eyes and nose were red, as if she'd been crying.

Monica smiled at a woman wearing a red turtleneck and a yellow slicker who handed her two jars of cranberry salsa. The woman pointed toward the bakery case. "And I'll take three of those gorgeous cranberry muffins if you don't mind."

"My pleasure." Monica smiled, pleased by the compliment, and slid open the door to the case. She grabbed a sheet of glass-ine, her hand hovering over the muffins. "Will these three do?"

The woman nodded and smiled at Monica. "I can't wait to have them with my morning coffee."

Monica selected three plump muffins and placed them in a white paper bag. "Bon appétit as the French would say."

"Is everything okay?" Monica whispered to Darlene as she rang up the woman's items.

Darlene sniffed and nodded curtly. "It's just that . . ." she began the moment Monica turned away.

Monica swiveled back toward Darlene and tried to put a

receptive look on her face. She was far more worried about all the customers still waiting in line.

Darlene sniffled and swiped a hand across her nose. "It's just that today is the two-month anniversary of my dear mother's, may she rest in peace, death."

"I am so sorry." Monica put a hand on Darlene's arm. "I had no idea."

"It's okay. It was before you got here."

"What happened?" Monica asked in a low voice as she smiled at the next person in line and put out a hand for their purchases.

"Heart attack. Mother didn't have any insurance, and we couldn't afford doctors. The doctor said that the heart attack was just waiting to happen." She gave a loud sniff.

Monica patted Darlene's arm again and silently vowed to be more patient with her in the future. "Would you like to go home? I think I can handle this." She motioned toward the people waiting in line.

Darlene shook her head. "I'll be okay. It's just hard for me sometimes."

Monica gave Darlene an encouraging smile, squeezed her arm again and turned her attention toward her customer, an older woman with a tight gray perm.

"I don't suppose you have any more of the cranberry coffee cake left?"

Monica looked in the case. The platter that had held the coffee cake was empty except for a few crumbs. She shook her head. "I'm afraid it's all gone. Would you like some scones instead?"

"Are they as good as the coffee cake?"

"I certainly hope so. I make them both."

"Fine. I'll take two of those then."

The double swinging door to the processing area opened, and Jeff stuck his head out.

"Monica? Could you come in here, please?"

He looked worried, Monica thought. What was going on?

"Can you manage by yourself for a minute?" she asked Darlene.

A look of panic crossed Darlene's face, but she nodded yes.

"I'll only be a minute, I'm sure."

As soon as Monica walked into the screening room behind Jeff, she realized whose car she had recognized outside. Detective Stevens was perched on a desk chair Jeff had wheeled out from the office for her.

She gave Monica a brief smile. "I'm sorry to interrupt your workday. But I need to get this case wrapped up as soon as possible." She indicated her belly with a rueful smile. "For more reasons than one."

Monica was too tense to even smile at the joke.

Stevens looked toward Monica. "I understand you were helping your brother with the cranberry harvest when the body was found, correct?"

Monica nodded. Her mouth had suddenly dried up, and her tongue was sticking to the roof of her mouth.

"You had a crew member by the name of Mauricio." It was a statement, not a question. "I also understand that this Mauricio took off before the police arrived on the scene."

Jeff looked as uncomfortable as Monica felt. He gave a small nod.

"And yet nobody thought to mention it to me?"

Monica cleared her throat. "We were all in shock. I'm sure you can understand that." She wasn't about to let this detective browbeat them, even if she and Jeff had been in the wrong. Monica shot a glance at Jeff then turned back to Stevens. "How did you . . ."

Stevens frowned. "I'm afraid I can't say. But I'm hoping you can give me some information. We're trying to track this Mauricio down. It's quite possible he's completely innocent, but until we talk to him, we can't rule him out as a suspect. Do you have his address? Has he been back to the farm here?"

Jeff ran a hand across his forehead. "No, he hasn't. And I'm afraid I don't know where he lives. All I have is his name and social security number."

Stevens raised her eyebrows.

Jeff shrugged. "We hire a lot of seasonal help. Some of them may not have a permanent address."

Stevens looked doubtful but didn't press the point. Monica almost opened her mouth to say something about Charlie Decker, but bit her tongue.

"Do you have any idea why Mauricio would be trying to avoid the police?"

Jeff quickly shook his head, and Monica hoped her face wasn't turning red. She figured it wouldn't be too long before Stevens put two and two together. She was obviously a bright woman.

Stevens looked from one to the other of them and then began to struggle to her feet.

"I hope you will be in touch if you hear from Mauricio." She handed them each a business card.

"We will," Monica assured her as she tucked the card into the pocket of her jeans.

Stevens nodded and made her way to the door.

The interview left Monica with a decidedly unsettled feeling. Was it because she knew more than she had admitted to the detective? She was definitely going to make a clean breast of it eventually. But if Stevens continued to focus on Mauricio, then she would leave Jeff alone. And Monica would have the chance to do a little investigating of her own.

Monica had invited Gina and Jeff for dinner that evening, but Gina had insisted on taking them to the restaurant at the Cranberry Cove Inn instead—her treat.

Monica pulled a deep green knitted dress from the back of her closet. She had a pair of black suede boots she'd purchased on impulse after seeing them in the window of a shop on Chicago's Magnificent Mile. That was when she was still with Ted, and their dates had often included fancy, five-star restaurants.

The dining room at Cranberry Cove Inn was as close as Cranberry Cove came to having a five-star restaurant. Monica hadn't been yet, but she'd heard people talking about it. Tourists dined there regularly—locals only went for special occasions like engagements, silver wedding anniversaries and fiftieth birthdays. And most of them avoided the place during tourist season, when they were apt to feel out of place despite the fact that the Inn was in their own backyard.

The Inn dated from the late 1800s, when tourists first discovered Cranberry Cove. It had been added on to and shored up many times in the intervening years. Some of the additions had been more successful than others. The main part of the Inn was white with black shutters and had a picket fence running along the front. It stood on a bluff above the lake and had a commanding view of the water.

Gina roared up to Monica's cottage in her Mercedes, half an hour late. She was in one of her over-the-top outfits with a short skirt, plenty of cleavage and her hair in its usual casual, but artfully arranged, disarray.

"Jeffie, darling, you don't mind driving, do you? I always think it's peculiar to see a car pull up with a woman driving when there's a perfectly capable man riding shotgun."

"No problem."

Jeff slid behind the wheel, and Monica thought he looked uncomfortable in his unaccustomed sport coat and tie.

Fifteen minutes later, Jeff pulled up in front of the Cranberry Cove Inn. The Inn boasted valet parking so Jeff handed the keys to an attendant in a short black jacket and white shirt.

"You be careful with my car, now," Gina called after him as he got behind the wheel of her Mercedes.

Monica couldn't help but notice Jeff wince slightly. Gina's perfume left a trail behind her as they followed her into the lobby, where one of the staff immediately came rushing forward.

"Good evening, Mrs. Albertson. How are you tonight?"

Monica felt the jolt she always did at someone other than her mother being called *Mrs. Albertson*.

"We've got reservations in the dining room," Gina said. "Although I'm afraid we're a wee bit late." She pouted prettily.

"No problem. The maître d' is holding your table. If you'll come this way."

The young man escorted them to the door of the dining

room and, with a flourish, turned them over to the care of the maître d'.

The maître d' led them to a table for four, which was strategically situated in front of a large window that overlooked the lake. If it hadn't been overcast, they would have had a beautiful view of the last rays of the sun as it set over Lake Michigan. Lights were coming on along the promenade that ran the length of the beach in back of the hotel, and they twinkled in the twilight.

"Isn't this nice? All of us together," Gina said as she took her seat.

Jeff ran a finger around the collar of his shirt and smiled wanly.

A waiter appeared to take their drink order, and Gina ordered a bottle of champagne.

The waiter reappeared in minutes bearing a silver ice bucket on a stand. The neck of a bottle of expensive champagne poked out the top. He set it down, deftly removed the cork and filled their glasses.

As soon as the waiter was finished, Gina raised her flute in a toast. "Here's to my new venture," she said before taking a sip of her drink.

Jeff choked slightly on his champagne. "New venture?"

Gina nodded. "Yes. I've really gotten to like it here in Cranberry Cove, and I don't have anything tying me to Chicago anymore."

By now Jeff was beginning to look really alarmed, and Monica, too, felt a sense of unease. They exchanged surreptitious glances.

"So I've decided to stay here." Gina punctuated her announcement with a sip of her drink.

"You mean for a couple of weeks?" Jeff asked hopefully.

Gina shook her head. "No. Permanently."

"But what will you do?" Monica asked, thinking of all the things that Gina was used to having at her disposal in a big city like Chicago.

Gina waggled her finger at them playfully. "I'm going to open an aromatherapy shop."

For a moment, Monica and Jeff sat in silence, stunned by Gina's announcement.

"What's aromatherapy?" Jeff asked, breaking the awkward pause.

"It's kind of hard to explain, but aromatherapy uses the scent of essential oils to bring harmony to the body and to make you feel good." Gina leaned forward, warming to her topic. "For instance, lavender relieves stress and is marvelous if you have a migraine. I absolutely swear by it when I get one of my headaches."

"But . . . but . . . where is this shop going to be?" Jeff fanned himself with the pages of his menu.

"You know that empty space down by the hardware store? I signed the lease today, and the carpenters begin work right away."

"This is so sudden," said Monica. The very thought of plunging into a venture like this with so little forethought made her panic. She could practically feel her throat closing up.

"You have to seize the moment." Gina picked up her menu. "Now, what are you all planning on ordering?"

They were halfway through the first course when one of the busboys approached Jeff.

"Aren't you living the high life tonight?" He slapped Jeff on the back.

Jeff's face broke into a broad smile. He jumped up from his seat and pumped the young man's hand. "Kevin! I didn't expect to see you here."

"And I sure didn't expect to see you," Kevin shot back.

Monica thought she had seen the young man before, but she couldn't place him. There was something about his curly blond hair that seemed familiar.

"Picking cranberries doesn't pay all that much," Kevin said with an impish glint in his blue eyes. "I have to moonlight."

Jeff hung his head. "I know. I wish I could pay you guys more, but until Sassamanash Farm is in the black . . ."

Kevin slapped Jeff on the back again. "It's alright, old man, don't worry about it. It's just that my girlfriend is out of work at the moment, and there's the rent to pay."

Jeff turned toward the table. "Gina, Monica, this is Kevin. He's on my crew at the farm."

Kevin nodded toward each of the women in turn. Suddenly Monica recognized him—he was the worker she had noticed who wore a knitted cap pulled down low over his curly blond hair.

"Didn't Ashley used to work here?" Jeff asked.

"Yeah. But that wretch Culbert got her fired."

Jeff's eyebrows shot up. Monica leaned closer so she could hear their conversation.

"She was having a bad night. Had stomach cramps and was coming down with a fever. She wasn't at her best. She accidentally spilled a drop of a drink on Culbert, and he was furious. Called the manager over—the whole show. Culbert insisted Ashley be let go. He's a big customer here—the manager didn't have any choice."

"I'm sorry to hear that."

Kevin shrugged. "She'll find something else. Maybe something better. She's a trained fitness instructor. There just isn't much call for them around here."

Kevin shot a look over his shoulder. He slapped Jeff on the back again. "I'll see you in the morning." He took off at a trot.

"He seems like a nice young man," Gina said.

They were quiet for a moment as they waited for the rest of their meal.

Monica had finally decided on the duck a l'orange. It wasn't something she ever made for herself, despite the fact that it was one of her favorite dishes.

Finally the waiter appeared, and slipped their entrees in front of them.

Gina lifted a forkful of salmon with dill sauce to her mouth. "It certainly seems that there were plenty of people out there with a reason to wish Sam Culbert six feet under."

"Let's talk about something else, alright?" Jeff threw his napkin down on the table. "Excuse me for a moment, please."

"Well!" Gina said as she watched Jeff walk away. She turned to Monica. "I hope you can be excited for me and my plans."

For a moment Monica couldn't find the words to respond. "Yes. Certainly."

Gina caught and held Monica's gaze. "It's just that there's nothing left for me in Chicago. I never planned to be a divorcee again at my age." She smiled ruefully. "I'm a little old to go back on the market. The only men who would be interested in me now are octogenarians, I'm afraid." She made a face. "And I can't bear being alone. Here I'd have you and Jeff."

Monica swallowed a piece of duck, and it went down the wrong way. She began to cough. She gulped some ice water.

Peg Cochran

"Of course we're pleased for you, Gina. And I'm sure we'll both enjoy having you here." The words stuck in Monica's throat much as the duck had done.

Gina beamed. "That's wonderful then!" She snapped her fingers and called for the waiter.

"Yes, ma'am," he said with a smile.

"Another bottle of champagne, please. We're celebrating."

# Chapter 10

Monica woke with a slight headache the next morning. That would teach her to overindulge in champagne. But it had been fun to get out for the evening and away from all the problems of Sam Culbert's murder, as well as the dwindling finances of Sassamanash Farm.

Sam Culbert's funeral was being held at St. Andrew's Episcopal church early that morning. Jeff felt he ought to go since he'd known Culbert and also because his absence would set tongues wagging. The townspeople didn't know Jeff had been cheated by Culbert, and he wanted it to stay that way. Not to protect Culbert's reputation, of course, but to keep people from realizing that Jeff had a good motive for Culbert's murder. Monica offered to go with him even though she'd never met Culbert, because she suspected Jeff could use some moral support.

Monica drove them in her Focus. The sun was shining,

which seemed at odds with the solemnity of the occasion. She glanced at Jeff, who looked just as uncomfortable in his jacket and tie as he had the previous night at dinner. His face was pinched, and she could see the muscle working in his jaw.

Beach Hollow Road was crawling with traffic, and their progress was slow.

Jeff pointed out the window. "Look at all these cars. You'd think it was the height of summer."

"I can't imagine sleepy little Cranberry Cove crowded with strangers."

Jeff turned to Monica. "You'll see when June gets here." His tone was ominous.

The parking lot was already filling up when they arrived at the church. For someone so disliked, it looked as if Culbert would have quite a crowd at his funeral.

St. Andrew's was set on a slight hill, back from the road, and surrounded by large trees that created a colorful canopy of red and yellow leaves over the old church's slightly leaky roof. A winding, badly cracked and uneven cement path led to heavy, ornate wood doors that had been thrown open for the occasion. Soft organ music drifted out as Monica and Jeff made their way up the path.

"Let's sit toward the back," Jeff whispered as they paused just inside the door.

An usher, whom Monica recognized as Bart Dykema from the butcher shop, came toward them. He looked odd without his white apron. He was wearing a black suit, and the buttons of his jacket strained against his ample stomach, as if he had purchased the suit when he was considerably slimmer. He led them to an empty pew.

Monica looked around the church. She was surprised to see

Darlene up front. But then she remembered that Darlene cleaned for the Culberts. Monica supposed she didn't want to miss the funeral. It looked as if everyone in Cranberry Cove had stopped what they were normally doing in order to attend.

Monica was reading through the program when she sensed someone sitting down beside her. She looked up to see the VanVelsen sisters sliding into the pew. Today they were wearing muted gray dresses and matching coats and hats.

Hennie smiled when she recognized Monica. "Quite a turnout, isn't it?"

"I'm rather surprised considering . . ." Monica hesitated.

"You mean considering Culbert wasn't very well liked?" Hennie shook her head. "Weddings, funerals, Fourth of July parades—anything that gives the residents of Cranberry Cove an opportunity to get together is going to be well attended." She waved a hand around the church. "I'm afraid all this has nothing to do with Sam Culbert."

There was a bit of a commotion at the front of the church, and Monica strained to see over the heads blocking her view. A woman was being led to the front pew. A tall, thin gray-haired man held her elbow solicitously. She slid into the pew, and he followed her.

Gerda touched Monica's arm. "There's Andrea Culbert, Sam Culbert's wife." She pointed to the woman. A handful of people had filed in behind the couple. "I wonder who that man is?"

Hennie leaned forward. "That must be her brother," she said with a hint of satisfaction in her voice. "You know Deirdre—she's the receptionist at the Cranberry Cove Inn?"

Gerda straightened her shoulders. "Of course I know Deirdre," she said, sounding slightly miffed. "Why wouldn't I?"

"I was talking to Monica," Hennie said with great dignity.

"Deirdre came in yesterday for a bag of those Swedish fish her sister likes, the poor thing. Her sister's been in a wheelchair ever since she had that accident in high school," she explained to Monica. "Deirdre told me that Andrea Culbert's brother had just arrived and had checked into the Inn."

Gerda scowled. "You didn't tell me that."

Hennie pulled her coat more closely around her shoulders. "I'm certain I did, dear. You just don't remember. You haven't been quite yourself lately."

Monica hid a smile. The VanVelsen sisters presented a united front to the world, but there was obviously some dissension between them in private.

Monica examined the woman who had been identified as Culbert's wife. Even from a distance, she could tell that Andrea's clothes were well made and expensive. Just then, Andrea raised a hand to her carefully coiffed hair, and the large diamond ring on her finger winked in the light coming through the stained-glass windows.

"I don't imagine she's any sorrier to see the end of Sam Culbert than the rest of us," Hennie whispered to Monica.

"Who? His wife?"

Hennie was about to answer when the organ music, which had been playing softly in the background, swelled, and the congregation rose to its feet. A hush settled over the crowd as a highly burnished wood casket was rolled down the aisle.

Hennie whispered in Monica's ear. "Culbert treated his wife very badly. Old Doc Hadley said one time he was called out to—" Hennie put a hand over her mouth. "I really shouldn't be telling tales out of school. Suffice it to say that any tears Andrea Culbert sheds will be crocodile tears."

• • •

Talk in the Sassamanash Farm store later that afternoon centered around Culbert's funeral and that evening's fundraiser—the spaghetti supper for Charlie's mother. To Monica, it sounded as if the whole town was going to be there, much as they had turned out en masse for Culbert's funeral. The event ought to bring in plenty of money for Debbie's medical bills.

Monica had been hoping to get Jeff to go with her. He needed to do something to take his mind off of everything that had happened, but he claimed he was too tired. He and his crew were still harvesting the crop and had several more bogs to do before the season would be over.

Gina had offered to pick Monica up, and Monica couldn't think of an excuse fast enough to say no. She just hoped Gina would wear something appropriate. Now that Gina was going to live in Cranberry Cove, she was going to have to give her wardrobe a makeover if she didn't want to stand out among the locals.

Then again, Monica had never known Gina to *not* want to stand out.

Gina arrived fifteen minutes late—early for her—and Monica was pleased to see that her outfit was at least partially appropriate. She was wearing her leopard-print trench coat but underneath she had on dark slacks and a bright red silk blouse. As far as Gina's outfits were concerned, this one was almost subdued enough for a funeral.

The supper was being held at the Central Reformed Church, where a lot of events in Cranberry Cove took place—from wedding receptions to funeral luncheons to meetings of the

Women's Garden Club. The church was a large, redbrick building just off the village green—as solid and stalwart as the members of its congregation.

Gina maneuvered her car down Beach Hollow Road. All the parking spaces were already taken, and cars lined the streets branching off from the village green.

"Looks like the whole town has turned out," Gina said as she went around the block again, hoping a space would appear.

"That's good news for Charlie, I guess."

"Oh, look." Gina pointed ahead of her, where there was an open space along the curb. She hit the gas, and they flew forward.

"Rats," Gina said when they got closer and noticed the bright yellow fire hydrant. "I have half a mind to park here anyway." But she continued slowly down the street, her eyes scanning the parked cars for an opening.

In the end they had to leave the car in the parking lot of the Cranberry Cove High School. It was a bit of a walk to the church, and Gina complained every step of the way.

"Maybe you should have worn different shoes," Monica finally said when Gina twisted her ankle on a bit of uneven pavement.

"I didn't realize we were going to have to hike to the supper," Gina shot back.

Monica was glad she'd worn loafers, and she was grateful for the pair of gloves she found tucked in the pocket of her jacket. The evening air was growing colder.

Finally they were in sight of the church.

"I wouldn't be doing this if it weren't for the fact that I'm about to open a business here," Gina grumbled. "I would have gladly settled for writing a check and sending it in, but I have to show the locals that I'm one of them."

Monica looked at Gina and her leopard-print coat, high-heeled peep-toe shoes and casually upswept hair and stifled a laugh. She had a feeling that Gina could live in Cranberry Cove for the next couple of centuries and still not fit in.

A handmade poster-board sign outside the church directed them around to the back, where a door was propped open and another handmade sign announced the spaghetti supper.

Monica and Gina descended the three cement stairs leading to the open door. Dried leaves were caught in the door well and crunched under their feet. The entrance led to another, longer set of stairs—metal with a bright red railing—that took them to the floor below.

Noise rose up the stairs to greet them—chattering voices, clattering plates and crying babies.

"Sounds like Kleinfeld's when they have their annual sale," Gina said as they paused in the open doorway.

It was a large room with windows placed high on the cinder block walls. Long tables were covered in white plastic cloths, with aluminum folding chairs placed as close together as possible around them. Another long table was set up at the back of the room in front of a pass-through to a kitchen. Several women stood behind it dishing out the evening's fare of spaghetti, salad and garlic bread on paper plates.

Monica and Gina hesitated in the entrance. Monica scanned the crowd for anyone they knew. The tables were crowded but there were still a few seats scattered here and there.

A woman with very dark hair, the sort of blue eyes that only came from colored contact lenses and bright red lipstick swept toward them. She was wearing a purple caftan and had a large crystal on a black silk cord around her neck. If possible, she looked even more out of place than Gina.

"You must be the new girl out at Sassamanash Farm," she said, shaking Monica's hand.

Monica was no longer surprised that everyone knew who she was. "Yes. I'm Monica." She turned to Gina. "And this is my stepmother, Gina."

The woman stuck out her hand to Gina. "Tempest Storm," she said in her deep voice. "I run Twilight, the New Age shop in town. I'm the town oddball, as I imagine you've already guessed." She smiled at them. "Welcome to Cranberry Cove."

She swept a hand around the room. "Looks like you'll get to meet all the locals at once. Sort of baptism by fire. They're not a bad bunch though—just suspicious of anyone who hasn't been here for at least three generations. Not that I blame them. Wait till summer when the tourists arrive from the four corners of the globe. We resent them at the same time we acknowledge we depend on their business." She fingered the crystal around her neck. "I hope you'll stop by the shop one day. We have yoga classes, too, if you're interested."

Monica made a noncommittal reply.

"There are some empty seats at my table. Why don't you join me?" She looked at Gina and smiled. "You look like a kindred spirit."

"I'd like to think so," Gina said. "I'm opening an aromatherapy shop. It's going to be down by the hardware store."

"You don't say?" Tempest said as they made their way through the packed tables.

Monica noticed more than one head swivel in their direction, following their progress across the crowded room.

A small boy with red hair and freckles came around the

corner full tilt and ran smack into Monica. A young woman in a faded flower-print dress was right behind him. She grabbed him by the strap of his overalls and pulled him to a halt. "Now, Freddie, apologize to the lady." She smiled shyly at Monica.

"That's okay—"

"No, no. He needs to learn to watch where he's going." The woman gave the boy a slight shake.

His face had turned bright red so that all his freckles looked as if they had blended together. "I'm sorry," he said, more to his shoes than to Monica.

"That's okay," Monica said again.

The woman beamed. "Good boy, Freddie. Now let's go get you some ice cream."

As soon as she let go of Freddie, he was off again as if he'd been catapulted from a slingshot. His mother gave Monica a rueful glance as she took off in pursuit.

They caught up with Tempest, who had turned to wait for them. "I'm right over there." She pointed to a table with three empty seats. "You go get your food, and I'll save you a place." She put a hand to her mouth. "I don't mean to strong-arm you. If you'd rather sit somewhere else, please feel free."

"We'd love to sit with you. Thanks for asking us."

Monica was glad of Tempest's invitation. She had been hoping to find Greg Harper there, but she didn't see him and was disappointed. Perhaps he had changed his mind about attending.

Monica and Gina joined the line of people waiting for their meal.

"I would still have rather sent a check," Gina whispered to Monica as they held out their plates.

A woman in an apron and a hairnet, her round face red

and perspiring, ladled a serving of spaghetti and meatballs onto each of their plates.

"Salads are over there. Help yourself." She looked up. "Oh. You're out at Sassamanash Farm, aren't you? How are you getting on? Got the crop harvested yet?"

Once again, Monica realized that living in a small town was not unlike living in the proverbial fishbowl.

"My brother is harvesting now."

"Got a good crop, has he?" The woman picked up a paper towel and wiped a spot of sauce off the tablecloth. She looked Gina up and down curiously. "We heard about the body." She put her hands on her hips and blew a piece of hair that had escaped from her hairnet off her forehead. "Not surprised. Nobody around here liked Sam Culbert. Threw his weight around if you know what I mean."

Monica nodded and smiled. "That's what I've heard."

"Practically everyone in town had a reason to want to see him six feet under. Especially that wife of his, poor thing."

"Really?" Monica could sense Gina's impatience to get moving, but she didn't want to lose any opportunity to learn more about Culbert.

The woman laughed. "I guess every woman would like to see her husband six feet under at some point. Still, we didn't expect Culbert to come to such an untimely end." She gave another laugh that shook her ample belly. "That enough for you?" She gestured toward Monica and Gina's plates.

Monica looked at the generous serving. "Plenty, thank you."

The woman nodded and reached for her spoon to serve the next person in line.

"Looks like everyone knows you already," Gina said as they heaped salad onto their plates.

"That's small town living for you."

A slightly worried look creased Gina's brow and was immediately gone. She probably didn't want to wrinkle her forehead, Monica thought. It was unnaturally smooth as it was, and Monica strongly suspected that Botox had been involved.

They made their way through the crowded room and back toward where Tempest was sitting.

They had just settled in with their plates when Tempest turned to Gina. "So you're opening an aromatherapy shop? It will be interesting to see what the locals make of that. I don't think a single one of them has ever darkened the doorway of Twilight. I'm sure they think I have two heads and cast spells turning men into toads." She laughed. "Although that's not such a bad idea if you ask me." She shook her head. "Even the yoga classes scare them, although I have a small but loyal following. I've assured the few others who have dared to ask about them that there's nothing necessarily mystical or pagan about twisting yourself into downward facing dog or triangle pose. If it were a couple of centuries ago, I'm sure they'd have burned me at the stake by now."

"Why stay in Cranberry Cove then?" Monica put her napkin in her lap.

Tempest leaned back in her chair and folded her hands on top of the table. "It's a long story. Short version—I spent the last three years caring for my mother. When she finally passed away, I wanted something completely new and different. I liked the idea of living by the lake, the shop was available and . . ." She spread her hands open. "Here I am. And you? I've heard you've come to help your brother with the farm."

Monica nodded.

"Do you think you'll put down roots here permanently?"

"I honestly don't know at this point."

"And what brings you here?" Tempest turned to Gina.

Gina patted her lips with her napkin. "The usual. Divorce. Finding myself at loose ends. Wanting to be near my son." She frowned. "I hope I've made the right decision." Gina looked around the room. "I must say, the people here sure do help their own."

Monica nodded. "It looks like they're going to raise a lot of money."

"It will help. But these suppers don't really bring in all that much money. Not when you consider the work involved. I tried to tell Karla that, but she didn't want to listen."

Tempest must have noticed the blank look on Monica's and Gina's faces.

"Karla organized the whole affair. She's Debbie's oldest friend. They met in the womb, or so they would like you to believe, and haven't been apart since. Organizing is what Karla does best. She'd organize the leaves falling off the trees in the fall if it were possible." She shrugged. "At least it looks as if we're making an effort to help, and I suppose that's what counts." She speared the last meatball on her plate, then glanced up at Monica and Gina. "I hope it isn't all in vain."

Monica stopped with a forkful of salad halfway to her mouth. "What do you mean?"

"They had to rush Debbie to the hospital the other night. I was still at the shop putting out some new stock when I heard the ambulance go screaming past. Charlie's beat-up old van wasn't far behind."

Monica was very still. "When was this?"

"Oh." Tempest blew out a puff of air. "It was the night before Culbert's body was found. I remember thinking about that old saying that things come in threes. I couldn't help but wonder what would be next."

"Do you remember what time it was?"

"Around ten o'clock maybe?" Tempest pushed her empty plate away. "I live above the shop—it isn't fancy but it sure is convenient. It was after midnight when I heard Charlie on her way home. That old rattletrap she drives makes a heck of a noise. I'd just turned off the television and was getting ready for bed when I heard it clanking and screeching down the street loud enough to wake the dead."

Monica and Gina exchanged glances. If what Tempest said was true, and Charlie was at the hospital with her mother that night, then Mauricio didn't have an alibi. Who was to say he didn't sober up long enough to leave Primrose Cottage, drive out to Sassamanash Farm and murder Culbert?

# Chapter 11

Monica and Gina lingered at the table even after Tempest had excused herself and left for home. The noise level in the room had diminished slightly and people were sitting with their empty plates pushed away from them, their elbows on the table, enjoying quiet conversation with those around them. It was obvious no one was in any hurry to leave. Monica had the sense that they were waiting for something.

Gina turned to Monica. "How do you suppose Mauricio knew that Sam Culbert was going to be out at the farm?"

"He didn't have to. Mauricio could have called Culbert himself and told him he had something important to discuss with him and could they meet out at Sassamanash."

Gina pursed her lips. "I suppose it's possible. It seems like a strange place to meet someone at night." She shivered. "It would certainly creep me out."

"But not the two of them. They were both familiar with

116

the farm, and they knew no one would see them there. Mauricio wouldn't want anybody to know about their meeting. Especially if he planned on killing Culbert. You've already seen how nosy a small town can be."

Gina straightened the collar on her silk blouse. "That's for sure."

A clanking noise came from the far corner of the room, and they both turned in that direction. The huge pots of spaghetti had been cleared from the table, and a very tall and robust-looking gray-haired woman was setting up a couple of deep fryers in their place.

"What do you suppose those are for?" Gina wrinkled her nose.

Monica shrugged. "I have no idea, but I suppose we'll find out soon enough." She smiled. "This has been fun, don't you think?"

"I suppose so. The pasta couldn't hold a candle to the farfalle with Bolognese sauce at La Traviata though."

Monica laughed. "I don't imagine it could. But I like the feeling of community. It's nice after being anonymous for so long in Chicago. Even the people who came to Monica's on a regular basis rarely ever acknowledged that we recognized each other."

Someone got up from one of the tables—a man with a very broad back in a plaid flannel shirt with the sleeves rolled up. Monica peered through the gap his absence had created.

"Oh, there're the VanVelsen sisters."

"The who?" Gina looked in the direction Monica was pointing.

"The VanVelsen twins. They own Gumdrops, the candy shop on Beach Hollow Road."

Gina squinted into the distance. "My goodness, the two of them look exactly alike!"

"They're identical twins."

"I thought I was seeing double," Gina said, echoing the reaction that Monica had had on her first visit to Gumdrops.

"I'm going to go over and say hello. Do you want to—"

Gina was already shaking her head. "I'll wait for you here. To be honest with you, I'm starting to get a headache."

"I'm sorry. Should we—"

Gina shook her head again. "No, no, I'll be fine. I'll pop a couple of aspirin while you go talk to your friends."

Monica felt a little guilty about leaving Gina behind at the table, but if she was going to fit into the community at Cranberry Cove, she had to take every opportunity to cement friendships.

The VanVelsen sisters were in their usual pastel-colored matching outfits—pale lavender tonight. Although, for the first time since Monica had met them, their faces didn't look exactly alike: Hennie looked much the same as usual but there were lines of fatigue on Gerda's face that hadn't been there before. It made her appear slightly older than her twin.

"Any news about Midnight?" Monica asked when she reached their table.

Gerda's mouth turned down. "I'm afraid not. I think we have to prepare ourselves for the worst." She retrieved a tissue from the sleeve of her sweater and dabbed at her eyes. She turned to look at her sister. "You don't think that someone from that Twilight shop might have taken her? For some sort of black magic?" She shuddered.

"I've met the owner, and she's very nice. I don't believe for a minute that she would do something like that." Monica smiled gently. "Besides, I don't think they're practicing black magic at Twilight. Just doing yoga and reading tarot cards and the like."

Gerda looked doubtful. "Mother would have said that those sorts of things are the work of the devil, designed to lead us astray."

Hennie nodded her head.

Monica realized it was pointless to try to persuade them that that was not the case. Their beliefs were too ingrained and long held to be changed at this point. But she had to defend Tempest against cat-napping.

"Don't you suppose that Midnight has simply wandered off to have an adventure?" Monica said.

Gerda shook her head and her permed curls quivered. "Midnight has never done that before. I hope that dreadful boy who likes to tease her hasn't stolen her." Her lower lip trembled.

"Billy Johnson?" her sister asked.

Gerda nodded. "He tied a can to her tail once. Poor little thing was nearly going crazy when I found her. I gave him a real talking-to, I can tell you that. He thought the whole thing was a joke. That boy is incorrigible. You mark my words." She shook her finger at Monica. "He's going to cause big trouble someday if a stop isn't put to his mischief now."

"You know what they say. Small children, small problems. Big children, big problems," Hennie said sagely. "Although I really doubt he's had anything to do with Midnight's disappearance, I'll have a word with his mother." She put a hand over her sister's. "Everything will turn out. I just have a feeling."

Gerda nodded but didn't look convinced.

Monica decided it would be best to change the subject. She pointed to the table where the deep fryers had been set up. The scent of hot oil and something sweet was beginning to fill the air. It reminded Monica of the smell at fairs and carnivals.

"What are they doing?" she asked.

A look passed between Hennie and Gerda. They were much too polite and well-bred to smirk, but their smiles suggested that Monica's question had been naïve or even downright humorous.

"They're making oliebollen for dessert, of course."

*Oliebollen?* It sounded like some sort of old-fashioned game. Monica pictured hoops and girls in crinolines and boys in short pants.

"What are oliebollen?"

Again that look passed between the two sisters.

"Well, oliebollen means *oil ball* in English, but that certainly doesn't sound very appetizing, does it?" Hennie laughed. "They're a sort of doughnut. But without the hole in the middle. The early Dutch settlers brought them here to the new world."

Gerda nodded. "And now you have your Dunkin' Donuts and your Krispy Kremes, all because of the influence of the Dutch and their oliebollen."

"They're normally eaten at New Year's and are a huge treat," Hennie confided. "Mother certainly never made them at any other time of year, but I imagine the organizers wanted to give everyone something special tonight. You'll like them. They're delicious."

Monica could hear the fat sizzling as the large woman with gray hair dropped balls of dough into the fryers. The smell was tantalizing. She pulled out a chair and sat down opposite the twins.

Hennie leaned toward Monica. "They'll dust them with powdered sugar after they've been fried." She rolled her eyes upward. "Heavenly." She tapped Monica on the arm. "The trick is to be sure the oil is hot enough, or they'll be greasy and tough."

Gerda had a worried look on her face. She was pleating the fabric of her skirt, running it between her thumb and forefinger. "I do hope Rieka checked the temperature of the oil before she started the frying."

Hennie patted her sister on the arm. "I'm sure she did. Rieka has been making oliebollen for years. It's going to be fine. You worry too much," she admonished. She turned toward Monica. "Sometimes they put currants or raisins inside." She sniffed. "Frankly, I prefer mine plain."

Monica had a sudden thought. Could she make oliebollen with cranberries mixed in? Probably not. It would be impossible to keep them fresh enough. By the time she got them from her kitchen to the store, they'd most likely be a sodden mess.

Hennie leaned closer to Monica. "Has there been any word about . . . you know?"

Monica had been afraid of that—people asking questions about the investigation. She almost hadn't come tonight because of it. Was the word around town still that Jeff was the culprit? She couldn't bear it if it was.

She shook her head and looked down at her hands. Surely she could bring up some topic that would steer the conversation in another direction.

"Oh, look. Cora is here," Gerda said. "I'm glad she could get away. That poor woman needs a break."

"Who is Cora?" Monica asked feeling at sea once again.

"She's a waitress at the Cranberry Cove Diner," Hennie said, her tone clearly indicating she was incredulous that Monica didn't already know that.

"She used to own a beauty parlor in town," Gerda confided. "She was one of the few hairdressers around who still knew how to do a marcel wave."

"Why did she close her salon?" Monica thought it was far preferable to run a hairdressing salon than being run off your feet all day at the Cranberry Cove Diner.

"It was such a shame." Gerda shook her head and her silver curls quivered again.

"Yes," Hennie agreed. "All because of greed." She looked at Monica. "How much money does one man need? Money is the root of all evil, they say."

"I don't understand—"

"It was all Sam Culbert's fault," Hennie said in a tone that suggested that *that was that.*

"He used to be such a nice boy," Gerda said. "He delivered our paper." She turned to her sister. "Do you remember, Hennie?"

Hennie nodded. "Yes. And he was quite the star on the Cranberry Cove High School football team, if I remember correctly. Don't know why he turned out the way he did."

Monica was busy trying to make a connection between Cora's beauty parlor and Sam Culbert.

"And she wasn't the only one." Hennie took a sip of her water. "There was the fishmonger George—what was his name?"

Gerda wrinkled her brow. "Kuipers, wasn't it? I wonder what happened to him?"

"He moved away, I think."

"I know Cora even went to Sam Culbert and begged him to reconsider."

"But what did Sam Culbert do—" Monica started to ask.

"He raised the rent," Hennie said in a tone that suggested everyone ought to know that. "He owns half the buildings on Beach Hollow Road. He put poor Cora's beauty salon out of business. The fishmonger, too. Don't know what happened to George, but Cora made the best of things by taking a job at the Cranberry Cove Diner."

"She didn't want to leave Cranberry Cove. Her mother is still alive, and Cora looks in on her every day," Gerda explained.

"She resented Sam Culbert something fierce."

Hennie nodded. "That's for sure. I don't imagine she's going to waste any tears over Sam's death."

But did Cora resent Sam Culbert enough to kill him? Monica wondered as she made her way back to where Gina was sitting. A gentleman was relaxing in the chair Monica had recently vacated. He was handsome with thick, wavy gray hair and a sharply chiseled profile. He was wearing a sport coat with suede patches on the elbows and a pair of expensive-looking leather driving shoes.

"Excuse me," he said, jumping to his feet as Monica approached. "I'm afraid I've taken your place." He turned to Gina. "It was lovely talking to you. I am sure we'll see each other again."

"Who was that?" Monica asked after he had left. She plopped into the chair. Gina was looking considerably brighter, she noticed.

"That's Preston Crowley. He's the owner of the Cranberry Cove Inn. He just stopped by to drop off a check for Debbie's fund."

"I guess Sam Culbert didn't own everything in town then." Monica looked over her shoulder at Gina's companion, who was making his way toward the exit. "He looks very nice."

"He is. He said he would take me sailing one of these days. He has a boat docked here in the marina." Gina smiled. "Things are looking up in Cranberry Cove, that's for sure."

Monica was about to ask Gina if she wanted to try some of the oliebollen—the smell had been tempting Monica long enough—when she felt a hand on her arm. She turned around. It was Lauren—the girl Jeff had been dating. Her face was drawn and she looked as if she might cry at any moment.

"Is Jeff here with you?" she asked. "I'd hoped to see him tonight."

"I'm afraid he was too tired to come with us. He just wanted to put his feet up in front of the television and eat one of those dreadful microwave dinners he subsists on."

Lauren gave a fleeting smile. She glanced at Gina then back at Monica. "Could I talk to you for a moment, please?"

"Sure." Monica started to get up from her chair.

"Don't mind me," Gina said. "I think a trip to the ladies' room to freshen up is in order. I'm sure I've bitten off most of my lipstick by now."

Lauren watched her go then slid into Gina's vacant seat. "It's about Jeff."

Monica could see the tears forming in Lauren's eyes. They hung on the edge of her lower lids, threatening to spill at any moment, like water over a dam.

Monica made a noncommittal noise. She cringed at the thought of getting involved in other people's business, especially when it involved romance. Her girlfriends used to talk for hours about the men they were dating—how often they called, what they said when they did call, what did it mean if they asked you out on Friday night but not Saturday. Monica had had no patience for any of it. She had been more than happy to retreat from the dating scene when she became engaged to Ted.

Lauren glanced around the room and then leaned closer to Monica. Her blond hair fell across her face, partially obscuring her expression.

"Do you have any idea what's up with Jeff?" Her lower lip began to quiver, and she bit it. "Is he seeing someone else?"

Monica saw Lauren's hands clench and her knuckles turn white.

"I'm so sorry," Monica said, feeling as if she needed to apologize for Jeff. She was silent for a moment debating how much to tell Lauren. She felt Lauren deserved the truth, but was it her place to reveal it?

Monica stared at her hands for a moment and then made up her mind. "No, there isn't anyone else." She looked up to see Lauren's face brighten. "The problem is with Jeff." Monica licked her lips to wet them. "He . . . he doesn't feel worthy of you. Because of his arm and the fact that the farm is skating on such thin financial ice."

Lauren's face brightened even more—like the sun coming out from behind a cloud. "Why would he . . . I don't care . . . that's ridiculous," she sputtered. "I mean I don't care about his arm. It doesn't make any difference to me and never has. And as for the farm . . ." She shrugged her shoulders. "If things don't work out, Jeff can always sell and move on to something else."

Monica had a sudden pang at the thought of Jeff selling the farm. It meant so much to him. And it was beginning to mean a lot to her, too.

"Will you talk to him?" Lauren stared into Monica's eyes. "Please?"

"I think it's a little more . . . complicated than that." How much should she say to Lauren? "I think," and again she hesitated, "I think that what Jeff really needs is some counseling. To come to grips with his injury and all the terrible things he must have seen when he was in Afghanistan. There's no shame in it—many returning veterans are doing the same." She looked up. Lauren was watching her intently. "As for the farm . . . I think it is going to be a success. Jeff needs to gain a little confidence that he can do it."

"What do you think I should do?" While they were talking, Lauren had shredded Gina's discarded napkin. She brushed the pieces together into a pile.

"Wait. I know that isn't the easiest thing to do and probably not what you want to hear. But I plan to talk to Jeff about seeing a therapist as soon as the time is right."

"So you don't think I should call him and—"

"No." Monica shook her head. "I think the best thing is to give him some space and, as hard as it is, some time."

Lauren looked both relieved and disappointed. "At least I know there isn't another girl." She attempted a smile. "I guess I'll just wait, like you said." She got up from her seat and turned to look at Monica. "Thanks. Thanks for telling me the truth." This time she gave a real smile. "Jeff is worth waiting for."

# Chapter 12

Monica was taking a batch of cranberry bread out of the oven when there was a knock on her back door. She pulled it open and was shocked to find Gina standing there. She looked at her kitchen clock, thinking for a moment that she had lost track of time and somehow it was already past noon.

"Surprise," Gina said as she followed Monica into the kitchen. "I know I'm not usually up this early, but if I'm going to be running a store, I'd better get used to it, so I thought I'd start practicing now. Besides, those darn birds make such a racket in the morning. And I thought the country was going to be quiet." She put a hand to her mouth to stifle a yawn. "I don't suppose you have any coffee?"

"Certainly." Monica opened a cupboard, grabbed a mug and filled it from the pot sitting on the warmer.

She was surprised to observe that Gina wasn't in her

trademark short skirt but rather had on black leggings, a long, knit sweater and a pair of low-heeled booties.

"I'm meeting the architect and the contractor at my shop this morning to go over our plans," she said, as if she'd noticed Monica's astonished glance. Suddenly she buried her face in her hands. "I just wish this whole thing with Jeff would be settled. It's keeping me up at night."

Monica poured herself a cup of coffee and joined Gina at the table. She took a closer look at her stepmother. Gina looked older than she had a couple of days ago—drawn and pale with dark circles under her eyes—the kind of tired that no amount of Botox could erase.

Monica cupped her hands around her mug to warm them. The old kitchen was drafty and chilly, even with the oven going. "Jeff can't be the only suspect. Mauricio doesn't have an alibi, as we've discovered. If Charlie was at the hospital with her mother, Mauricio could have easily left the Inn and no one would have been the wiser."

Gina's face brightened slightly.

"Sam Culbert wasn't very well liked," Monica continued. "The VanVelsen sisters—"

Gina looked blank.

"They're the identical twins who were at the spaghetti supper last night."

"Of course. I'm afraid I'm never going to keep all these names straight."

"According to them, Culbert put the local beauty salon out of business when he raised their rent. The former owner, Cora, is now working at the Cranberry Cove Diner."

"That sure would make me angry." Gina drummed her fingers on the table.

"Also, according to the VanVelsens, Culbert's wife probably isn't too sorry to see him gone. Sounds like he was something of a bully and an abuser." Monica took a sip of her coffee.

"Those sisters really have their ear to the ground, don't they?" Gina pointed a finger at Monica. "If they're right about the wife then I'm betting she did it. A woman can only stand so much before she snaps." Her face brightened considerably.

Monica smiled. "We don't exactly have any proof. I thought I would go by the diner later and talk to this Cora."

"Good plan. Are you going to check to see if she has an alibi?"

"I can hardly come right out and ask her. But maybe I can get a feel for what she's like and how much she really hated Sam Culbert."

Monica finished her coffee and got up to put her mug in the sink.

"I wish I could go with you, but I've got my meeting." Gina looked at her watch. "In . . . five minutes ago." She stood up and took her empty cup to the counter. "Let me know what you find out."

Monica closed the door behind Gina and began to pack her baskets full of the goodies she'd baked that morning. She certainly hoped she'd learn something from Cora because even though she didn't want to admit it, she was as worried about Jeff as Gina was.

Monica crested the hill into town and paused for a moment. Dark clouds were moving in from the west, hovering over the lake menacingly, and an increasingly strong wind was whipping the water into white-capped waves. She wasn't surprised—she had felt the sharp edge in the air when she went out to her car. She shivered thinking of Jeff and his crew standing thigh deep in cold water.

There were a few drops of rain on her windshield as she turned onto Beach Hollow Road. One of the VanVelsen sisters—Monica couldn't tell them apart without their name tags—was out in front of Gumdrops sweeping up the dried autumn leaves that had collected in the corners of the shop's doorway.

A red pickup truck backed out of a space in front of the Cranberry Cove Diner, and Monica quickly pulled in. The smell of bacon frying hit her as soon as she opened the car door. She felt her stomach grumble. Breakfast had been at six thirty a.m., and it was now almost noon. Maybe today she would have a chance to treat herself to a bowl of the diner's famous chili.

The cook, Gus, was behind the grill flipping burgers and frying eggs with casual ease while keeping his eye on a pile of hash browns and some French fries spitting and sizzling in the fryer behind him. He had wavy dark hair, strong forearms and a broad chest and shoulders. He gave Monica a barely perceptible nod. Monica was pleased to note that since she was now living in Cranberry Cove full time, she warranted some personal acknowledgment of her presence from Gus. But the VanVelsen sisters had warned her that it would be years, if ever, before she got the smile that Gus reserved for locals. According to them, he had a complicated hierarchy of greetings ranging from none at all for the summer tourists right up to coming out from behind the counter to shake someone's hand and slap them on the back. Apparently, there were only one or two people in all of Cranberry Cove who merited that level of enthusiasm. The irony that Gus himself was a transplant was no doubt lost on him.

A counter with stools ran in front of the grill. Two men sat at one end nursing cups of coffee with newspapers spread open in front of them. The red leather booths on the other side of the room were already filled with customers eating lunch. A waitress with short, gray-streaked hair was leaning on the counter waiting for her order. *Cora?* She had a pencil behind one ear and a weary expression on her face. Gus slid a dish in her direction, and when she didn't immediately pick it up, he stabbed a stubby finger toward it and scowled at her.

All heads had turned in Monica's direction when she walked in. She was still a stranger as far as the people of Cranberry Cove were concerned, especially those whose families had been living there for generations. Suddenly Monica heard someone call her name. She glanced toward the booths to see Greg Harper sitting in one of them. He had a plate of bacon and eggs in front of him and the newspaper propped open on the table. He motioned to Monica.

"Good afternoon," he said, then glanced quickly at his watch. "Well, it will be shortly. The noon whistle will be going off in five minutes." He pointed to the seat opposite him. "Please join me," he said as Monica hesitated.

Monica slid into the other seat as Greg folded up his newspaper and tucked it beside him.

"I was sorry to miss you at the spaghetti supper the other night."

Greg made a face. "What a nightmare! I was getting ready to leave the store when one of my bookshelves collapsed. Guess I shouldn't try to stuff so much on them. The manufacturer claimed they were heavy duty, but obviously they're not." He gave a rueful smile. "It took me until almost midnight to repair the shelves and reorganize the books."

Monica thought back to her visit to Book 'Em. *Organized* wasn't a word she would use in conjunction with the haphazard array of stock in the store.

"But enough about my sad tales of woe. How did you like the Agatha Christie? Have you finished it yet?"

Monica laughed. "One of the benefits of country living is that the lack of nightlife leaves plenty of time for reading."

"Do you miss Chicago?" Greg put a hand toward his fork and then paused.

"Please don't stop eating on my account." Monica leaned back as a waitress, not the one Monica had noticed earlier, slid a glass of water and a napkin-wrapped bundle of silverware in front of her.

"To answer your question," she said when the waitress left after dropping a menu on the table, "sometimes. I enjoyed city life—the museums, concerts, art galleries and things like that—but the country does have its compensations."

"I hear you," Greg said, forking up the last bite of his eggs. "I moved here from Minneapolis myself, and while it's not as large as Chicago, it's still a long way from Cranberry Cove."

"What brought you here?" Monica took a sip of the ice water the waitress had left. "If you don't mind my asking," she added hurriedly.

Greg grimaced. "I was a victim of the dot-com bust. A friend and I had the mistaken notion that we could take on Amazon. We started an online bookstore, but neither of us had any experience in fulfillment."

"What's that?"

"In a nutshell, getting the product to the buyer in a somewhat timely fashion. I'm afraid we failed spectacularly."

"But why Cranberry Cove? There must have been a lot more opportunities in Minneapolis."

Greg ducked his head briefly. "Frankly, I was embarrassed, so I crept away with my tail between my legs. I couldn't keep up with the friends I'd made in the city—successful lawyers, bankers and other professionals. I came here to lick my wounds. The bookstore was for sale, and I used what little money I had left to buy it. And you know what?"

Monica shook her head.

"I like dealing with real books a lot more than virtual ones. It's a lot more satisfying to interact one-on-one with a customer. Plus I get to talk about my favorite subject all day long—authors and their books." He pushed his plate away and leaned his elbows on the table. "Speaking of which, you didn't say. How did you like the Christie?"

"I liked it very much. I've been meaning to stop by to pick up something new."

"Looks like we have our own mystery right here in Cranberry Cove. Has there been any more news about Sam Culbert's murder? There wasn't much of anything in the paper."

"Nothing new that I know of, I'm afraid."

Greg glanced at his watch again. "Sorry. I'd better shove off. I've got this young girl working for me part time, and she expects to go to lunch on the dot of noon, even if the store is full of people and there's a line at the register. Good help is hard to find."

Monica thought of Darlene. "That's for sure."

"Let's get together one of these days. I'll give you a call." Greg tapped her on the shoulder as he walked past and headed to the cash register.

Greg was paying his bill when the gray-haired waitress

stopped by Monica's table to take her order. Monica glanced at the name tag pinned to her uniform. *Cora* was written on it in fading letters.

Monica ordered a bowl of chili and an iced tea then opened her mouth to say something to Cora, but she had already turned around and was scurrying to the counter to place the order.

Monica looked out the window while she waited. She saw Bart Dykma hurry past, looking more like himself in his butcher's apron than he had in his somber black suit at Culbert's funeral. From this angle she could see the empty storefront next to the hardware store Gina was renting for her aromatherapy shop. She was going to have to depend on business from the tourists because Monica couldn't see the locals going for it. They were down-to-earth folk with old-fashioned values. Many of the shops, like Danielle's Boutique and Twilight, were open only on weekends during the winter, their only business being the tourists who came to see the Christmas decorations.

Monica didn't have long to wait for her order. Cora was back almost immediately with a steaming bowl of chili and a frosted glass of iced tea. She placed them in front of Monica. Monica spoke quickly, before Cora could turn around.

"I want to ask you about Sam Culbert."

Cora looked startled and glanced over her shoulder at Gus, who was plating a hamburger and fries.

"What about him?" Cora's mouth set in a bitter line. "He was a miserable wretch, pure and simple. What else can I tell you?"

Cora looked over her shoulder again. Gus had the plate ready and was looking for Cora.

"Listen, I've got to go. Gus doesn't like it if we spend too much time talking to the customers, especially not when we're busy."

Monica looked around. The booths were full and all but one of the stools at the counter was occupied.

"I'd like to talk to you. Can we meet after you're finished working?"

Cora sighed and pulled her order pad from the pocket of her apron. She wrote briefly, tore the sheet off and handed it to Monica. "Here's my address. I get off at five. Come by any time after. I don't have plans for the evening. By the time I get home from here, I'm too tired to go anywhere."

Gus cleared his throat and Cora scurried off. Monica put the paper in her purse and started in on her chili.

The locals were right—it was some of the best chili she'd ever had.

Monica finished eating, fished some bills out of her purse and took the check to the counter. Several people were waiting in line for takeout orders, and Gus was really hustling behind the grill flipping burgers, toasting buns and checking on the French fries.

Monica was about to leave when she spotted Darlene in the takeout line.

"I thought you were supposed to be at the shop this afternoon." Monica glanced at her watch.

Darlene shrugged. "I've got to eat, don't I? Jeff said it was okay."

Jeff was way too easy on his employees, Monica decided as she walked back to her car. She would have to speak to him about it.

• • •

Monica spent the afternoon struggling with the farm's accounts. Now she understood the expression *robbing Peter to pay Paul*. If they were going to meet the payroll for the week, she was going to have to put off sending the check for the electric bill until after it was due. Monica pushed away from the kitchen table where she'd set up her laptop and took a mug from the cupboard. She filled the kettle with water and while it was heating, got out a tea bag. As she was closing the cupboard door, she noticed the bottle of Scotch. It was certainly tempting to take Gina's advice and spike her tea. Looking at the bleak numbers on the computer screen had given her a headache.

Monica gave herself a mental shake. Things were going to turn around. As soon as this crop was in and sold, the picture would be a lot rosier. And she kept meaning to talk to Jeff again about getting an auditor to go over the books. If they could prove Culbert had been embezzling funds, then perhaps they could sue his estate for what they were owed.

Monica was still bent over her computer when her back door opened. It was just Jeff, but she made a mental note to be more careful about locking up in the future.

Apparently her stress was obvious, because Jeff put his hands on Monica's shoulders and began to rub them. "You're all knotted up."

Monica opened her mouth to say something about the farm's financial situation but then closed it again. Jeff already knew things were bad. Why worry him more? But she did want to talk about Culbert.

"Would you like a cup of tea?" she asked. Jeff was rubbing his hands together as if they were cold.

"Sure." Jeff pulled out a kitchen chair, turned it around and straddled it.

"You know, I've been thinking," Monica said while she had her back to her brother. "We really need to get someone to go over the farm's books. If I'm right, and Culbert was embezzling money—and I'm pretty sure he was—we need to report it."

"What good is that going to do now?"

"We might sue his estate for the return of the money. Besides, it's theft and whether he's alive or not doesn't change things."

"I suppose."

Monica slid a mug of tea across the table toward Jeff. He cupped it in his hands.

"Is the farm really doing that badly?"

Monica bent down and pretended to tie her shoe. She'd never been good at lying, and she didn't want her face to give her away. "Things are fine. It just doesn't seem fair for Culbert to get away with it."

Jeff grunted. "I suppose so. Although it seems to me he already got what was coming to him." Jeff shivered. "I wouldn't want to go like that."

"I'll do some research online, check if there have been any similar cases and how they were handled, okay?"

"Sure." Jeff picked up his mug and gulped down the remainder of his tea. He looked at his watch. "I've got to get going. I'm meeting some of the guys from the crew for a beer and burger."

She'd already brought up one touchy subject; Monica decided she might as well go all out. "Have you ever thought about getting some counseling?" she blurted out as Jeff put on his jacket.

"Counseling?" His face was blank. "What kind of counseling? What for?"

Monica clenched her fists until her nails dug into her palms. "To deal with . . . some of the things you experienced in Afghanistan?"

Jeff's face twisted into a bitter expression. "You mean like this?" He lifted his left arm with his right and then let it drop again.

"Yes," Monica said, more firmly than she felt. "You can't let it hold you back from . . . from doing things."

"Like what? It seems to me I'm doing just fine. I'm keeping up with the rest of the crew when it comes to harvesting my crop."

"You are." Monica hastened to reassure him. "But you can't let it hold you back from forming . . . relationships." There. She'd said it.

"You mean like with Lauren?"

"Yes. Or any other woman for that matter."

"Look, Sis, I've already told you. I'm a lousy prospect as a husband. I'm handicapped, and I'm barely getting by. All the counseling in the world isn't going to change that."

The slamming of Monica's back door punctuated his statement as Jeff stomped out of the cottage.

Monica glanced at the clock on her kitchen wall. It was after five o'clock. She powered off her computer and shut her eyes. She'd been staring at numbers for so long she could still see them dancing on her closed lids. She needed to take a break.

It was almost dinnertime, but she wasn't hungry yet.

Monica pushed her chair back. She would go see Cora instead. Cora ought to be home from the diner by now.

Monica grabbed her fleece jacket from the coat tree by the front door and slipped it on. The nights were getting progressively colder, and it wouldn't be too much longer before the landscape was blanketed in snow.

As Monica drove toward town, she noticed the leaves were quickly changing to brilliant reds, oranges and yellows. The locals were already complaining about the tourists on color tours who were taking over the town—their large tour buses belching exhaust into the fresh, clean air and clogging traffic on Beach Hollow Road. But the shops were full and the cash registers ringing, so that took the sting out of it. They'd have Cranberry Cove back for themselves soon enough.

Cora lived in a mobile home park just outside of town. Monica found it easily enough. A sign at the entrance announced it as the Park View Estates, although Monica could see nothing resembling a park—unless you counted the small playground ringed by a few trees—nor did she see anything that could even remotely be called an estate.

The place was very tidy, however, and Monica was surprised. She'd expected to see run-down trailers and lawns that were more dirt than grass, but everything was shipshape— the trailers were all in good repair with fresh paint and the miniature yards were well tended. The cars in the driveways were older but clean. Cleaner than her Focus, she thought ruefully.

It was very quiet. The playground was empty, and no one was outside sitting on their deck or doing work in the yard. Monica imagined everyone was inside having dinner or preparing it. Somewhere a dog—it sounded like a small one—began to bark shrilly, breaking the silence.

She followed the numbers until she found Cora's trailer. It was the second from the end of a row of similar looking mobile homes. She was about to turn into the driveway when two boys zoomed past her on their bikes, forcing Monica to brake hard.

Her hands were shaking slightly as she pulled in behind a green Taurus that she assumed was Cora's car. Certainly that must mean that Cora was at home.

Monica mounted the three steps to the deck and approached the door, where a cheerful-looking yellow print curtain was pulled across the window. Hopefully she could get this over with quickly—her stomach was beginning to rumble. She pressed the bell and waited. After two or three minutes, Monica rang again. The trailer was a double-wide, and it couldn't possibly take Cora that long to get to the door.

There was still no answer a minute later. On the off chance that the bell was broken, Monica decided to knock.

She had just rapped on the door when someone called to her from the neighboring trailer. A woman was standing on her deck smoking a cigarette. She was in a T-shirt and had her arms wrapped around herself for warmth. Her hair was unnaturally black, and there was a colorful tattoo peeking out from under the sleeve of her top.

"Looking for Cora?" She called in a husky voice.

"Yes."

"She ought to be home. Her car's there," she pointed her cigarette at the Taurus, "and I didn't see her go out." She took a puff on her cigarette and let the smoke out in a stream. "You'd better knock again."

"I will."

The woman stubbed her cigarette out in an aluminum ashtray that was propped on the deck rail. "Of course she might be in the shower and can't hear you."

Monica hoped that wasn't the case. She knocked again and waited. Still nothing.

Perhaps she couldn't hear her for some reason, but she could peek in the trailer and see if Cora was there. There was a window over the deck with the curtain pushed to the sides. For once Monica was glad of her height. She stood on tiptoe and peered in.

She was looking into Cora's living room. It was as tidy as the outside of the trailer, with a floral patterned sofa and a round, tiered table crammed with ceramic figurines.

An armchair in the same floral pattern was at right angles to the sofa. Cora was sitting in it, slumped over and lifeless.

# Chapter 13

Monica's first instinct was to scream, but she managed to stifle it, and it came out as more of a whimper. She didn't want to alert the entire neighborhood. There was still the possibility that Cora had simply fallen asleep sitting in her chair. Monica could remember occasions when she, herself, had been so tired after a long day at the cafe that she had fallen asleep sitting bolt upright on the sofa.

She rapped hard on the window. There was no movement from Cora. Monica knocked again as hard as she could—it hurt her knuckles—but no response.

She needed to get inside to see if Cora was okay. Somehow, Monica had the feeling that she wasn't.

Hopefully Cora wasn't the sort who locked up tight every time she went inside. Monica tried the door, and the handle turned. Her heart was hammering hard against her ribs. She wasn't particularly squeamish, but despite finding Culbert's body in the bog, she was hardly accustomed to being confronted with corpses.

Cora's living room was as tidy inside as it had looked through the window. There was a mug with what appeared to be tea in it on the coffee table in front of her. Monica called Cora's name as she approached the chair where Cora was sitting, but she already suspected it was hopeless. There was an unnatural stillness to Cora's body—no rise and fall of her back to suggest she was breathing, and no whistling sound of her breath, either.

As soon as Monica touched her, she knew Cora was dead. She backed away from the body quickly and fumbled in her purse for her cell phone. The call went through quickly, and Monica managed to keep her voice steady as she explained the situation to the dispatcher.

The dispatcher promised to send someone over immediately, and it wasn't long before Monica heard the sound of sirens in the distance. She went out on the deck to wait.

The fresh air felt good. Monica grasped the deck rail as she breathed deeply, trying to steady the frantic beating of her heart. She heard a movement behind her and turned around. The woman next door was standing outside her back door lighting a cigarette. Monica suspected she was more interested in what was going on than having another smoke.

The sirens got louder, and a minute later a patrol car came roaring down the quiet street. It pulled into Cora's driveway and stopped. Both front doors flew open at the same time, and two uniformed patrolmen jumped out. They weren't the same policemen who had arrived at Sassamanash Farm when Culbert's body was discovered—they were both thin and wiry, and to Monica, they looked like rookies. They were too young to be anything else.

They took the stairs to the deck in one giant step and stood uncertainly in front of Monica.

"You okay, ma'am?"

Monica wondered just when she'd segued from being *miss* to *ma'am*? It made her feel very tired all of a sudden, and she sagged against the deck rail.

"You going to faint, ma'am?" the one cop asked, a look of alarm on his face.

"No. I'm fine," Monica reassured him. She waved a hand toward Cora's door. "She's . . . she's in there."

Both policemen tried to get through the door at the same time. The one with the glasses scowled at the other, who dropped back to let his partner go first.

Monica looked up to find the woman across the way staring at her. She was leaning on her deck rail, both arms crossed, a cigarette burning unheeded in her fingers. She jerked her head toward Cora's trailer.

"What's going on?"

Monica didn't know what to say. She shook her head. "I don't know. I think Cora has taken ill."

"Is it her heart?" The woman took a deep drag on her cigarette and then dropped the butt over the side of the deck. "My name's Dawn by the way."

"Nice to meet you, Dawn," Monica said, trying to convey with the tone of her voice that she didn't want to prolong the conversation.

It had no effect on Dawn. She started down her deck steps and headed in Monica's direction. Monica could smell the smoke on her as soon as she got close, and it made her feel slightly sick.

"I'm not surprised she's had a heart attack," Dawn said, crossing her arms over her chest. "She puts in a lot of hours at that diner. The owner's a slave driver."

Monica gave a noncommittal smile.

"I'm guessing since the cops are here that she's . . . well, that there's not much hope."

"I'm afraid not."

"Sad." Dawn didn't look particularly distressed as she pulled a fresh cigarette from the waistband of her sweatpants.

By now several people had come out of their homes and walked down to stand in front of Cora's trailer. Dawn assumed a superior air, as if she was somehow in the know. She waved to a couple of people and smiled smugly.

Monica didn't want to go inside, but she didn't want to stand out here any longer with everyone staring at her, either. A couple of the women were still wearing their aprons, and one of the young boys had what Monica hoped was ketchup all down his shirt.

Finally another car came down the street and pulled up to the curb outside Cora's trailer. Detective Stevens heaved herself out of the driver's seat. Monica thought she looked even bigger than the last time she'd seen her.

Stevens mounted the three stairs to the deck, pulling herself up by the handrail. She was a little breathless as she stood in front of Monica.

"Want to tell me what's happened?" Suddenly she spun around. "There's no need for you to be here," she said to Dawn.

Dawn looked sulky but she took off for her own trailer without complaint.

Stevens turned to look at the crowd that had gathered in

front of Cora's. "You can all go home now. There's nothing to see. A woman took ill, that's all."

Monica could hear the group muttering as they slowly dispersed and made their way home.

"Ghouls," Stevens said as she watched them leave. She turned back to Monica. "You look cold. Do you want to go inside?"

Monica wasn't anxious to spend any more time in a room with a dead body, but her teeth were beginning to chatter, although she suspected it was more from shock than cold. She followed Stevens through the door.

"Try to touch as little as possible," Stevens said. "We don't know what we're dealing with here yet. Although two murders in Cranberry Cove in less than a week is a bit hard to swallow." She turned to the patrolmen. "Did you check for a pulse?"

"Yes, ma'am," they chorused. "Nothing."

Stevens looked at Monica. "Do we know who she is?"

"Her name is Cora Jenkins. She works at the Cranberry Cove Diner."

Stevens approached the body and looked it over carefully. She pulled a pair of gloves from the pocket of her trench coat and slipped them on.

Monica turned away and looked out the window. The small crowd that had dispersed previously had gathered again at the end of Cora's driveway with Dawn right in front. She still hadn't donned a coat or jacket and was about to light yet another cigarette.

Finally, Stevens was finished with the body. She stripped off her gloves and turned to Monica. "Why don't we go into the kitchen?"

Cora's kitchen was spotless. A small round table by the window was covered with a clean white lace cloth with salt and pepper shakers painted to look like Kewpie dolls in the center. Ironed dishcloths printed with cranberries hung from the oven door handle. Monica wondered if Cora had purchased them at Sassamanash Farms.

Stevens looked all around the room. She came to a halt in front of the sink. "That's odd." She pointed inside the sink. "Look. There's a dirty mug in here."

"There was a cup of tea on the coffee table in front of the . . . in front of Cora, too."

"Did you have tea with her?" Stevens jerked her head toward the sink.

"No. She was already . . . dead when I got here."

Stevens glanced around the room again. "Not a thing out of place," she said almost to herself. "Why would Cora leave a dirty mug in the sink?" She pointed to the dishwasher. "Why not put it in the dishwasher?"

"Maybe she was in a hurry to leave this morning?"

Stevens shook her head. "She was sitting in the living room with a fresh cup of tea. Surely while the water was heating she would have dealt with the dirty mug. No, I think she had a visitor, and she gave that person a cup of tea. And that person brought the mug out to the kitchen and left it in the sink. What we don't know is, did that person also kill Cora?" She was thoughtful for a moment. "Assuming Cora didn't die of natural causes. There's no evidence of trauma—no wounds, no bleeding. Maybe she merely had a heart attack or a stroke. That would certainly make my job easier." She rubbed her belly absentmindedly and gave a gusty sigh. "We'll find out soon enough when the autopsy is done."

By the time Monica turned her Focus into her own driveway, she was shivering again. This time she knew it was nerves—she had had the heater going full blast the whole way home but to no effect. She would make a hot cup of tea and this time she would spike it with the last of the Scotch in the bottle.

She was getting out of the car when Gina's Mercedes pulled in in back of her. Monica groaned. She'd been looking forward to a quick dinner, some reading and then early to bed. But she put a smile on her face and waved.

"Gina. Hi." She almost asked what Gina was doing there but bit her tongue at the last minute.

"I hope you haven't eaten." Gina slammed her car door shut. She was carrying a plain white shopping bag.

"No, I haven't."

"Perfect. The chef at the Inn put together a little care package for us." She followed Monica inside.

"A care package?"

"Yes." Gina put the bag down on the kitchen table and began to remove the contents—several aluminum tins and a bottle of wine. "He's sent chicken Marsala." She opened the lid on one of the containers and breathed deeply. "Doesn't that smell heavenly?"

Monica had been sure that she would be too upset to eat, but she had to admit that the aroma drifting from the pans was enticing.

"There's also a side of pasta, a green salad and a huge piece of tiramisu we can split for dessert."

Monica grabbed some plates from the cupboard and a handful of silverware and quickly set the table.

"Where's your corkscrew?" Gina held up the bottle of wine.

Monica rummaged in a drawer. "Here it is." She handed it to Gina.

Gina opened the bottle and poured each of them a glass.

Monica took a sip. It was just what she needed, and as they sat down to eat, she realized that she was actually starving.

Gina pointed her fork at Monica. "Tell me what's been going on."

Monica finished her bite of chicken Marsala. "Like I told you I've been trying to track down some of the other people in Cranberry Cove who had a bone to pick with Culbert. I decided I would pay a visit to Cora Jenkins who is . . . was the waitress at the Cranberry Cove Diner."

"Was?" Gina said, her eyebrows raised.

"I'll explain. I went over to the diner at lunch to see if I could talk to Cora, but she was busy. She gave me her address and suggested I come by her place after work." Monica put down her fork. Her appetite had suddenly deserted her. "I did, but she couldn't tell me anything. She was dead."

Gina gasped. "Another murder!"

Monica held up a hand. "Not necessarily. Detective Stevens said it could have been a stroke or a heart attack or some other natural cause. We won't know until the autopsy is completed."

"When will that be?"

Monica shrugged. "Stevens said they would make it a priority, so hopefully soon."

Gina unwrapped the piece of tiramisu. "Do you think Mauricio did it?'

Monica pursed her lips. "Mauricio? I can't imagine why. I don't know if he even knew Cora."

"But don't you think it's a little too coincidental? I mean, two murderers in the same small town?"

"We don't know if Cora was murdered."

Gina licked some whipped cream off her upper lip. "True, but let's face it—the whole setup smells. Two murders in Cranberry Cove seem pretty unlikely, but it's just as unlikely that Cora suddenly dropped dead from some heart issue at the same moment she was about to talk to you. My guess is she had more to tell you than just her opinion of Culbert."

"You're probably right." Monica picked at her piece of tiramisu. "I suppose we'll have to wait to see what the autopsy reveals."

"I'd bet anything it's going to show that foul play was involved."

# Chapter 14

Monica gathered up the remnants of her dinner with Gina. She threw the containers in the trash, tied the plastic bag closed and opened the back door to take it out to the garbage can. A strong breeze caught the edge of the open door and nearly yanked it from Monica's hand. She hesitated, feeling the chill wind. Should she get her jacket? The can was only a few yards outside the back door. She would brave it.

By the time Monica got back inside, she was shivering. The sharp edge of the wind had cut straight through her sweater and turtleneck. It wasn't particularly late, but the thought of crawling into bed with the news magazine that had just come in the mail was too enticing to resist.

The second floor of the cottage was noticeably chillier than the first floor. *Wasn't heat supposed to rise?* Monica thought. She opened the hall closet and pulled out a second down comforter and spread it out on the bed. She washed her face, brushed her teeth and filled the hot water bottle she kept for nights like these. She tucked it into the bed to warm the sheets while she changed into a pair of flannel pajamas.

Monica didn't last long. The soothing warmth from the hot water bottle and the coziness of her bed had her eyes closing before she knew it. She tossed her magazine onto the bedside table and turned out the light.

She woke abruptly several hours later. She glanced at her alarm clock—it was one a.m. Had she heard something? Or had the noise been part of a dream? She could hear the wind whistling and rattling the old cottage's windows but otherwise it was quiet.

She put her head back on the pillow and burrowed deeper under the covers. It must have been a dream. She'd barely finished the thought when she heard a noise again. This time it was obvious someone was pounding on her door.

*Who on earth . . . ?*

Monica grabbed her robe and quickly tied the belt around her waist. She turned the hall light on and was nearly blinded as she made her way down the stairs. The knocking was coming from the back door. Monica felt her way through the darkened kitchen. She stubbed her toe against a chair leg and winced but kept on going as the knocking intensified.

"Who is it?" she called when she was within earshot of the door.

"It's Jeff. I need your help."

*Jeff?* Monica's heart began to pound. Was something wrong with him? She pulled open the door, and the wind tried to snatch it from her hand, as if they were playing some sort of game.

"What's the matter—" Monica began but Jeff was already talking.

"There's been a frost warning. I know it's a lot to ask, but I can't rouse any of the crew, and I need help checking the sensors in the bogs that we haven't harvested yet."

"Of course," Monica said, even though she dreaded the thought of going out on such a bitter night. "I'll be dressed in a minute."

"Here." Jeff thrust a battery-operated lantern at her. "Take this with you. You know where the pump house is?"

Monica nodded.

"Meet me there, and I'll show you where to go."

Monica was about to shut the door when Jeff stopped her. "And bring your cell, okay?"

Monica went back upstairs and began pulling on her warm-est clothing—thermal undershirt, turtleneck, heavy wool sweater and socks, corduroy pants. She shivered as she listened to the wind knocking at the windows and felt the draft working its way around the edges of the old, ill-fitting panes.

She pulled on a pair of boots, her down jacket, a fleece hat and a pair of gloves and stood hesitating by the back door. She really didn't want to go out there—her bed had been so warm and cozy—but Jeff needed her help. She reso-lutely pulled open the door and flinched as the cold air hit her. It certainly felt as if a frost was imminent. She hoped they were in time to save the berries.

The moon was bright and lit the dirt path quite well, but when a cloud floated across it, obliterating the light, Monica turned on her lantern. The ground was uneven and slightly spongy beneath her feet, and she had to move slowly to avoid tripping. She thought she saw a glint of light from the corner of her eye. It came through the trees over toward the rutted dirt road that led past the farm. But who would be out at such an hour? It was probably just the moon flickering through the trees.

Finally, Monica could see the pump house looming like a grotesque shadow in the distance. The old boards were weather-beaten and peeling. Monica knew that giving the structure a fresh coat of white paint was on Jeff's summer agenda.

Jeff came around the side of the pump house and called out. "Over here."

Monica aimed her flashlight in the direction of Jeff's voice and could just make out his face.

"I can't thank you enough—" Jeff began when Monica got there, but she waved him to silence.

"Just tell me what to do. It feels as if the temperature has dropped just while I've been walking here."

"Remember I showed you where the sensors are in each of the bogs?"

Monica nodded, hoping she'd be able to find them in the dark.

"Just check the temps on the three bogs that haven't been harvested yet, then call me with the numbers. I'll turn on the sprinklers if they're needed." He gave a wan smile. "And be sure to get out of the way first. I don't want you getting soaked."

Monica shivered at the thought. Her teeth were already on the verge of chattering.

She headed in the direction Jeff had indicated, down a path with the bog on one side and the irrigation ditch on the other. Even with her lantern, it was rough going. A thick cloud had obscured the moon, and although it was slowly drifting past, it would be a while before it had moved enough for the moonlight to shine through and light the way.

Monica tripped on a tangled root that was embedded in the dirt and forcing its way to the surface. She thought she was going to go down but caught herself in time. She bit her lip. She would so much rather be back at her cozy cottage, tucked up warm in bed clutching her hot water bottle. But, she reminded herself, if Jeff didn't get the berries protected they would freeze, which would turn them mushy and worthless. Sassamanash Farm was already in debt enough as it was. They needed every single berry from this year's crop to survive.

The moon peeked out for a brief moment and shone on the murky waters of the irrigation ditch to Monica's right. Water on the farm was used and reused—moved from one bog to another through a series of canals that depended on rainwater for replenishment. It was very important to protect the wetlands that the farm stood on, as well as the adjacent water sources—several small lakes and ponds that bordered the farm.

The thick cloud covering the moon shifted again and light shone on the path, but then it was gone almost as quickly as it had appeared. Monica thought she heard a noise behind her, and she whirled around. She felt slightly foolish. The dark night, the oily waters of the irrigation ditch and the black hole of the bog were working overtime on her imagination. She had walked the streets of Chicago alone late at night plenty of times with only the sound of her own footsteps for company. But this was different. In Chicago there had been street lamps every few feet to illuminate the sidewalk, the occasional group of tipsy people spilling out of the bars just before closing and the odd store owner pulling down the metal grate over his window for the night. Here she was truly all alone.

She reminded herself that there was nothing to be frightened of. No wild, predatory animals roamed the farm, nor were there any serial killers on the loose and certainly not any boogeymen. Of course there *was* a murderer at large in Cranberry Cove, but whoever it was was unlikely to be out at the farm on such an inhospitable evening. Given her druthers, Monica would certainly have been tucked up in bed herself instead of out in the cold searching for a temperature sensor.

Silence descended again, and she assumed the noise had been a figment of her imagination. She slowed her steps— she thought she was approaching the area where she would find the first sensor. She was about to head into the bog when there was another noise.

Before Monica could even spin around to determine the source of the sound, a searing pain shot through her head and blackness darker than any night she had ever experienced enveloped her.

Monica heard someone frantically calling her name, but it seemed to be coming from a long distance away. It was far more tempting to settle back into the warm, delicious oblivion that was calling her, beckoning her like the sirens beckoned Odysseus. Someone shook her by the shoulders, and she wanted to tell them to stop—that she preferred to return to that state of unconsciousness that had been deeper and more satisfying than sleep.

But whoever it was would not give up, and eventually Monica roused, breaking through to reality like a swimmer breaking through the surface of the water.

"What?" she mumbled. Her lips felt thick and were difficult to move.

"Are you alright?" Jeff was leaning over her, his face creased with concern.

"Of course," Monica said, half of her still in the dreamlike state that had been caused by the blow to her head.

She stretched out an arm and was surprised to find herself lying on the ground. "What am I doing here?" she asked as she rubbed a hand across her forehead.

"I don't know." Jeff frowned. "Did you fall?"

"I don't think so." Monica tried to think, but everything was enveloped in a thick fog. What else could have happened? "I guess I must have." She ran a hand through her hair and was shocked to discover a huge bump on her head.

"No!" she blurted out suddenly. "I heard a noise behind me and the next thing I knew there was a terrible pain in my head." She rubbed the sore spot again and her hand came away with blood on it. "There's a big lump."

"Where is it?" Jeff held out his hand, and Monica grasped it and guided it toward the goose egg rising from the crown of her head.

Jeff snatched his hand back. "You didn't fall." His expression was grim. "Someone hit you over the head."

Monica struggled to prop herself up on her elbows. The damp was slowly penetrating her jacket, sweater and turtleneck, and she could feel her teeth beginning to chatter.

"We've got to get you to the hospital."

"No! I'll be fine. We need to see to the cranberries."

"The cranberries aren't important," Jeff said shaking his head. "You are."

"I'm fine," Monica insisted. "Go check the temperature in the bog and then do what you have to do. I'll head back to the cottage."

She began to struggle to her feet.

Jeff hesitated.

"Go on!"

He stuck out a hand and pulled Monica to her feet. She swayed briefly. Jeff still didn't move, and Monica gave him a gentle shove. He nodded curtly and plunged into the bog.

As Monica made her unsteady way back home she heard the hiss of the sprinklers coming on. She crossed her fingers. Hopefully Jeff had been in time to save the last of the crop.

By the time Monica reached her cottage, her head was pounding. She went into the tiny powder room off the kitchen and flicked on the light. She was shocked when she saw that blood had trickled down the right side of her face and was matted in her hair.

She opened the medicine chest, shook two ibuprofen out of the bottle and went into the kitchen for a glass of water.

She was swallowing the two pills when a thought occurred to her. The night Culbert was killed, Jeff had said there'd been a frost scare. Monica remembered him saying how tired he was because he'd been out checking the sensors. He could have easily lured Culbert to the farm somehow and then hit him over the head. And who else knew she would be out alone tonight . . . ? Monica shook herself. The blow to her head was obviously affecting her thinking. Jeff wouldn't harm her, and as mad as he'd been at Culbert, he wouldn't have harmed him, either.

Monica had just sat down at the kitchen table when the back door opened and Jeff walked in. He had his cell phone in his hand.

"I've called the police."

"What? Why?" Monica half rose from her seat.

"Someone tried to hurt you. They hit you over the head and could have killed you. If you had fallen unconscious into the irrigation ditch . . ." The unspoken words hung in the air between them.

"If I was attacked, do you think it's related to Culbert's murder?" Monica watched as Jeff retrieved a bag of frozen vegetables from her freezer.

"Here. Put this on your head." He handed her the bag of peas. "You've been going around asking questions. Someone saw or heard you and got spooked. They wanted to be sure you couldn't do any more snooping."

"But how would they know I'd be out on the farm at one o'clock in the morning instead of in bed where any sane person would be?"

"I don't know. Either they were here for some reason—to break into the farm store or steal equipment maybe—and it was just their luck to find you wandering alone in the dark. Or," Jeff opened a cupboard and got out two mugs, "they knew that with a frost in the forecast, we'd have to turn on the sprinklers. And maybe they took their chances that you would be out helping me."

Monica shifted the bag of peas on her head. "That would seem to argue that Mauricio is behind this. He would know about the frost, and he can probably find his way around the farm in the dark better than I can."

Jeff filled the mugs with water, placed them in the microwave and stood with his back against the counter. While they waited for the water to heat, Monica told him about Cora.

"I can understand why Mauricio might have wanted to kill Culbert, but Cora?"

"Maybe there's a connection we don't know about."

Jeff was retrieving tea bags from the cupboard when there was a brisk knock on the door. He pulled it open.

Detective Stevens stood on the doorstep. Her hair was rumpled and she was wearing a pair of sweats with a corduroy jacket open over them.

"Sorry to get you out so late," Monica said.

"It doesn't matter." Stevens ran a hand over her belly. "I might as well get used to being woken up in the middle of the night."

"Tea?" Jeff was already reaching for another mug.

"Sure. A little caffeine shouldn't hurt." Stevens plopped into one of Monica's kitchen chairs with a sigh.

"Is this your first?" Monica took the mug Jeff handed her.

"Yes. And something of a surprise. My husband and I thought we were too old, but obviously Mother Nature didn't think so." She ran her hand through her hair. "My first husband and I never had any kids, which was fortunate. He was the reason why I joined the force. I saw firsthand how too many cops ignored domestic violence. I hoped I could change that."

Monica didn't know what to say. She took a sip of her tea and winced when the scalding liquid hit her tongue.

"So." Stevens pulled a small notebook from the pocket of her jacket. Suddenly she was all business. "Want to tell me what happened?"

Monica told her about hearing a noise and then being hit over the head. Her hand went to the bump on her skull.

Stevens looked up from her pad, a puzzled look on her face. "What were you doing out on the farm in the middle of the night?"

"That's easy." Jeff jumped in to answer the question. He

explained about the frost and the need to check the temperature in the bogs.

Stevens looked up at Monica. "And you're sure you didn't get dizzy or trip and fall and bang your head? Then, when you came to, you couldn't remember what happened and jumped to the conclusion that you had been attacked?"

Monica stiffened. "No. I'm positive. Someone hit me on the head." She snapped her fingers. "I remember something else. As I was walking to meet Jeff by the pump house, I saw a light. Just a brief glint, and I thought it was coming from the moon, but maybe it was coming from the road. It might have been someone's headlights penetrating the thick cover of trees."

Stevens nodded and made a note but didn't say anything.

"It seems obvious to me that this is somehow connected to Culbert's murder, don't you think?" Jeff paced the small room with his hands behind his back.

"What about Cora?" Monica looked at Stevens.

Stevens scrubbed a hand across her eyes, then stifled a yawn. "The ME did the preliminary autopsy. Of course, the toxicology reports won't be back for a while yet. If they keep cutting the budget and laying people off, there won't be anyone left to run the tests." Stevens sighed. "But I called in a favor, and hopefully we'll be moved to the top of the list. The ME has ruled out the obvious—heart attack, stroke, aneurysm, cancer . . . along with stab wounds, gunshot wounds, strangling, drowning, asphyxiation and the like. It seems that Cora was a reasonably healthy middle-aged woman, and there was no cause for her to drop dead while sitting in her own living room. Of course, until the tox reports come back, we can't rule out poisoning. The ME did find a needle mark on her right bicep. Just the one, so I think we can safely assume she wasn't a junkie. Besides, my guys searched that trailer from top to bottom and didn't find any evidence that she was a user. She'd probably just gotten a flu shot. It's that time of year." Stevens stifled another yawn. "Of course they didn't find any other useful evidence, either."

Monica frowned. "That certainly is strange."

Stevens nodded in agreement. "It's a real puzzler, that's for sure."

# Chapter 15

Monica was surprised when she glanced at her alarm clock and saw that it was already past eight o'clock. She was about to leap out of bed when she remembered it was Sunday. She sank back against her pillows and pulled the comforter up to her chin. Her bed felt warm and delicious, and she decided to indulge herself for a few minutes. She was used to rising before dawn. While she'd been running her café, she would get the first batch of muffins or scones in the oven by four thirty a.m., and now at Sassamanash Farm, she had to get an early start on making the salsa and the fresh-baked goods for the store.

Monica ran a hand through her hair and winced. Why was her head so sore? Almost immediately the events of the previous evening came flooding back. The pitch-black night, her flashlight creating only a narrow band of light ahead of her, the noise she thought she heard . . . then nothing. Monica touched the spot again—more gingerly this time. The lump was still there, but it was smaller than it had been. She was grateful that she didn't have a headache to go along with it.

Jeff had been concerned that she might have suffered a concussion and had wanted to spend the night on her sofa so he could check on her every hour, but Monica had convinced him to go back to his apartment. She was grateful because the thought of being woken up every hour and asked what day it was or who the president was had been decidedly unappealing.

Ten minutes later, Monica realized she was bored with lying in bed and she reached for her robe and slippers and padded down to the kitchen. She got the coffee going and pulled open the back door to retrieve the Sunday paper from the mat where the paperboy had tossed it. She shivered as the icy wind blasted her in the face. She glanced at the sky. The clouds were moving swiftly, buffeted by the strong breeze, and there was a sliver of blue visible to the west. Hopefully that was the portent of a sunny day.

Monica dropped the newspaper onto the table. She poured herself a cup of coffee, popped a cranberry muffin in the toaster oven to warm it and sat down at her kitchen table.

The paper was still cold to the touch as she flipped through the various sections. As usual, the Sunday edition was full of circulars. Monica was about to toss them aside when her eye caught the one for Fresh Gourmet, a national chain grocery store just outside of town that featured a lot of organic products, healthy frozen food items and hard-to-find ingredients.

Monica paged through the insert. Lamb from New Zealand, coffee beans from Tanzania—Monica nearly gasped at the price—smoked salmon flown in daily from Scotland

and other items she couldn't afford. She was about to toss the section in the recycling when a thought occurred to her. Why shouldn't Fresh Gourmet carry Sassamanash cranberry salsa? If it was good enough for the Cranberry Cove Inn, then wouldn't it be good enough for Fresh Gourmet?

Her laptop was already open on the table. Monica pushed the papers and the remains of her breakfast to one side, and pulled the computer closer. She quickly found the website for Fresh Gourmet. Her mouse hovered over the bottom of the screen until she found the link for vendors. She clicked on it and brought up the relevant page.

If Fresh Gourmet agreed to carry the farm's salsa, it would be a source of revenue year round. They could add on to the screening house and build a kitchen. Monica imagined they would need all the appropriate permits as well as be ready to pass health inspections in order to produce the salsa in greater quantities.

She read through the information on the Fresh Gourmet website—the first step was to submit an application to the regional office. Monica was dismayed by the length and breadth of the information required—packaging, labeling, market research and more. First she would have to make sure that the farm's product was right for the store. If they already sold a number of homemade salsas, then they would most likely not be interested in hers. As soon as she was dressed, she'd take a drive to the nearest Fresh Gourmet and scope it out. And she'd pick up something for dinner—assuming she could afford anything more than a can of corned beef hash.

Monica pulled on a fresh pair of jeans, a sweater and then, thinking of her destination, added a decorative scarf to her outfit. She looked in the mirror. She wasn't ready for the Magnificent Mile in Chicago, but she thought she looked good enough for Fresh Gourmet.

Beach Hollow Road was deserted as Monica drove through town, although the parking lot of St. Andrew's was full. The church bells began to peal as she drove past, and she saw a couple walking arm-in-arm scurry through the doors just as they were being closed.

Monica felt guilty about not being in church. She vowed that the following weekend she would be in the front pew at St. Andrew's. But right now she was on a mission to save Sassamanash Farm, and she hoped God would be okay with that.

Fresh Gourmet was located in a strip mall about five miles outside of Cranberry Cove. A green-and-white striped awning hung over the entrance and two huge terra-cotta pots holding ficus trees flanked the door. Like the shops on Beach Hollow Road, the store was most crowded in the summertime and on weekends, but it was a popular chain and people were willing to drive down from Grand Rapids to frequent it. Despite it being Sunday morning, there were already a dozen cars in the parking lot.

Monica parked the Focus and went inside. The interior smelled of ripe cheeses, smoked meats and freshly baked bread. It was intoxicating, and Monica found herself drifting toward the section where the sign reading *Charcuterie* hung over the cases. She was halfway there before she reminded herself that she was on a mission, and it wasn't to indulge in gourmet food items she could ill afford.

She stopped in her tracks and scanned the overhead signs trying to decide where they would be likely to display fresh salsa. The deli counter seemed the most logical place, and she was rewarded when she found a refrigerated case of salsa, hummus, cheese spreads and dips.

The salsas were pedestrian fare, or so it seemed to her— tomatoes, peppers, cilantro—all the usual ingredients. She felt her heartbeat quicken. Sassamanash Farms' cranberry salsa could really take off here. She had a lot of work ahead of her, but all of a sudden she was confident she could pull it off.

When she turned away from the refrigerated case, she knew she had a smile on her face. She hadn't gone more than three feet when she bumped into Greg Harper.

His face lit up at the sight of her. "Good morning. I didn't know you shopped here."

"I don't," Monica admitted. She explained about the salsa.

"That's a wonderful idea," Greg said.

He smiled and moved his cart out of the way of a stern woman who shot him a dirty look. Monica noticed Greg had selected several of the gourmet frozen meals and a jar of olives. She recognized bachelor fare when she saw it.

Greg gestured toward his cart disparagingly. "I'm not much of a cook, I'm afraid. And I don't have much time for it." He looked at Monica's face and laughed. "These frozen meals aren't all that bad. You don't have to feel sorry for me."

Monica had been cooking since she was a child—dragging the stepstool to the counter to help her mother as she prepared for one of the many dinner parties her parents used to give. She'd even had her own miniature apron that she had treasured more than any of her dolls or stuffed animals.

"And speaking of food," Greg hesitated briefly and looked down at his feet. "Have you eaten yet? The Cranberry Cove Inn does a great brunch."

Monica's smile broadened. "I had a muffin several hours

ago, and after smelling all the delicious aromas in here, I'm starving."

"Splendid." Greg's smile widened as well. "I'll check out and meet you there in ten minutes." He dug in his pocket and pulled out his cell phone. "I'll just call ahead to make sure we get a table. It's a popular place on a Sunday morning."

As Monica headed toward the Cranberry Cove Inn she wondered if her outfit was up to snuff. Greg had been dressed just as casually in corduroys and a sweater. There was probably no need for her to worry, but she was glad she'd taken the time to add the silk scarf and to dab on some lipstick. She put a hand to her hair. Hopefully it wasn't in too much of a tangle. Fortunately Greg didn't seem like the type who cared. His own hair, more often than not, was a rumpled mess. Adorable, to be sure, but definitely not every hair in place.

Judging by the number of cars in the Cranberry Cove Inn parking lot, Greg had been wise to call ahead for a reservation. There was a line of people ahead of Monica waiting to be seated by the hostess. Monica peered into the dining room but it appeared as if Greg hadn't arrived yet. She perched on the edge of a white wicker settee by the front door.

Greg strode in moments later, slightly breathless, his hair having blown into even greater disarray by the strong breeze coming off the lake.

"Sorry you had to wait. I stopped by the store to pick up this." He handed Monica a book. "It's a first edition Louise Penny—*A Fatal Grace*. I think you'll like it."

Monica didn't know what to say—it was so unexpected. "Thank you. That's terribly kind of you."

"Have you read her before?"

Monica shook her head.

"Harper?" the hostess called, a stack of menus clutched to her chest.

"Here."

Greg raised a hand, and he and Monica followed her to their table.

"A table by the window." Monica smiled. "I'm impressed."

"I have clout, you know." Greg laughed. "Not really. We just got lucky I guess."

Monica looked around. The dining room was nearly full, with several of the larger tables being the only ones unoccupied. Animated chatter, along with the melodic clinking of silverware, filled the room. Monica found herself relaxing for the first time in a long time.

Greg pointed toward the window. "Looks like another storm is brewing."

Monica followed his gaze. Angry-looking dark clouds hovered on the horizon, and the waters of Lake Michigan were whipped into a froth.

A waitress in a pink apron appeared at their table and filled their coffee cups. "Ready to order?" she asked, holding the pot out to the side.

"I think so?" Greg looked at Monica.

Monica nodded her head.

"I'll be right back." The waitress turned and put the pot of coffee down on a warmer at the side of the room.

"I'll have the eggs Benedict," Monica said when the woman returned, order pad in hand.

"The waffles with strawberries for me." Greg handed the waitress his menu. "I've got an insatiable sweet tooth," he said to Monica.

"I'm more the savory type myself."

They chatted easily until the waitress slid plates of food in front of them.

"I heard about poor Cora," Greg said as he poured a puddle of syrup over his waffles.

Monica looked surprised.

"The tom-toms have been working overtime in the village lately. News like that won't stay under wraps for long." He forked up a bite of his breakfast. "I wonder if there's any connection between her death and Culbert's?"

Monica leaned back as the waitress refilled her coffee cup. "Mauricio—he's the fellow who was working on my brother's crew—seems the most logical suspect in Culbert's murder."

The waitress moved around to the other side of the table and held the pot of steaming coffee over Greg's cup. "More coffee?"

"Yes, please," Greg said.

"Culbert was forever threatening to report Mauricio because he didn't have his papers," Monica continued. "And he acted suspiciously when the body was found. But as far as I know, there's no connection between him and Cora at the diner."

The waitress had finished pouring Greg's coffee and was about to turn away when she stopped. "You're talking about that Portuguese fellow, right? I mean, there can't be more than one person in Cranberry Cove with that name."

Monica was startled. "Do you know him?"

"Sure. He used to work here but left for some reason. Went to work at the Cranberry Cove Diner. I can't imagine the tips there would be as good although I gather he wasn't there long either."

"I wonder why he left the diner?" Monica said when the waitress moved away.

Greg stirred a spoonful of sugar into his coffee. "Maybe Gus got cold feet about his lack of papers."

"Or, maybe there was another reason. Maybe he did something . . . something not quite right, and Cora caught him. And then she told Gus about it."

"You could be right, Miss Marple," Greg said with a smile.

Monica laughed. "I guess I am playing amateur detective." Her expression grew serious. "It's not that I don't trust Detective Stevens to get to the bottom of things. I'm sure she knows what she's doing. But until she does solve this, people in Cranberry Cove will continue to think my brother had something to do with the murders."

Monica enjoyed her brunch with Greg, but for some reason, it left her feeling restless. She paced her small living room unable to settle down to anything—her book, the Sunday crossword or a favorite old movie that was showing on television.

She couldn't stop thinking about what Greg had said— that Cora and Mauricio had worked at the Cranberry Cove Diner at the same time. Now she really wished she'd had the chance to talk to Cora.

Monica was making a cup of tea when the thought struck her. She hadn't been able to talk to Cora, but maybe she could talk to someone *about* Cora. Perhaps there was someone Cora had confided in—a friend or relative. Monica had no idea who that might be, but she knew where she was going to start— Cora's next-door neighbor. She was obviously nosy and perhaps she had managed to worm some information out of Cora.

Monica had had an acquaintance like that in college. No matter how much you wanted to keep something a secret, she had a way of badgering you until you finally gave in and told her everything. More than once Monica had sworn to keep her mouth shut, but then the next thing she knew she was spilling the beans. She hoped Cora's neighbor Dawn would turn out to be the same way.

Monica finished her tea and put the empty cup in the sink. She needed to empty the dishwasher, but she didn't feel like doing it now. It wasn't something she would normally let go, but all of a sudden, she couldn't wait to talk to Dawn.

She was halfway there when she had to turn on her windshield wipers. The rain was coming down heavily, drops bouncing off the window, when she turned into Park View Estates. The narrow streets were deserted, as Monica had expected. She pulled up in front of Dawn's trailer, edging the car as close to the side of the road as possible.

Dawn was standing outside, huddled under the green-and-white striped metal awning that hung over her front door, a cigarette in her hand. She looked up when she heard the slam of Monica's car door.

Her face held a look of curiosity as she watched Monica pick her way up the uneven stone path that led to the entrance to the trailer.

"I didn't think I'd be seeing you again," Dawn said, but her voice was friendly enough.

"I'm sorry to bother you—"

"It's no bother." Dawn waved her hand, and smoke drifted toward Monica's face.

It was cramped with both of them sheltering under the

awning. Water dripping off the edge trickled down Monica's back.

Dawn stubbed out her cigarette with the bottom of her shoe. "Come on inside."

The interior of Dawn's trailer was clean and tidy, with the scent of bleach lingering in the air. A large black leather sectional, placed in front of a flat-screen television, took up most of the room. A teenaged boy was stretched out on it.

The walls were hung with original paintings—stark land-scapes that were very striking. A painting in progress sat on an easel in the corner of the room.

"Are these yours?" Monica gestured toward the oils.

Dawn ducked her head. "Yeah. It's a little hobby of mine. I took it up the last time I quit cigarettes in order to keep myself busy." She shrugged. "It didn't work. I went back to smoking but continued with the painting."

"These are very good." Monica looked around the room again. Dawn's oils were as good as anything she had seen in galleries in Chicago. "Have you had any exhibitions?"

"You're kidding, right?"

Monica shook her head. "Not at all. There's a gallery in town. You should show them your stuff."

"I don't know. . . ." Dawn twisted the edge of her T-shirt in her hands as if she were wringing out wet laundry. "Do you really think . . . ?"

"I do."

"I'm sorry. I should have asked you to sit down." Dawn turned toward the sofa. "Shoo, Terry, go watch TV in your room. And turn that off." She pointed to the set.

The young man unfolded himself from the sofa, a sulky

expression on his face. He had long, shaggy hair with bangs that hung in his eyes.

Dawn shook her head. "I can't believe how big he's getting. He's taller than I am now. And he's eating me out of house and home." She laughed. "Sit." She pointed toward the sofa.

Monica perched on the edge of one of the cushions.

"You want something to drink? I got some cold beer in the fridge. . . ."

"No, I'm fine. But thank you."

"I imagine you wanted to talk to me about something?" Dawn gestured toward the easel in the corner. "I hope you don't mind if I continue working. I don't want it to dry before—"

"No, no, not at all. I realize I'm interrupting." Monica looked down at her hands folded in her lap.

"Hey, I'm glad for some company." Dawn picked up a brush and applied a dab of red to the painting on the easel.

"I wanted to talk to you about Cora."

"Cora?" Dawn jerked her head toward the trailer next door.

"Yes."

"She was a good neighbor. Quiet. Kept her yard up. She brought us a plate of cookies every Christmas." Dawn frowned as she dabbed the brush against her canvas. "She used to be a hairdresser, you know. She still did hair for people in the park—the older ladies would go to her for their permanents." Dawn wrinkled her nose. "I don't know how she could stand the smell of that stuff."

"It sounds like she was a hard worker."

"You can say that again. Put in long hours at the diner. Did double shifts when one of the other gals didn't show up. Gus works his employees hard." Dawn took a step back from the painting and considered it. "Of course, she had her own business until Sam Culbert raised the rent so high she could no longer afford it. I told her she needed to raise her prices, but she said people around here didn't have that much money, and she couldn't take advantage of them. She didn't attract the summer trade." Dawn squeezed more paint onto her palette. "She was too old-fashioned for them. Still used rollers and sat people under the dryer." Dawn laughed. "Frankly, when I heard Sam Culbert had been murdered, I half wondered if Cora had gotten up the gumption to do it herself."

"Did you notice if she had any visitors yesterday?"

"You know the police asked me the same thing," Dawn said, wiping her hands on a rag. "I was hardly looking out the window the whole time, but I didn't see any cars in her driveway. And I went out every half hour for a smoke." She jerked her head toward the far wall. "Don't want the kid breathing in all those noxious fumes. I keep trying to quit but so far no luck."

"Did you happen to notice what time Cora got home? She told me she was getting off work at five."

Dawn nodded her head. "She got home just a bit after. I was on the deck, and she waved hello."

"And I got here around five thirty, maybe a few minutes later."

"If someone had stopped by for a visit, I would have seen the car. I'm sure of it."

"Did she ever mention someone named Mauricio?" Monica asked, holding her breath.

Dawn tilted her head to one side. "The name sounds familiar."

"Apparently he worked at the diner with Cora."

Dawn stabbed a finger into the air. "That's why it sounds familiar. Yeah, he worked with Cora. I remember she told me."

"Did she say anything else about him?"

Dawn stood holding her brush in the air. "Now that you mention it, she did. She told me she thought he was taking money from the cash drawer."

"What happened?"

Dawn shrugged. "I think she told Gus about it, but I'm not sure."

Cora must have, Monica thought. And Mauricio had harbored a grudge. Otherwise he would have had no reason to kill her.

# Chapter 16

Monica thought about what Dawn had told her as she drove back to Sassamanash Farm. The rain had stopped, and the faintest rainbow hung over the lake. She hoped that was a good omen.

She felt conflicted. As much as she wanted to solve Sam Culbert's murder—and Cora's, if it did indeed turn out to be murder—she had been hoping the killer wasn't Mauricio. She had instinctively liked him.

Monica groaned when she saw Gina's car in her driveway. *Not now.* She was tired. But she plastered a smile on her face as she opened the back door.

Gina was sitting at the kitchen table with an open bottle of wine and a glass in her hand. Next to her were several suitcases.

The smile on Monica's face grew stiff until she was quite certain it looked more like a grimace than a smile.

"Surprise!" Gina declared.

Gina was always a surprise, Monica thought. She devoutly hoped that the bottle of wine was meant to be the surprise, but she doubted it.

"I've come to stay with you for a bit." Gina put her glass down and jumped up from the table. "Would you like some wine?"

Monica nodded weakly and sank into one of the kitchen chairs.

"What's wrong with the Cranberry Cove Inn?" Monica resisted the temptation to put her head down on the table and bang it.

"Someone booked the suite I was in. Not to mention the entire Inn. Apparently there's a wedding next weekend at the Cranberry Cove Yacht Club, and the bride, her mother and an entire posse of bridesmaids are arriving early. There weren't any decent rooms left." She handed Monica a glass of wine. "It's only for a bit. I hope you don't mind."

Monica took an enormous gulp of her drink and began to choke. Gina patted her on the back.

"Where will you be staying . . . permanently?" Monica asked with extreme trepidation.

Gina's face split into a huge grin. "I'm going to have the most wonderful space," she crowed. "Above my shop. The architect has plans to turn it into a showplace." She looked down into her glass of wine. "I've never had my own place, you know." She looked up at Monica with an expression of intense yearning. "Before I married your father, I shared apartments with girlfriends because I could never afford the rent myself. Then your father and I had our condo in downtown Chicago for weekends and the big house in Evanston.

But I never really owned any of it. This place is going to be *mine*!"

Monica had to ask, although she wasn't sure she was going to like the answer. "When will the apartment be ready?"

"A couple of weeks. They're going to take out a few walls to give the space a more open-plan feel. And of course, the kitchen and bathrooms need to be completely redone."

Monica had been adding up days in her head. She switched to adding up months instead. If this renovation project was going to be like most, there would be delays, changes of plan, wrong measurements, and who knew how many other catastrophes.

It looked like Gina was going to be around for a while.

Monica was up early the next morning and had the first batch of cranberry muffins in the oven before six A.M. She was surprised when Gina wandered into the kitchen as she was taking them out thirty minutes later.

She was wearing jeans and a turtleneck sweater. Her hair hadn't been combed, and she had no makeup on. It made her look strangely vulnerable.

"Coffee?" Monica grabbed the pot from the warmer and held it out.

Gina nodded.

"You're up early," Monica said, pushing a mug across the table to Gina. "I hope you weren't too uncomfortable last night."

Monica's guest room, if it could even be called that, was strictly bare bones. If Gina had found the only room at the Inn unacceptable, Monica couldn't imagine what she thought of these accommodations.

"It was fine." Gina yawned and took a sip of her coffee. "I'm up early because I'm meeting the contractor at seven thirty."

"Do you want anything to eat? I have some muffins hot from the oven."

Gina shook her head and yawned again. "I never eat breakfast. I can't stand the thought of food before noon."

No wonder, Monica thought. Gina usually wasn't up until noon.

Gina took her coffee upstairs with her to finish dressing, and Monica cleaned up the kitchen.

She packed up the muffins and as she added the salsa she'd made the evening before, she vowed that tonight she would get started on the product application for Fresh Gourmet.

It was the kind of crisp, clear fall day that made Monica glad to be alive. She whistled under her breath as she walked the path to the farm store. She'd never been any good at carrying a tune, and she was glad there was no one around to hear her.

Monica was approaching the store when she stopped whistling. Two people were dead. What right did she have to feel so upbeat?

Darlene had arrived just ahead of her. She was hanging up a fleece jacket that was pilled around the collar and nearly worn through at the elbows. Monica knew Darlene didn't have much, and she felt sorry for her. She smiled, trying to put a note of enthusiasm in her voice.

"Good morning. Gorgeous day, isn't it?" she said as she hung up her own jacket.

"Yes. I suppose so." Darlene straightened her glasses. "I thought it was a little chilly myself."

Some people would always be glass half empty, Monica thought.

The store was no longer as busy as it had been right after Culbert's murder, when sensation seekers had come to satisfy their curiosity, even making road trips from as far as two and three hours away.

Monica stowed the salsa in the refrigerated cabinet, noting that there were two containers left from yesterday. She bit her lower lip. The brisk sales they'd experienced had been nice, even if they had come at the expense of Sam Culbert's life.

Darlene wriggled her way behind the counter, and when she turned toward Monica, Monica noticed she had tears in her eyes.

"What's wrong?" She put a hand on Darlene's arm. "Has something happened?"

"It's just that I'm missing my mother." Darlene took off her glasses and dashed a hand across her eyes. "She would have made me that special cake I liked today—German chocolate cake. I know it's not traditional for birthdays, but she knew it was my favorite." She gave a loud sniff and wiped her nose on her sleeve.

"It's your birthday?"

Darlene nodded.

"I didn't know. I'm so sorry. Happy birthday." Monica smiled. "Do you have anything special planned?" She realized, as soon as the words were out of her mouth, that it was the wrong thing to say.

Darlene gulped back a sob and shook her head. "There's no one to celebrate with now."

"Your friends . . . ?"

Darlene scowled. "I don't have any friends. I mean, I

know a couple of girls who were in my youth group from church, but not all that well."

"You should throw yourself a birthday party!" Monica declared. "Invite some of those girls to go out to dinner with you. It would be fun."

Darlene scowled again. "I can't afford to go out for dinner. I get my lunch once a week at the diner, and that's it."

The door opened and a customer walked in. Monica was relieved that the interruption put an end to such an uncomfortable conversation. She felt sorry for Darlene, she really did. But on the other hand, she also wanted to shake her.

She decided that as soon as she could, she would run into town and pick up a little something to give Darlene as a present. Maybe that would cheer her up.

Shortly after ten A.M. Monica decided it was safe to leave the store in Darlene's hands. They'd only had half a dozen customers, and it didn't seem likely they would get much busier.

She untied the cranberry-themed apron she wore behind the counter. She'd insisted Darlene wear one as well, although Darlene had protested at first. But the aprons gave them a uniform look and kept their clothes clean.

"I'm heading into town to run some errands. Is there anything I can get you?"

"Maybe." Darlene reached for her purse and pulled out her wallet. She counted out some singles one by one, the tip of her tongue caught between her teeth and her brow furrowed as if the exercise were a particularly challenging one. "Here." She handed the stack of bills to Monica. "I should have enough there for a hamburger and a pop from the diner. It is my birthday," she added somewhat belligerently.

"What do you want on your burger?" Monica asked as she stuffed the money into the pocket of her pants.

Darlene looked heavenward as if searching for inspiration. "Mustard, ketchup, mayo, lettuce and tomato and onion." She pursed her lips. "And if there's enough there," she pointed to Monica's pocket, "can you bring me a cola?"

Great, Monica thought. Now Darlene would be breathing onion fumes all over the customers all afternoon. She patted her pocket. She had already decided that she would treat Darlene to lunch and give her the money back. She nodded. "Got it. A cola."

The sun made the interior of Monica's car toasty, but when she cracked a window, the brisk edge to the wind was a reminder that September was almost over.

There were few cars parked along Beach Hollow Road when Monica got there. The town was generally quiet this early in the week, with traffic building as it got closer to the weekend. Tourists would be arriving in earnest again now that the leaves were changing, and Monica planned to get most of her errands done before that happened.

There was a space in front of Book 'Em and, without thinking, Monica pulled into it. Was she hoping to run into Greg? Yes. Why not? As Gina said, Ted had been gone long enough, and it was time for her to live again. Monica glanced at her left ring finger. Upon moving to Cranberry Cove she'd put her engagement ring in a safe deposit box at the bank. The slight indention that had circled her finger had filled in, and it was no longer obvious that there had been a ring on that hand.

She got out of the Focus and beeped the door locked. She couldn't resist pausing in front of the window of Book 'Em. Greg had arranged a display of classic English mysteries—books by Josephine Tey, Dorothy Sayers, Agatha Christie, Patricia Wentworth and Ngaio Marsh. Monica remembered reading many of the titles herself.

A movement beyond the display caught her eye, and she saw Greg beckoning for her to come in.

A bell over the front door tinkled melodically as Monica pushed it open.

"This is a pleasant way to start the week," Greg said with a smile.

Monica returned his smile. "I came into town to run a few errands."

"I won't keep you . . . much as I'd like to."

Greg edged his way around the counter. "I wanted to give you this." He handed Monica a piece of paper. "We're starting a mystery book club here at Book 'Em," he said, gesturing to the flyer. "I thought you might be interested. We'll begin in a couple of weeks."

"I think I would like that very much."

Greg accompanied Monica outside and waved as she walked away.

"See you soon," he called after her.

The wind grabbed the edges of Monica's jacket as she walked out of Book 'Em. She stopped to pull up the zipper and fish her gloves out of her pocket. As usual, tantalizing smells wafted out from the Cranberry Cove Diner next door. Monica wondered if the air in front of the diner didn't permanently smell of frying bacon. She would go back for Darlene's lunch order once she'd picked out a gift.

She stood on the sidewalk for a moment, enjoying the warmth of the sun on her face. What to get Darlene? She glanced back at Book 'Em, but she didn't know what kinds of books Darlene liked. Or if she even read at all. So many people didn't these days.

She started walking—past Twilight, where an elaborate display of tarot cards was set up in the window. She doubted she'd find anything for Darlene in there. She continued on and hesitated briefly in front of Danielle's Boutique. The usual swimsuits and fancy cover-ups in the window had given way to hand-knit-looking fishermen's sweaters, an exclusive brand of all-weather jackets and a colorful array of silk scarves. All to tempt the tourists on color tours and the ones who would arrive at Christmastime to admire the charming decorations. Monica doubted there was much of anything in the store that she could afford or that would suit Darlene.

Next was Gumdrops. She stopped in front of the store. Perhaps a selection of candy would make a nice gift.

Hennie came rushing forward as Monica pushed open the door.

"Lovely to see you, dear."

Hennie smoothed down her sage green cable-knit sweater. Monica wondered if the VanVelsen sisters' wardrobe changed color with the seasons.

"I need a gift for someone," Monica said, peering into one of the cases. She looked up at Hennie. "It's for Darlene who works in the farm store."

"Darlene Polk?" Hennie sniffed. "I doubt that girl will ever make anything of her life. Her mother's fault, you know. She babied her. While all the other kids in town worked at summer jobs, she sat around reading romance novels." Hennie sniffed again. "Putting notions into her head that she didn't need—waiting for Prince Charming to come riding down Beach Hollow Road on a white horse, no doubt."

"I do feel sorry for her though," Monica said. "Losing her mother. She doesn't seem to have any other relatives or even any friends."

Hennie nodded curtly. "I know. It is a sad case. Her mother passed way too young. She had the sugar, you know. Diabetes. Never did take proper care of herself. It led to her heart attack, I heard."

Monica smiled. She doubted there was much of anything that happened in Cranberry Cove that Hennie and Gerda didn't *hear*.

"Now what should you get for your gift?" Hennie furrowed her brow and pursed her lips. "Chocolate is always good. We have De Heer chocolate bars—milk chocolate and dark." She pointed to a selection of candy bars in orange wrappers in the glass case. "Or the Verkade milk chocolate."

Monica peered into the glass. The candy bars were arranged with near military precision, and she suppressed a smile.

"Of course there are always the Droste pastilles." Hennie gestured toward the pyramid of colored boxes. "It's a shame Droste doesn't make their chocolate orange balls anymore. Of course they didn't come out until the holidays. We used to get them in our stockings at Christmastime."

"I think the pastilles are a wonderful idea. The boxes are so pretty and colorful. Perhaps a selection?"

"Excellent choice." Hennie beamed at her like a teacher regarding an exceptionally bright pupil. "We do have a box of assorted flavors." Hennie pointed to a stack on the shelf behind the counter. "That way you get some of each, and the box makes a lovely presentation."

"Perfect. I'll take one of those."

"Would you like me to wrap it, dear?"

"If you wouldn't mind."

"Not at all. It would be my pleasure."

Hennie turned to a roll of wrapping paper behind the counter and tore off a piece.

Monica heard the beaded curtain to the stockroom move and glanced over to see Gerda entering. She had been wondering where Hennie's twin was. She couldn't recall ever having seen one without the other.

"So lovely to see you," Gerda said when she noticed Monica. "Have you come for some of your peppermints?"

"Not this time." Monica pointed to the box Hennie was wrapping. "I needed a gift for someone."

"That Darlene Polk," Hennie said over her shoulder. "You remember her, don't you?"

"Of course. She used to come in every week with her allowance to pick out something. Odd girl." Gerda shook her head.

Monica looked down to see a glossy black cat weaving its way in and out of Gerda's legs.

"Midnight's come back!" Monica exclaimed.

"Yes." Gerda swooped the sleek black cat up in her arms. Midnight looked less than pleased about being held captive. Her long tail swished back and forth impatiently.

"Where was she? Where did you find her?"

"We didn't exactly find her ourselves," Hennie said, brandishing the beautifully wrapped package. "A young man brought her back."

Gerda nodded. "Imagine that! He found her in a deserted barn outside of town. How she got there, we'll never know. It's a good five miles away."

Hennie put the box of chocolates in a Gumdrops bag and set it on the counter. "Someone took her, I'll bet, and then let her loose out there. We've had threats before, you know. Just because poor Midnight doesn't have a smidge of fur on her that isn't black."

"That's horrible." Monica fished in her purse for her wallet. "Do you think the fellow that brought her back is the one who took her? Maybe he felt guilty?"

"Oh, no," Gerda said as Midnight jumped down from her arms and went to take up a position in the sunbeam slanting through the front door. "He was terribly kind and most concerned."

"He said he saw some of Gerda's posters around town. That's how he knew where to bring our precious baby."

They all glanced in Midnight's direction. The cat preened and began to groom her front paw.

"Did you know this fellow?" Monica asked. There wasn't anyone in Cranberry Cove that the VanVelsens didn't know.

Hennie leaned her arms on the counter. "No. We'd never met him before. But he reminded me of that young man you were asking about a couple of days ago."

"Yes. The foreign-looking one with the dark hair," Gerda said.

"Mauricio?"

"Yes," the sisters chorused. "That was his name."

"When was this?" Monica asked with a sinking feeling.

"Yesterday."

"You don't happen to remember what time do you?"

"Must have been near a quarter after five," Hennie said. "We were getting ready to go home. I was counting out the register while Gerda swept the front steps. You should have heard her scream when she saw the young man walking towards her with Midnight in his arms."

"I didn't scream," Gerda said huffily.

Hennie ignored her.

"How long did he stay?" If the sisters found Monica's questions odd, they were much too polite to say.

"We invited him to dinner," Gerda answered. "We were so thrilled that he'd brought our Midnight back."

"He looked like he could use a good meal," Hennie added, taking the twenty-dollar bill Monica handed her. "I think he may have been roughing it out in that barn."

"So he got here at around five fifteen and went home with you for dinner?"

"Yes." Hennie handed Monica her change. "We'd made a big pot of erwtensoep, so there was plenty."

Monica must have looked confused because Hennie added, "Pea soup."

"So Mauricio was with you from five fifteen until . . ."

"After seven, I would say, wouldn't you, Gerda?"

"Oh, yes. *Jeopardy* was just coming on as he was leaving."

"It's our favorite show," Hennie explained.

"But you must see our surprise," Gerda said, clapping her hands. She gestured for Monica to follow her into the stockroom.

Midnight rose from her spot in the sun and scooted past them, her tail twitching and swishing briskly in the air.

The stockroom was every bit as neat and organized as the front of the shop, which didn't surprise Monica in the least. Gerda took her arm and led her over to a large cardboard box.

Midnight leapt over the side of the box and curled up in the corner, giving them all a disapproving look.

Monica peered into the box. "Oh!" was all she could say.

"Aren't they darling?" Gerda bent and stroked one of the tiny kittens. "This one looks just like Midnight." She pointed to a black kitten sleeping in the corner.

"So Midnight was pregnant!"

"Yes, we had no idea. Thank goodness that young man found them. With the weather getting colder . . ." Gerda shivered.

"Would you like one of them?" Hennie smiled at Monica.

Monica had never thought about having a pet. She'd been too busy in Chicago to contemplate anything more needy than a houseplant. But now, why not? A cat would love being on the farm with so many mice and other small creatures to chase.

"I don't know which one to pick." There were three in the litter—the black one and two black-and-white ones.

"You don't have to choose now. They have to stay with their mother for a few more weeks."

"Yes," Hennie added. "They'll have more personality then, and you can see which one suits you the best."

Monica gave a last look at the kittens and bid the sisters good-bye, the white Gumdrops bag swinging from her hand. The information they'd given her put Mauricio in the clear for Cora's murder. So now she was back to square one. But was she looking for one killer or two?

# Chapter 17

Monica was walking back toward her car when she heard someone call her name. She turned to see Gina waving furiously at her.

She walked over to where Gina was waiting on the sidewalk, wearing a construction helmet, which she somehow managed to make look feminine and like the latest fashion. She was standing in front of an empty store, and Monica could hear the sounds of banging and drilling coming through the open door.

"Come see what we're doing," Gina said, taking Monica by the arm and leading her into the building.

Monica followed, stepping carefully over a couple of two-by-fours. The smell of sawdust filled the air, and she could see particles of it floating in the beam of sunlight coming through the dusty front window.

Two burly construction workers in jeans and flannel shirts nodded at Monica.

"What do you think?" Gina asked. "This is going to be my new shop. I'm calling it Making Scents."

"It's kind of hard to tell what it's going to look like at the moment." Monica glanced around. The interior of the shop had been gutted down to the studs, with only two-by-fours creating the suggestion of separate rooms.

"The stockroom will be back here." Gina walked through a roughly sketched opening. "I'm going to have a small kitchen area where I can make coffee and have a bite to eat without having to leave the shop."

She grabbed Monica's arm and led her to a staircase. "These stairs will go up to my apartment above the shop. They'll be starting on that next week. It will be an open-plan kitchen and living room. I'll be able to see the lake through the living room windows. There'll be a bedroom, of course. Not very large, but I wanted room for a walk-in closet and an en suite bathroom. I'll have a small powder room for guests off the kitchen."

"It sounds lovely," Monica said, wondering how long all of this was going to take. The renovations seemed extensive to her.

The two workers had stopped momentarily and were leaning against one of the beams sipping coffee from Styrofoam cups.

Gina gave Monica a coy look. "I saw you talking to that fellow who owns the bookstore. He seems like a nice guy. Kind of cute, too. I went in there the other day to pick up a book Jeff had ordered."

"Greg Harper," one of the workers spoke up. "He's the owner, and he is a nice guy. Ran for mayor a couple of years ago."

The other worker put down his cup, took off his construction helmet and ran his hands through his hair. "Wasn't there some big flap about the election?"

"Yeah," his coworker answered. "There were rumors that Culbert cheated. That he bought votes or something like that."

"Frankly, I wouldn't put it past him."

Knowing what Culbert had done to Jeff, Monica wouldn't put it past him, either.

"I voted for that Harper guy. He had some great plans for Cranberry Cove. All Culbert wanted to do was ride around on a float in the Memorial Day and Fourth of July parades and wave to the crowd."

The two of them snickered.

Obviously there were any number of people in Cranberry Cove who weren't sorry that Sam Culbert was gone.

Gina followed Monica outside to the sidewalk, where she nudged her in the side playfully.

"So are you two going out?"

Monica was confused. "What two? What do you mean?"

"You and the fellow from the bookstore. Are you dating? Or is that too old-fashioned a word? I think the kids call it hooking up these days."

"No!" The word burst from Monica before she could stop it.

"Why not? He seems nice enough, and he's rather cute with the way his hair is always a little rumpled."

"We had brunch together on Sunday, but I don't think that—"

"So you *are* going out!"

"I don't think it was a date exactly. We ran into each other, and we were both hungry so . . ."

"So you went to brunch together. He wouldn't have suggested it if he didn't like you."

"True," Monica said, her lips curving into an involuntary smile.

Gina nudged Monica again. "Give him a little encouragement, and I'm sure he'll ask you out."

Monica started to protest but then closed her mouth. Why not? She liked Greg, and she wouldn't mind spending more time with him. She was a little unsure as to how she was supposed to encourage him beyond being friendly, but she knew better than to ask. She doubted she would like Gina's answer.

Monica bid her stepmother good-bye and headed to the diner to pick up Darlene's lunch. It looked as if Cora had left rather large shoes to fill. The new waitress, a young girl with a tattoo of a butterfly on her ankle, looked harried and flustered. A lock of hair was matted to her cheek with perspiration, and she kept looking over her shoulder at Gus, who glowered at her from behind the counter.

Monica placed her order and decided to treat herself to a hamburger, too. They were both ready with astonishing swiftness, and Monica picked up her package from the take-out window and left.

She was about to head to her car when she had a flash of inspiration. She would stop at the bakery and pick up a couple of cupcakes. Darlene would have her birthday party after all.

Before Monica even reached Sassamanash Farm, the interior of her car was redolent of the smell of hamburger and French fries, subtly overlaid with the scent of sugary buttercream icing. She parked in the farm store parking lot and was headed toward the door when she noticed a movement out of the corner of her eye.

Someone was standing in the field to the right of the store. Monica squinted. Two someones. One of them was Jeff. She didn't have to see him clearly to recognize his stance and his movements—the way he tilted his head when he was listening and used his hands when he was talking.

Jeff stepped to one side, and Monica could see that his companion was a female. She was quite sure it was Lauren. Maybe they were hashing things out? Monica crossed her fingers. She hoped so.

Darlene was leaning on the counter with a sulky look on her face when Monica entered.

"I'm hungry," she said, reaching for the white bag from the diner that Monica handed her.

"Sorry," Monica felt compelled to say. "I guess I took longer than I meant to."

Darlene sniffed, peered inside her bag, and pulled out her burger. "Did you bring me a cola?"

"Yes. I think our drinks are in this bag." Monica pushed it toward Darlene. She dug in her pocket and pulled out the bills Darlene had given her earlier. "Here, lunch is on me since it's your birthday."

Darlene looked truly startled and, Monica thought, almost touched as she put out a tentative hand to reach for the money. She ducked her head as if to say *thank you*.

The shop was empty so they unwrapped their burgers and fries and ate them side by side at the counter. It was the most companionable Monica had ever felt with Darlene. Finally they were finished and Monica scrunched up the wrappings from their meal and tossed them in the trash.

"Thanks," Darlene said, looking as if the words stuck to the roof of her mouth.

Monica waved a hand. "You deserved a birthday treat so . . ." She pulled the white bakery bag out from under the counter like a conjurer performing a magic trick.

Darlene's mouth dropped open. "What . . . what . . ." was all she could manage to say.

Monica then pulled the Gumdrops bag out from where she had stowed it. Darlene was agog; her eyes as round as saucers, her mouth in a startled *O*.

Monica handed the Gumdrops package to Darlene. "Just a little something to say happy birthday."

Darlene dashed at the tears that had formed in her eyes, and pulled the bag toward her. She peered inside and then pulled out the box of Droste chocolates.

"This is for me?" she asked incredulously.

"Yes," Monica assured her.

Darlene started to fumble with the box.

"But wait. Before you open that . . ." Monica pulled the cupcakes out of the bakery bag. "I think I have some plates in the back."

Darlene rubbed her eyes. "I'm really having a birthday after all."

Monica smiled. She was glad she had gone to the trouble of arranging something for Darlene.

They finished their cupcakes, threw their paper plates and wrappers in the trash, and Monica swept the last of the crumbs from the counter into her hand.

"I hope you enjoy the chocolates. I thought of getting you a book, but I wasn't sure what you liked to read."

"That's okay." Darlene held the box of candy to her chest as if Monica was going to snatch it back. She fingered the velvet bow tenderly. "You know that guy who owns the bookstore?" she asked suddenly.

Monica nodded.

"He ran for mayor against Sam Culbert a couple of years ago."

"Yes, I've heard. Someone told me."

"Did they tell you that Culbert cheated in the election? Paid people to vote for him, I heard."

"They did mention something about that. But they were just rumors."

Darlene gave her a sly look. "I don't know about that."

Monica raised her eyebrows. "Why do you say that?"

Darlene shrugged her shoulders. "On account of the fight."

"Fight?" Monica wanted to scream. Couldn't Darlene just come out with it? She was like a miser with a purse full of coins—reluctantly doling them out one at a time.

Darlene nodded. "Yes, they got into a fight."

Monica suppressed a sigh. "Who is 'they'?"

"Sam Culbert and that bookstore owner, of course," Darlene said with exaggerated patience.

Monica felt herself become very still. "Sam Culbert and Greg Harper got into a fight?"

"Yes. Right in the middle of Beach Hollow Road. They were shouting something fierce and circling each other like two dogs ready to attack. And you know what?"

"No," Monica said, trying not to grind her teeth.

"That Harper fellow threatened to kill Culbert."

"Don't you think that was just an idle threat? Made in anger in the spur of the moment?"

Darlene looked confused and pulled at her lower lip.

"What I'm saying is that Greg probably didn't mean it," Monica said. "People say things in anger that they have no intention of carrying out."

But how well did she know Greg Harper, really? A couple of brief conversations and one brunch together hardly meant you knew someone.

Monica decided it might be best to change the subject. "Are you still cleaning for the Culberts?" she asked. "I guess I should say for Mrs. Culbert now."

"Yes, of course." Darlene turned toward Monica. "I don't make enough money working here, do I?" She looked at Monica accusingly.

Monica stiffened. How had Darlene managed to go from making her feel warm toward her to being aggravated with her in the space of a couple of minutes?

Darlene seemed able to handle the slow flow of customers that began to arrive toward late afternoon, so Monica decided to head back to her cottage to work on the product application form for Fresh Gourmet.

Darlene gave Monica a panicked look when Monica began to put on her jacket.

"We're not very busy," Monica said pulling up her zipper. "I'm sure you'll be fine."

Darlene had her deer-in-the-headlights look, but Monica ignored it and said a firm good-bye. She drove back to her cottage, sun streaming through her windshield. She knew the weather would be changing soon—the nip in the air told her that—and the landscape would be covered in snow. Fortunately Monica enjoyed all the seasons and looked forward to each in turn.

A familiar car was in the driveway when Monica pulled

in. Stevens was leaning against the hood, her hands stuffed in the pockets of her open coat.

"Please don't say it," Stevens said with a smile as Monica pulled alongside her and got out of the car. "If one more person says 'oh, you're still here,' I will positively scream."

Monica laughed but inside she was worrying. What did Stevens want now? "Would you like to come inside?" she asked the detective.

"Please." Stevens turned up the collar on her coat. "It's getting rather chilly. The temperature must have dropped a good ten degrees since this morning."

Monica led the way into her tiny living room. Once again Stevens eschewed the overstuffed sofa and chose one of the armchairs.

"I'm glad you're here," Monica said as she sat down opposite Stevens.

"Now that's something I don't hear very often." Stevens smiled.

"I have some information for you."

Stevens raised her eyebrows and pulled a battered spiral notebook from the pocket of her raincoat.

"It's about Mauricio," Monica began.

Stevens removed the ballpoint pen that was stuck through the spiral on the notebook and clicked it. She held it poised above the paper.

"It makes sense that the same person that killed Culbert also killed Cora, don't you think?"

Stevens shrugged noncommittally.

Monica knitted her fingers together in her lap. "I mean, it seems somewhat incredible that Cranberry Cove could have two murderers on the loose." She took a deep breath.

"I have proof that Mauricio couldn't have killed Cora." Monica looked down at her hands. "I should have called you right away. I'm sorry."

"Seriously?" Stevens's expression changed from one of near amusement to something more serious.

"Yes. I talked with the VanVelsen sisters—"

"Who are—"

"They're the twins who own Gumdrops on Beach Hollow Road."

"Okay. Go on."

"Their cat Midnight had been missing for almost a week when a young man returned her the night Cora was killed. They were so grateful that they invited him to dinner. The young man was Mauricio."

"And I'm gathering that the timing puts him at the house of these sisters during the period when we suspect Cora was killed?"

Monica nodded.

"Do you mind if we go over a few things? I just want to check some facts." Stevens smiled.

"Certainly." Monica tried to relax her hands in her lap. She didn't want Stevens to see how nervous she was.

"You arrived at Cora's home when?"

What had she told her? Monica momentarily panicked. But then she realized she had nothing to fear. She was telling the truth. "It was around five thirty P.M. or a little after."

Stevens made a note. "And you went directly to Cora's, knocked on her door and then opened it?"

"Yes. No. I had a brief conversation with that neighbor of hers—Dawn. She said she had noticed Cora arriving home from work and hadn't seen her go out again."

"And Cora's car was in the driveway?"

"Yes. If she'd gone out it would have had to have been on foot."

"Dawn tells us that she didn't see anyone in or around Cora's trailer between the time when Cora got home from work and when you arrived."

What was she getting at? Monica wondered.

Stevens suddenly changed tack. "The ME performed the autopsy." She pinched the skin on the bridge of her nose with two fingers. "Of course it's inconclusive. Everything rests on the toxicology report now. However . . ." She paused and looked Monica in the face.

"Yes?"

"I managed to get him to hazard a guess. And that's not easy, I can tell you. It appears as if she had a seizure before she died. That, combined with the puncture mark on her arm, suggests she might have been injected with something. Something like insulin, maybe. An overdose would cause extremely low blood sugar, which could lead to a seizure and ultimately death."

Monica nodded to show she was listening.

"So Cora arrived home and apparently did not leave her house. And," Stevens rubbed a hand over her stomach, "we suspect she had a visitor based on the mug found in her sink. But the neighbor didn't see anyone go in or out." She leveled a gaze at Monica. "Except you."

"Me?" Monica pointed at herself. "Why would I want to kill Cora? I didn't even know her."

"Please." Stevens held up a hand. "I'm not saying you killed Cora. But it does seem rather odd, doesn't it?"

# Chapter 18

Monica set her laptop on the kitchen table and powered it on. She brought up the product application from the Fresh Gourmet website and began scanning the questions. She rubbed her forehead. She was finding it hard to concentrate. Detective Stevens's visit had unnerved her more than she wanted to admit.

Half an hour later, Monica was no further along than when she had started. She was about to turn off her computer and put the task off until another day when she decided to visit her long-neglected Facebook page. She rarely posted anything, but it was amusing to see what old friends from Chicago, or even as far back as high school, were doing.

She scrolled through her timeline, laughing occasionally at the cartoons and jokes or frowning over the bad news—a high school classmate had died from cancer, an acquaintance from Chicago had been laid off, someone's daughter had developed diabetes.

Other posts were more upbeat—pictures of vacation spots with impossibly blue water and white sand beaches, and snapshots of happy family reunions or important wedding anniversaries.

Someone had posted a quiz. Monica usually ignored those, but she needed something to take her mind off things. This one created your punk rock band name by combining the color of your pants and the first object to your right. Well, she was wearing blue jeans . . . she glanced to her right. It looked as if her group was named The Blue Teacup. She laughed to herself. That sounded more like a senior citizen knitting club than a rock band.

Monica scrolled some more and came upon another quiz: *What Animal are You?* She clicked through the questions . . . "What is your favorite night out?" Staying in wasn't an option so she chose dinner and a movie. Then, "What's your favorite item of clothing?" Monica didn't really have one, but she chose her ratty old bathrobe because it was certainly the garment she'd had the longest. She finished the rest of the questions and then clicked on the tab to get the results.

According to her answers, she was a dog—faithful, loyal and protective. Monica laughed. Well, that was certainly true enough, although not terribly exciting or romantic. On the other hand, she'd hardly expected to be a lynx, jaguar or cougar. She was powering off her computer when the back door opened.

"It's just me." Gina pushed open the door and walked in. She plopped into the chair opposite Monica.

Gina's casual updo was in disarray, but not the artful sort of disarray created by spending hours in front of the mirror—this time it was real. Her top had a fine dusting of sawdust on it, and there was a smudge of dirt across the bridge of her nose.

"What a long day," she said, as she rotated her neck and flexed her fingers. "How did yours turn out?"

Monica fiddled with the latch on her laptop. "Detective Stevens was here again."

Gina started. "What? Again?" Her face clouded over. "She wasn't after Jeffie, was she?"

"No. This time I seem to be the prime suspect."

"You? But that's ridiculous."

"That's what I told her, although not in those exact words, of course." Monica gave a wry smile.

"If she can't see you're innocent, she's a fool."

"The problem is," Monica pushed her laptop away and leaned her elbows on the table, "neither Jeff nor I have an alibi. He was here for dinner, but unfortunately Culbert's murder took place sometime after that."

"But what about that Mauricio fellow?" Gina rubbed her hands over her face, smudging her mascara. "His alibi didn't hold up in the end, and why would he lie if he wasn't guilty?"

"The problem is, he didn't kill Cora." Monica pushed her chair back, got up and went over to the refrigerator. She opened it and rummaged around inside. "Would you like some cheese and crackers?" she called over her shoulder to Gina.

"Sure. Now that you mention it, I am getting a bit hungry."

Monica retrieved a box of crackers from one cupboard and a cheese plate from another. "I'm afraid all I have is a block of common, garden-variety cheddar."

"That's fine." Gina twisted around in her seat to look at Monica. "You've said Mauricio didn't kill Cora, but how do you know?"

"He has an alibi. He was rescuing the VanVelsen sisters' cat and bringing it back to them. He was with them from the time Cora supposedly arrived home from work till past the time I found her body." Monica placed the cheese and crackers on the table.

"Well, rats." Gina smacked the table, rattling the plate. "It would be so convenient if he were responsible."

"I know. Although I'm glad he's not. He seems like a nice young man." Monica pushed the cheese plate toward Gina. "Help yourself."

Gina cut a slice of cheddar and balanced it on a cracker.

"Darlene told me something interesting today. I'm not sure what to make of it," Monica said as she fixed a cracker for herself.

"Mmmm?" Gina mumbled around the food in her mouth.

"You remember how that carpenter at your shop told us about the mayoral election and how Greg Harper, the bookstore owner, lost to Sam Culbert?"

Gina nodded and brushed some crumbs off her top. "And he said Culbert cheated, which doesn't surprise me in the least."

"Me neither."

"So what did Darlene tell you?"

"She said that Greg and Culbert got into a huge fight about the election results."

Gina's eyes widened. "You mean they actually came to blows over it?"

"Just short of that, I gather. But apparently Greg threatened to kill Culbert."

Gina snorted. "From what I've heard, half the people in town have done the same thing."

"Yes, but Darlene seems to think he meant it."

Gina stabbed a finger in the air toward Monica. "But

what about Cora? You're forgetting about Cora. Why would Greg Harper want to kill her?"

"Who knows?" Monica shrugged. "We didn't think there was any connection between Mauricio and Cora, either, but we were wrong."

"True." Gina made a face. "But I don't want it to be him."

Monica laughed. "We can't just choose who we want to be the murderer!"

"I know," Gina said. "I was just making a joke." She looked at Monica for a minute. "You look very tense."

"I am."

"Twilight is having a yoga session tonight that's focusing on relaxation. Why don't we go?"

Monica hesitated but then thought, why not? It would probably do her good. She'd gone to a few yoga classes in Chicago and had enjoyed them.


Monica dug around in her dresser until she found an old pair of leggings. There was a small hole in the knee, but she didn't really care. She pulled them on along with a T-shirt that said *Monica's* on it. She'd had the shirts made to drum up business for her café. Seeing it now was bittersweet. She missed having her own business, but she felt good about helping Jeff, and she enjoyed life in Cranberry Cove. Although she could have done without the murders, of course.

Gina was already downstairs by the time Monica was ready. She was wearing a psychedelic-looking pair of leggings with swirls of pink and mauve and a matching pink tank top.

"Ready?" she said when she heard Monica enter the room.

She screwed the top back on the bottle of polish she'd been using to touch up her nails.

"Yes." Monica grabbed her coat from the back of the kitchen chair. A wave of tiredness nearly overwhelmed her, but it was too late to back out now.

Gina drove them—one hand on the wheel, the other gesturing wildly as she described her day and the construction at her new shop. A couple of times she turned and looked at Monica for so long that Monica had to remind her to turn her attention back to the road. Monica was a little embarrassed by the frightened mewling noises she made several times as Gina veered a little too close to the oncoming traffic.

Fortunately they arrived at Twilight in one piece. Monica couldn't imagine who in Cranberry Cove would be attending a yoga session, so she was surprised to see that quite a few people had already unrolled their mats on the floor of the room in the back of Tempest's shop. It was a diverse group of both young and old—everyone from the new waitress Monica recognized from the diner to the woman who sewed the tea towels and napkins for Sassamanash Farm. There was even one gentleman—he had long, frizzy gray hair tied back in a ponytail and was lying on his mat doing a very complicated-looking stretch. Monica hoped she'd be able to keep up with the class.

Scented candles flickered around the periphery of the room, and a fountain trickled softly in the corner next to a stack of folded blankets. Some sort of New Age music was barely audible in the background.

Monica and Gina unrolled their mats in the back and lay down on them. Monica hoped she wouldn't fall asleep before the class started. She had to suppress a yawn and was struggling to keep her eyes from closing.

Tempest took up a position next to Monica. She was wearing black yoga pants, a long-sleeved turquoise top with an Indian-inspired design on the front and had a matching wide, cloth headband holding back her dark hair.

Monica barely had time to say hello before the instructor took up her position in the front of the room. Monica was surprised to see that she was an older woman with gray hair pinned back into a tight bun. She led them through an hour of poses, and Monica marveled at her flexibility. Her own muscles were tight and stiff in comparison. Halfway through the class she found her mind quieting, and a sense of well-being washed over her. She was almost sorry when the class was over and the instructor bid them Namaste.

"What did you think?" Tempest asked as she rolled up her hot pink mat.

"I enjoyed it more than I expected," Monica said.

Tempest turned to Gina. "You have a good practice. You've obviously been doing yoga for a while."

"It helps to keep the stress level down," Gina responded. "Otherwise I'd have to go around with a cask of brandy around my neck like one of those Saint Bernard dogs."

Tempest threw back her head and gave a full-bodied laugh. "Things have been unusually stressful in Cranberry Cove lately, haven't they? Two unsolved murders—can you believe it?"

"Speaking of the murders," Monica began. "I've been told that Greg Harper, the owner of Book 'Em, ran for mayor against Sam Culbert and lost."

"That's true." Tempest looked at Monica curiously. "Greg's a nice guy. I had my eye on him myself when I first got here, but I think I'm at the wrong end of forty for him."

She shrugged. "But surely you don't think that he had anything to do with the murders?"

This time Monica shrugged. "I heard that he and Culbert got into a huge fight about it. Right in the middle of Beach Hollow Road. And that Greg threatened to kill Culbert."

"Really? That's the first I'm hearing of it." Tempest turned and waved good-bye to an older woman who had a bright yellow mat rolled up and tucked under her arm.

"So you don't know anything about the fight?" Monica asked.

Tempest shook her head. "No, and frankly I can't imagine Greg Harper threatening someone like that. I'm sure he didn't mean it, but even so, it doesn't fit with the little I know of him."

"That's what I thought."

"Do you think that girl is embellishing the story just a teeny bit?" Gina asked. "She doesn't seem like the brightest crayon in the box, if you know what I mean. I used to know someone like her back when I was working at Neiman Marcus. Always dramatizing events. I think she was bored, poor thing. Never went out as far as I could tell." Gina shuddered. "She lived in this pathetic one-room apartment and spent her nights eating in front of the television."

Monica felt her spirits lift. She really didn't want to think Greg capable of murder, and what Gina said made sense. Darlene was just the sort to make something like that up. Half the time she couldn't tell if Darlene was telling the truth or not.

By the time they got back to Monica's place, Monica was starving. She opened the refrigerator and scanned the contents.

"Would you like some pasta?" she called over her shoulder to Gina.

"Thanks, but Jeff is picking me up for dinner. He wants me to meet Lauren."

Monica paused with her hand on the open refrigerator door. "That must mean they're getting back together."

"You'd think so, wouldn't you? Jeff made some cryptic reference to 'working things out.'"

"It's a good sign at least." Monica pulled a half-full jar of pasta sauce and the makings for a salad from the fridge and pushed the door shut with her knee.

"I guess I'd better get ready." Gina glanced at the clock. "I didn't realize how late it had become."

Gina disappeared upstairs, and Monica began to boil water for her spaghetti. She was cleaning lettuce for a salad when Gina reappeared in a gauzy top over a pair of reptile-print leggings. Monica couldn't help but stare.

Gina must have noticed. "When I was with your father, I had to wear all these conservative clothes like those buttoned-up St. John's knit suits. Now I can let my own personality out." She circled in front of Monica. "Like it?"

Monica managed to stifle her initial reaction. "It's certainly . . . creative," she said finally, searching for a word that she could use with a straight face and that could still be considered complimentary.

"Thanks." Gina perched on the edge of one of the kitchen chairs, her foot jiggling in its customary fashion. "I wonder where Jeffie is?" she asked a few minutes later. "He was supposed to be here ten minutes ago."

"He may have gotten held up by something." Monica looked

out the kitchen window. It was already dark—Jeff was unlikely to still be out at the bogs.

Another ten minutes went by, and Gina's foot was now jiggling double time. She pulled her cell phone from her purse and tapped in the number with the tips of her manicured nails.

After several seconds she lowered the phone and looked at Monica. "No answer." She frowned. "This isn't like Jeff. It's not like him at all."

Monica had to agree, but she didn't want to sound alarmist. Jeff was only twenty minutes late—there could be any number of perfectly ordinary reasons why.

Monica finished putting her dishes in the dishwasher. She turned toward Gina. "Do you want something to eat . . . ?"

"No, thanks. I'm too wound up." As if to corroborate that, Gina's foot jiggling picked up even more speed, nearly becoming a blur.

Ten minutes later, Gina was pacing around the kitchen. "Maybe we should go check on him? Maybe he's ill or hurt or . . . something?"

"You know Jeff—if we do that he'll think we're babying him because of his injury. Why don't you try calling him again?"

"Okay." Gina stopped moving long enough to dial. She pressed her phone to her ear so tightly, Monica could see her knuckles turning white.

"Anything?"

Gina shook her head. A tear trickled down her cheek, and she swiped at it impatiently. "It's just that Jeff is all I have. Your father left me, my parents are long gone. I have no sisters or brothers. My father had a sister, Aunt Clarice, but she's in a nursing home somewhere in Iowa." She made a circular motion around her temple with her finger. "Dementia. I tried calling her once but she had no idea who I was—thought I was her long-dead mother." Gina collapsed into her chair. "What am I going to do?" She burst into full-fledged tears.

Monica was at a loss. She'd never been very good at dealing with other people's upsets. Her parents had considered emotions to be messy things that other people indulged in, but not them. She ran to the powder room to fetch a box of tissues and pushed them across the table to Gina.

"I think we're both worrying for no reason."

Gina grabbed one and blew her nose loudly. "I'm sorry. I shouldn't be burdening you with this." She looked up at Monica with tear-swollen eyes. "You mean a lot to me." She reached out and grabbed Monica's hand. "I know you don't approve of me, and I don't blame you for being bitter that I broke up your parents' marriage—"

Monica was already shaking her head. "No, you didn't." She squeezed Gina's hand. "Now that I'm older I can see that it was over before Dad ever met you."

Gina gulped and gave a thin smile.

They both jumped when the front doorbell rang.

Gina's smile got even bigger and she leapt to her feet. "That must be Jeff now. I wonder why he didn't come to the back door the way he usually does?" She picked up her purse and slipped into the jacket she had draped over the back of the kitchen chair.

Monica frowned. Gina was right—it wasn't like Jeff to ring the front bell. He normally just walked in and gave her that lopsided grin that had been melting her heart since he was a toddler. She feared that Gina was going to be disappointed. She hadn't said anything—she didn't want to worry Gina even more—but she was getting very concerned about Jeff herself.

Monica made her way to the front hall, Gina tight on her heels. She pulled open the door, and they both stood there for a moment, stunned.

It wasn't Jeff on Monica's doorstep but Lauren, her face pinched with worry. Her car was pulled up in front of Monica's cottage in such a way that it looked more abandoned than parked.

"I'm sorry to bother you," she began.

"It's no bother," Monica assured her. "Come in. It's getting cold out there."

The wind had picked up and dried leaves were swirling around the driveway, making a sharp rustling sound.

"What's wrong?" Monica asked as soon as they were inside.

"It's Jeff."

"I knew it," cried Gina, stuffing the knuckles of her right hand into her mouth.

"Please, sit." Monica pointed at the sofa. "Can I get you anything?"

Lauren shook her head and perched on the edge of the sofa. "Jeff was supposed to pick me up for dinner," she said, gripping the fabric of her trousers with both hands. "He was late, which isn't like him. I tried calling him, but there was no answer. I thought maybe I misunderstood and was supposed to drive to his apartment myself." Lauren took a big gulp of air. "He wasn't there. I didn't know what to do so I thought I would come here. I hope you don't mind." She looked from Monica to Gina with pleading eyes. "I was hoping he was here, and we'd just gotten our signals crossed."

Gina collapsed into the armchair. "I'm afraid he's not. We don't know where he is." She looked at Monica.

"Let's not jump to conclusions," Monica said, although she had already jumped to plenty of them herself. But this was no time to engage in her customary honesty.

She had barely finished speaking when her phone rang. They all looked at each other and then Monica sprinted toward the kitchen with Gina and Lauren right behind her.

"Hello?" She snatched the receiver from the cradle. "Jeff! Where are you? We've all been so worried."

"I'm sorry. I didn't mean to worry you, but there was no time to call."

"Has there been some sort of accident?" Monica tried to loosen her grip on the phone—she was getting a cramp in her hand.

"No, nothing like that. But one of the guys on the crew— Peter—has a brother who's a cop. His brother told him that there was a warrant out for my arrest. When I saw Detective Stevens pull into my driveway as I was getting ready to go pick up Lauren, I panicked."

"What do you mean you panicked?" Monica was panicking herself—her heart slamming against her ribs, her mouth dry.

"I didn't answer the door, and when Stevens went back to her car, I took off."

"Where are you now?"

"I don't want to tell you. That way if the police question you, you can be honest and say you don't know where I am."

"Jeff, I think you're making a mistake." Monica looked up to see Gina staring at her. She put up a hand to indicate that everything was going to be okay.

"I can't go to jail. I can't let them lock me up."

"You're not going to go to jail," Monica said firmly. "Even if it's true that they plan to arrest you, we'll call a lawyer and post bail."

"How? We don't have any money. The farm is operating on borrowed time as it is."

"Just tell me where you are." Monica thought that if she could talk to Jeff face-to-face she could drill some sense into him.

"I can't tell you. Just let Mom and Lauren know that I'm okay. Please?"

"Jeff—" Monica said, but the dial tone cut her off.

# Chapter 19

"What's going on? What did Jeff say?" Gina grabbed Monica's arm.

Monica took a deep breath. "Jeff is fine, but he's . . . he's gone into hiding."

"Hiding? What on earth for?" Gina sputtered.

"He seems to think that the police are about to arrest him."

Lauren had become paler and paler during this exchange.

"Are you okay?" Monica moved toward her and put a hand on her shoulder.

"Yes." It was barely a whisper.

"What are we going to do?" Gina asked.

"There isn't much we can do. He won't tell me where he is."

"We have to find him then."

Monica chewed on the edge of a ragged cuticle. "Going into hiding is only going to make things worse for him."

"We have to find him and persuade him to turn himself in." Gina thumped the sofa cushion next to her. She jumped to her feet. "Once he explains things, everything will be alright."

"But he doesn't have an alibi for Culbert's killing," Monica pointed out. "He was out checking the temperatures in the bogs that night. The police could easily use that against him."

Gina's posture stiffened. "I hope you don't think Jeffie did it."

"No!" The word burst from Monica like an explosion. "Of course not. I'm just trying to put myself in the position of Detective Stevens."

"Aren't people supposed to be innocent until proven guilty?" Gina shot back.

"Yes, of course they are," Monica responded. "But the police have to go by clues and check alibis and things like that."

"What about that woman who was killed?"

"Cora?"

"Yes, her. Jeffie had no reason to harm her. Not that I'm saying he had anything to do with Culbert's murder, either." Gina crossed her arms over her chest.

Monica didn't want to be at odds with Gina. Things were difficult enough as it was. She went over to Gina and put her arms around her. Such physical demonstrations weren't the norm for Monica, and she wasn't entirely comfortable with it. Fortunately it seemed to do the trick because she could feel Gina relaxing slightly.

"I'm just trying to see things from Detective Stevens's perspective so that we're prepared for whatever may happen."

Monica glanced at Lauren. The poor girl had been following the entire conversation, her head snapping from

Monica to Gina and back again. Monica was surprised she hadn't sustained a nasty case of whiplash.

A knock on the front door made them all bristle, and for a moment no one moved.

"I bet that's Jeffie." Gina made for the door. "Maybe he's come to his senses."

Lauren's face brightened at Gina's words, but Monica was doubtful, and she wasn't surprised when Gina flung open the door and uttered a startled cry at finding Detective Stevens standing on the doorstep.

"Yes, I'm still here," Stevens said by way of greeting. She was panting slightly from the walk from her car to the door.

"Would you like some water?" Monica asked.

Stevens shook her head. "I'm fine. I wanted to see if your brother is here."

"Why? So you can arrest him?" Gina took an aggressive stance in front of Stevens.

Stevens gave a weary smile. "I merely want to talk to him. If he's not here," she looked around, "can you tell me where he is?"

"We don't know where he is."

Stevens looked doubtful. "Has he been in touch at all?"

"No," Monica said a little too quickly.

Stevens's brows rose.

Monica fidgeted with the cuff of her sweater. Now she understood why Jeff hadn't wanted to reveal his whereabouts. He knew she wouldn't be able to pull off lying convincingly to the police.

"It would be better for him if he came to us willingly. Maybe you can pass that message along to him next time you talk to him," Stevens said as she made her way toward the door.

Monica went to the window and eased the curtain aside. "I guess she didn't believe us," she said as soon as Stevens had gotten into her car and started down the drive. "We've got to find Jeff."

"No," Gina said. "Jeff is right. You're terrible at lying. You'd never be able to convince Stevens that you didn't know where he was."

Monica had pretended to agree with Gina—that it was better if she didn't know where Jeff was hiding. But that didn't mean she wasn't going to go looking for him. She had an idea of where he might be, but she would have to wait till Gina went to bed or became occupied with the television before she could sneak out.

Monica made Gina some tea and toast—all she wanted—and pretended to settle down in front of the television to watch one of those shows where people sing in front of a panel of judges. Monica had never been much of a television watcher—she'd always been too busy, and when she had downtime she chose to pick up a book, preferably a mystery. But although she lounged in her chair with her feet up on an ottoman, the picture of ease, she was far from relaxed. Her mind was whirling. Was Jeff hiding where she suspected? And when would she be able to sneak out of the house to test her theory?

The television show was nearing the end. Monica glanced at Gina. Her eyes were closed, her breathing even. One arm lolled over the edge of the chair and her head was tilted slightly to the side.

Monica got up slowly, making as little noise as possible.

She would creep upstairs and close her bedroom door. If Gina woke and wondered where she was, she would assume that Monica had gone to sleep.

Monica crept back down the stairs and out to the kitchen. She eased open the drawer by the sink and took out the large, powerful flashlight Jeff had given her. She grabbed her jacket from the hook by the back door and silently slipped out.

The moon was full and bright, creating a well-lit swath across the grass. The wind was sharp, and Monica pulled her collar up and fished her gloves from her pockets. Tree branches swayed in the wind, creating looming shadows that danced menacingly across her path. She shivered but continued walking.

She was headed toward the old pump house. There wasn't much room inside—just enough space to put down a sleeping bag or small mattress. And although the boards were old and creaked with every puff of the wind, they kept out the worst of the cold. It wouldn't be a pleasant place to spend the night, but Jeff was no doubt used to much worse.

The wind made a loud whistling noise as it came through the trees, and Monica had to force herself to go on. She remembered all too well the night someone hit her over the head, and even the slightest noise made her jump and whirl around. She would have much preferred to be tucked up warm and safe in her bed, but she had to find Jeff before the police did.

Time seemed to be standing still, and she felt as if she had been walking for an eternity before the pump house finally came into view. It looked even more ramshackle in the moonlight, and Monica shivered at the prospect of spending the night there.

She approached as quietly as she could, pausing for a

moment to listen for the sounds of any movement from within. All she heard was the wind soughing through the branches of the swaying trees.

She turned the handle to the pump house door as slowly and quietly as possible and eased it open. The interior was pitch black. Monica aimed the beam of her flashlight at the dirt floor then carefully moved it around the small enclosure. Nothing. And no sign anyone had been there either. Monica's shoulders sagged with disappointment. She had been so sure that that was where Jeff was hiding.

She closed the door, not worrying about making noise now. If Jeff wasn't in the pump house then where on earth was he? Sleeping in his truck somewhere? If that was the case, she'd never find him.

Monica was passing the bog where Culbert's body had been found. She averted her eyes, half expecting to see his lifeless corpse floating faceup in the water. Of course, the bog had already been drained and the water channeled to another bog.

The gnarled roots from the trees lining the path had spread and were bursting through the ground, making walking treacherous. Monica kept her flashlight aimed at the ground and her eyes down. Even so, she nearly tripped twice, causing her heart to begin thudding so loudly she could hear it in her ears.

The beam of her flashlight picked up something that glinted in the light. Monica poked at it with the toe of her shoe. It looked like a piece of jewelry. She bent and picked it up. It was a ring.

It was a circle of gold with a large ruby or garnet— Monica couldn't tell which in the dim light—set deep into the band. Monica looked at the inside of the band to see if there was any inscription, but the light wasn't bright enough. Who could have lost such a valuable ring out here by the bogs? Maybe it was Gina's? But she hadn't mentioned anything about losing something so valuable.

Monica tucked it into the pocket of her jacket and continued on. The beam from her flashlight began to waver and then, after she had taken several more steps, it went out. Fortunately her cottage was already in view. She hurried the last few yards, breathing a sigh of relief when her hand touched the knob to the back door.

Gina was waiting in the kitchen, a glass of wine in her hand. She jumped when Monica opened the door, and wine splashed out of her glass and onto the table.

"Oh, you gave me a fright. What on earth were you doing outside?"

Monica didn't have an excuse ready so she was forced to admit the truth. "I was looking for Jeff. I thought he might be hiding in the pump house."

"Pump house?"

"It's where all the equipment for the water pumps is housed. There's just enough space to lay down a sleeping bag."

"He wasn't there?" Gina asked with a hint of hope in her voice.

"No. Unfortunately not."

Monica pulled off her gloves and went to stuff them in her pocket when her fingers touched the ring. She'd almost forgotten about it.

She pulled it out and handed it to Gina. "I found this on the ground. Is it yours?"

Gina took the ring and examined it. She shook her head. "No, it isn't mine. It's lovely though. And expensive. That's a very fine ruby. See how vibrant the color is?" She pointed to the stone mounted in the center of the circle of gold.

*Trust Gina to know her jewelry.*

"Are you going to keep it?"

"No. I have to find the owner. Is there any inscription?"

Gina held the ring to the light. "There's something here. Very faint though—the letters are partly worn through."

"Maybe it's very old?"

"Could be." Gina handed the ring back to Monica. "Are you going to put an ad in the paper?"

"Maybe. First I'll ask around and see if anyone recognizes it. Maybe Jeff—" She stopped, the words catching in her throat.

"Go on, say it." Gina jumped up from her chair. "Jeff is gone and we don't know where he is. We don't even know if we'll ever see him again. If the police find him . . . well there are plenty of people in jail for crimes they didn't commit just because they couldn't prove their innocence."

Monica's stomach clenched at the thought. Gina was right. No matter how good the system, there were still plenty of miscarriages of justice.

"Don't worry." She put an arm around Gina's shoulders. "We'll get to the bottom of this. We'll find out who really did it, and then life can go back to normal."

Monica was up early after a night of tossing and turning. When she did doze off, her sleep was filled with nightmares. She was more than happy to leave her warm bed for a change. The tangled sheets and the half on, half off comforter were a testament to her restless night.

She wrapped up in her old robe and crept down the stairs

to the kitchen. She didn't want to wake Gina. Frankly, she didn't want any company yet.

The kitchen was cold so Monica turned the heat up a notch and put on the kettle for some tea. When it was done, she carried her cup to the kitchen table, where she'd left her laptop. She would use the time to finish the application for product placement for Fresh Gourmet.

Sun was beginning to peek through the curtains when Monica hit send on the e-mail to which she'd attached her completed application. She crossed her fingers and sent up a silent prayer, then stretched her back and tilted her head from side to side. She hadn't realized how still she'd been sitting or how cramped she'd become.

It was time to begin baking the day's goods. Monica glanced at the clock. Past time really. She should have started a half hour ago. Fortunately the shop was rarely busy first thing in the morning. As a matter of fact, she'd thought of suggesting to Jeff that they adjust their hours and open slightly later during the week. The thought of Jeff gave her a pang, and she hurried to get busy and occupy her mind with something else.

With the muffins and coffee cake finally in the oven, Monica went upstairs to get dressed. The door to the spare bedroom was closed so she supposed Gina was still sleeping. Hopefully Gina had had a more restful night than she had, but given the circumstances, Monica doubted it.

She pulled on some jeans and a warm sweatshirt with *Loyola University* on it. It was from Monica's college days and she supposed she ought to get rid of it, but it had sentimental value. Besides, it was very warm.

The oven timer pinged just as she walked into the kitchen. She pulled out the muffins and coffee cake and put them on a wire rack to cool. As soon as she could handle them, she would pack them in her basket and take them down to the store. Any early customers would be treated to warm baked goods this morning.

Gina still hadn't woken up by the time Monica was ready to leave for the store. She scribbled a note, ripped the piece of paper from the scratch pad and left it on the kitchen table, propped against the salt and pepper shakers, where she hoped Gina would see it.

Monica began the walk to the farm store, her shoulders hunched against the cold. She passed the spot where she'd found the ring. It had been near the dirt path that had been worn between the cottage and the store. Whoever dropped it had been walking between the two. But who else could that have been except for her, Gina, Jeff and the members of his crew? It wasn't a man's ring—it was too small and too feminine-looking—so it was unlikely it belonged to one of the men working for Jeff.

Darlene was just unlocking the door when Monica arrived at the store. Instead of being in its accustomed ponytail, Darlene's hair hung down her back, and Monica noticed she had had her bangs trimmed. She gave Monica a shy smile.

Well, Monica thought—the money she'd spent on the birthday gift and lunch had obviously been money well spent.

"Can I help you with that?" Darlene asked after they'd both hung up their coats.

"Would you?" Monica handed her the baskets of baked goods. "There's something I want to check."

Darlene began arranging the muffins with slightly more care than usual, and Monica was pleasantly surprised.

As soon as Darlene's back was turned, Monica pushed open the door into the screening room. The lights were off and the machinery was idle and silent. Monica bit her lip. With Jeff in hiding, they were going to be behind on the harvest, and they could ill afford that. They needed the check from the sale to the cooperative as soon as possible.

Monica flicked on the lights. She knew it was a long shot but perhaps Jeff had spent the night in here. She looked around, but the room was empty, and there was no sign that anyone had hunkered down there for the evening.

She went back through to the store, grabbed her apron from the hook and had just finished tying it when the door opened and a woman walked in. She had on an expensive all-weather jacket like the ones in the window of Danielle's Boutique in town. Her dark brown leather boots were polished to a gleaming shine, and her hair was styled in such a way that Monica guessed she'd had it done at a salon in Chicago or some other big city.

Darlene sidled toward the woman at her customary snail's pace. Monica hovered nearby in case Darlene needed any help. The woman asked for an entire coffee cake. Monica thought she said it was for her book club.

Darlene retrieved the cake from the case and slid it into a white bakery bag. Monica made a mental note to order bags that had *Sassamanash Farm* written on them as soon as they ran low on the plain ones.

The woman pulled off her leather driving gloves, retrieved an ostrich-skin wallet from the depths of her Coach handbag and slid her credit card across the counter to Darlene.

Monica couldn't help but notice the large diamond ring on the woman's finger. It made the one Gina wore look like something from a Cracker Jack box. It also reminded Monica of the ruby ring in the pocket of her jacket.

As the woman gathered her purchases together and prepared to leave, Monica went to her jacket, stuck her hand in the pocket and retrieved the ring. She would show it to Darlene and see if she possibly recognized it.

"Can I show you something?" Monica asked.

"Sure. What is it?" Darlene blinked rapidly several times.

Monica put the ring on the counter. "I found this on the path between here and my cottage."

Darlene gave a bitter laugh. "Well, it isn't mine, that's for sure."

Monica suppressed a sigh. She hadn't expected it to be Darlene's. Sure enough to bet the farm at any rate.

"Do you recognize it at all?"

Darlene tilted her head to the side, regarding the ring from all angles. Finally she plucked it from the counter and held it in front of her nose. "It looks familiar. I think I might have seen one like it before."

"Really? Could it belong to one of our customers?"

Sightseers on a tour of the farm could conceivably have taken that path to the bogs. Someone might have dropped that ring. Monica knew that the colder weather tended to make rings looser. Her engagement ring used to twirl around and around her finger in the winter, even though the jeweler had sized it appropriately.

Darlene continued to stare at the ring, the tip of her tongue showing between her teeth. She put the ring back on the counter.

"I think it belongs to Mrs. Culbert. I've seen one like it on her dressing table when I was in her room dusting."

Monica froze. "Are you sure?"

Darlene bobbed her head. "Yes. I remember thinking it

was pretty." She put out a finger and reverently touched the ring. "I like the red stone. Red is my favorite color." Darlene sniffed. "Must be nice having fancy jewelry like that. Of course poor Mrs. Culbert had to pay for it."

"Pay for it? You mean she bought it for herself?" Monica wondered where Darlene had gotten such information. Perhaps she and Andrea Culbert had become close?

Darlene rolled her eyes and smiled smugly, as if for once she was one up on Monica. "I didn't mean actually pay for it. Like with money. I meant she had to put up with Sam Culbert." Darlene rolled her eyes again.

"I've heard he was . . . difficult."

"Yes. Everybody knows that. And he was even worse at home. Everything had to be just so. Mrs. Culbert used to get so nervous when she heard his car pulling in the driveway. I stayed clear of him myself, that's for sure."

"Why didn't she divorce him?" Monica was all for trying to work things out, but that didn't sound possible in this case.

"She wanted to." Darlene lowered her voice although they were all alone in the store. "She told me she'd been to see a lawyer. The problem was the money. I heard them arguing one time." Darlene lowered her voice even further. "And he told her that if she left him, he'd make sure she didn't get a single penny."

Darlene shuddered. "That Sam Culbert scared me. I'm glad I don't work there anymore."

"You quit?"

Darlene shook her head. "Mrs. Culbert said she didn't need me anymore." Darlene's eyes shifted away from Monica's. "She said that all their assets—I guess she meant her money and stuff like that—were tied up until they did something about the will. She told me what it was, but I can't remember."

"Probate? Until the will was out of probate?"

"Yes, that's it. I don't know what it means. All I know is it means I'm out of a job for the moment. Mrs. Culbert did say she'd call me the minute they were done doing . . . what you said."

The shop door opened and a woman came in. She went to the bakery counter and motioned for Darlene.

While Darlene waited on their customer, Monica straightened up the display of tea towels and pot holders. She kept thinking about what Darlene had said. If Darlene was right, and the ruby ring did belong to Sam Culbert's wife, then that meant she had been at Sassamanash Farm. Had she been there the night Culbert was killed? And had she decided that murder was a lot more expedient than a divorce?

# Chapter 20

Monica retrieved a clean handkerchief from her purse, wrapped the ring in it and tucked it back into her pocket. She would have to take it to the police and let them sort it out. Would it yield any useful fingerprints? The one thing she was certain of—the ring couldn't possibly incriminate Jeff in any way. He'd never been to the Culbert's house, and Monica knew there was no way he would have stolen such a valuable piece of jewelry.

Monica was about to leave the store when she heard her cell phone ringing from the depths of her purse. She rummaged around until she found it, pulled it out and held it to her ear.

"Hello?"

"Monica? It's Gina."

"What's wrong?" Gina sounded terrible—her voice was thick, as if she had been crying.

"Nothing really. It's just that I had this idea where Jeff

might be hiding. I'd given him a key to my new shop—you know how I am about losing things, and I thought it would be safer that way. Jeff never loses anything. He must get that from his father."

There was a long pause. "Yes?" Monica asked.

"I thought he might have let himself in to spend the night." She made a noise that sounded halfway between a sob and a hiccough. "As a matter of fact, I was sort of counting on it. I didn't want to say anything in case I was wrong." She gave an unmistakable sob. "And I was. There's no sign of him and no sign that he's ever been here."

"Gina," Monica pleaded. "Listen to me. Wherever Jeff is, you know he's fine. He managed to take care of himself in Afghanistan, didn't he?" Monica pushed thoughts of Jeff's paralyzed arm out of her mind. "I'm sure he can take care of himself here in Cranberry Cove. Even if it means sleeping rough for a couple of nights."

Gina sniffed. "You're right. I'm being silly. It's just that I'd gotten my hopes up . . ."

"Why don't I come into town, and we'll go get a cup of tea at the diner."

Gina laughed. "A drink would be more like it."

"The only bar likely to be open at this early hour is Flynn's, and I never want to set foot in that place again."

"That makes two of us. The diner it is."

Monica clicked off the call, grabbed her purse and slipped on her jacket.

Ten minutes later she was driving down Beach Hollow Road. She had to lower her visor against the bright sunlight coming through the window of her Focus. A car was pulling out of a space in front of the bookstore, and Monica pulled up, waiting patiently, her blinker going to let others know she was claiming the space. The station wagon finished backing up and took off down the road. Monica quickly maneuvered the Focus into the space.

A white van with *Book 'Em* in red lettering was double-parked just beyond where Monica had pulled in. The back doors were open, and Greg was busy unloading armfuls of books. He waved Monica over to where he was standing.

"I must be covered in dust," he said as she approached. "I've been to an estate sale. Old Mrs. Pickering who owned that big house just outside of town, overlooking the lake, passed away, and her nephew thought I might be interested in some of her books. She had quite a collection. The house had a proper library, complete with floor-to-ceiling bookcases, and still they were tumbling off the shelves and stacked in huge piles on the floor. I think she was more of a hoarder than a collector."

"Did you find anything good?" Monica tilted her head so she could read the titles of the books in Greg's arms.

"Believe it or not, I did. She had an entire set of Ngaio Marsh. First editions, too, and in good condition. The nephew refused to take any money for them. Said he was grateful to have someone cart them away, but I couldn't let him do that. I wouldn't have been able to live with myself if I hadn't given him a fair price for them." Greg freed one hand and scratched his nose. "There were plenty of other treasures, too, but the Ngaio Marsh set is a real find."

"She's always been a favorite of mine. I think I have something of a crush on Roderick Alleyn."

"Really?" Greg laughed. "She was passionate about the theater, you know. A fascinating woman all around."

"Listen," Monica said on impulse. "I know this is last minute, but would you like to come to dinner tonight?"

A huge grin swept across Greg's face. "I'd love to." He glanced down at his feet. "I'll bring a bottle of wine. Red or white?"

Monica thought for a minute. "Red?"

Greg nodded. Monica started to give him directions, but he interrupted her.

"I know where Sassamanash Farm is, don't worry."

They settled on a time, and Monica reluctantly said good-bye. As she was walking down the street toward Gina's shop, she wondered what on earth had gotten into her. It wasn't like her to be so spontaneous. She was the one who planned things well in advance, who made checklists of her checklists and stuck to a timetable no matter what happened. It was freeing though, and she rather liked the feeling at the same time that it scared her.

She could hear hammering and sawing as she approached Gina's shop. Hopefully they were making progress and would soon start on Gina's apartment.

Gina was deep in conversation with a man in khakis, a crisp blue shirt and a hard hat when Monica poked her head into the open doorway. They were leaning over a counter examining a sheet of unrolled papers.

Gina scurried over to where Monica was standing.

"Hi, sweetie. It was so nice of you to come, but the architect is here, and we're reviewing some possible changes to the plans."

"That's fine." Monica studied Gina's face. She seemed to have recovered from her earlier upset, although there were still lines of strain evident on her face, but overall she was looking brighter than Monica had expected. "I've got to pick up something for dinner anyway. Greg is coming over."

"Greg? The fellow from the bookstore?" Gina's face brightened even more. "You've invited him to dinner?"

Gina sounded rather incredulous, and Monica bristled slightly. Did Gina really think she was so hopelessly socially inadequate?

"Yes," Monica said with a tart edge to her voice. "And I have no idea what to feed him."

"A steak," Gina said decisively. "You can't go wrong with some red meat for a good old red-blooded American man." Gina turned and held up one finger to signal to the architect that she'd only be another minute. "I'll make myself scarce tonight, don't worry. I've got a key to Jeffie's apartment so I can go in and wash up and then take myself out to dinner."

"I'm sorry." Monica twisted her hands together. "I didn't intend to kick you out—"

Gina held up a hand. "Don't give it another thought. I'm just glad that you're starting to live again." She reached over and hugged Monica.

"Do you still want to get a cup of tea or are you going to be alright?"

Gina put a hand on Monica's arm. "I'm okay. Besides, the architect is here, and since he's probably going to charge me for this visit anyway, I'd better talk to him." She squeezed Monica's hand. "But thanks. I appreciate the offer, I really do."

Gina went back to where the architect was standing with his plans, and Monica headed two doors down the street to the butcher shop.

Bart was behind the counter wearing a fresh white apron and sharpening a long-bladed knife. He had a slender piece of beef on the butcher block in front of him. He put the knife down and leaned with his palms flat against the board when he saw Monica. His shirtsleeves were rolled up, and Monica could see the sinewy muscles in his forearms.

"Hello there. Fine day we're having, isn't it?" He jerked a shoulder toward the window. "What is it you're after today? I've got some beautiful loin pork chops in that case over there, and we just finished making some darn fine Dutch rookwurst, if you're interested."

"Actually I was after a steak," Monica admitted. "What's that you have there?" She pointed to the piece of meat arrayed in front of Bart.

"This is your beef tenderloin." Bart patted the meat affectionately. "Very tender, but not that much flavor." He poked at the meat again. "People tend to confuse tenderness with flavor. If it's flavor you want, go with one of your other cuts. The tenderloin is a small muscle that's hardly used. Very little myoglobin, and it's the myoglobin that gives your meat its flavor." He gave the tenderloin a little shake. "Of course, the more myoglobin your piece of meat has, the longer and slower it has to cook to break down the connective tissue and get it to what people like to call *falling off the bone* tender."

Monica's head was spinning, but she did know she didn't want long and slow. She didn't have time for that.

"I guess I was thinking along the lines of your basic steak." *Was there such a thing?* "Like maybe a sirloin or porterhouse?" Monica grasped at two of the only names she remembered from visits to restaurants.

"I take it you're cooking dinner for a man?" Bart smiled and ran his hands down the front of his apron.

"Yes, how did you—"

"Ladies usually go for the filet mignon, or worse, a chicken breast."

Monica laughed. "What's wrong with a filet mignon?"

Bart pointed at the tenderloin on his board. "Your filet mignon comes from this shorter end of the tenderloin. Very tender, but little flavor. It needs a good sauce to round it out."

"I guess I want something more . . . robust . . . then."

"Who is your lucky dining companion?" Bart started to poke around in one of the cases.

Monica's first instinct was to tell him it was none of his business, but he was just being friendly and that would make her look churlish.

"Greg Harper," Monica admitted.

"Thought so," Bart said, his head half stuck in one of the cases. He pulled out a tray of meat. "Will one of these do? These are some pretty fine porterhouses. It's a man-sized cut if that's what you're after." Bart plucked one from the tray and held it out toward Monica. "Name's supposed to come from some restaurant or hotel, but no one knows for sure if that's true or not."

"That looks fine." Monica hoped Greg would come with a good appetite. Bart was right; it was certainly a man-sized cut of meat.

"I'll just wrap this up for you then." Bart tore a piece of butcher paper from the roll next to the counter. "Greg's a nice guy," he commented as he placed the meat on the paper. "Known him for a long time. I'm a good ten years older, but I helped coach the little league team he was on."

Monica was confused. "I thought Greg was from Minneapolis. At least that's what he told me."

Bart stopped with a piece of string stretched between his

hands. "He did go to Minneapolis for a number of years, but then he came back again. I think he wanted to get away after what had happened."

Monica wanted to tread lightly so as not to dry up this well of information, but knowing Bart's propensity for gossip, she figured that was highly unlikely to happen.

"I'm afraid I don't know anything about that," Monica said in an offhand tone.

Bart put the paper-wrapped steak down on the counter. He hadn't fastened the string yet, and his careful wrapping began to slowly flutter open.

"Back then, when they were both in junior high school, Greg and Sam Culbert were friends. It was an odd combination, I can tell you—Harper being on the bookish side and Culbert an athlete and something of a cutup."

Monica's eyes widened in surprise. Greg and Sam friends?

Bart gave a nod as if he sensed her disbelief. "They hung out together all the time—at least whenever Greg didn't have his nose buried in a book and Sam wasn't at practice for one sport or another." He paused and licked his lips. "One night they really got up to mischief. I always believed Culbert was responsible, but Harper got the blame."

Monica waited as Bart took a breath.

"Someone set a fire out at an old abandoned barn on the edge of town. Luckily it never really took hold, and the fire crew was able to put it out easily enough. It was mostly a lot of smoke, but it did do some damage, and they ended up pulling the whole structure down right afterward. A bunch of teenaged boys had been seen hanging out around the barn, no doubt smoking cigarettes and taking nips of liquor from bottles stolen from their parents." Bart picked up the abandoned piece of string and began to tie up Monica's steak. "Someone told the police they'd caught a glimpse of Culbert on the scene, which didn't surprise anyone. If there was mischief to be had, he was always right in the thick of it."

Bart tightened the string and tied an expert knot. "Culbert claimed he'd been at the barn that night, but he'd left before the fire was started. Told the police it was Harper's idea and that he, Culbert, wanted none of it." Bart looked thoughtful. "Oddly enough, Harper said much the same thing, only that the fire had been Culbert's idea, and he had left early, before the first match had even been lit."

"Nothing was ever proven either way, but it put a cloud over Harper's head from that day on. He'd been the golden boy, on his way to class valedictorian and all that. People began to look at him funny—well, you can guess the rest. Took off for college and never came back to Cranberry Cove until a couple of years ago, when he suddenly showed up and opened that bookstore."

Bart placed Monica's wrapped steak in a white butcher bag and handed it to her. "Anything else I can do for you today?"

Monica shook her head, thanked him and left the shop. She was so deep in thought she nearly walked straight into a no parking sign along Beach Hollow Road. Why hadn't Greg told her he was born in Cranberry Cove instead of making it sound as if he'd only just arrived there from Minneapolis? Monica already knew he had a reason to feel bitterly toward Sam Culbert because of the mayoral race, but what Bart had just told her gave him an even better reason to hate the man.

Had he hated him enough to kill him?

# Chapter 21

Monica thought some more about what Bart had told her as she drove back to Sassamanash Farm. She certainly didn't believe that Greg had been the one to set that fire in the old abandoned barn. She even found it hard to believe that Greg and Culbert had once been friends. She couldn't imagine two people who were less alike. But literature was filled with odd couples, so there were bound to be plenty of them in real life as well.

The sun was heating up in the interior of Monica's car, and she cracked the windows slightly. She took a deep breath. The air was fresh and clean, and she thought she could detect the faint tang of the lake on the breeze. Despite the murder and despite everything that was going on, she felt a lift to her spirits, and she began to whistle. Tunelessly, that was for sure, but there was no one to hear, so why not?

By the time she pulled into the driveway in front of her cozy cottage, she was singing a robust version of some pop song whose name she had forgotten and whose lyrics were more than a bit hazy in her mind.

The cottage seemed exceptionally quiet this afternoon. Monica was looking forward to having one of Midnight's little kittens for company. She would have liked to have had a pet when she was living in Chicago, but her hours were too uncertain, and it wouldn't have been fair to anything other than a goldfish. Even her plants had been neglected.

She put the steak in the refrigerator. It had cost her a pretty penny—she hoped she could manage to cook it properly. She certainly knew her way around a kitchen, but meat could be tricky, and she was having last-minute jitters about having Greg to dinner. She also had salad fixings and was planning on baking potatoes—nothing out of the ordinary, but easy to do and something men usually liked. She'd been experimenting with a cranberry cake and planned on that for dessert.

Monica looked at the clock. She might as well get started on the cake. Lauren had offered to help out in the store since fewer people were coming to tour, so she had the afternoon to get ready. This would be the first time she'd entertained a man since Ted, and she was excited but also a little nervous.

Monica was sifting flour when her front doorbell rang. Odd. She wasn't expecting anyone—not even any deliveries. She wiped her hands on her apron and went through to the foyer.

A strange man was standing on the doorstep. He was wearing tan slacks and a sport coat and was carrying a briefcase, but his weathered skin suggested he spent a fair amount of time outdoors.

"Can I help you?" Monica said when she opened the door. At least he didn't look as if he was selling anything.

"I'm looking for Jeff Albertson? I understand he owns Sassamanash Farm?"

Was he some sort of bill collector? Monica wondered. She was quite certain they were up on almost everything. Certainly the electric company wouldn't send someone out just because payment was a few days late.

"I'm afraid he's not here," Monica said. What would she say if the man asked her where Jeff was?

"I've been trying to get hold of him. He hasn't returned any of my calls. Do you know where I can find him?"

That was the sixty-four-thousand-dollar question, Monica thought.

"Not at the moment, but I'd be happy to take a message. I'm his sister."

The man looked abashed. "I'm sorry. I should have introduced myself. Drew Tompkins. I'm with the cranberry cooperative. I wanted to have a word with your brother."

Monica felt her stomach take a nosedive. Was something wrong? Everything depended on selling this crop. Without that sale, Sassamanash Farm would be finished.

The fellow cleared his throat. "There have been rumors that a body was found in one of the cranberry bogs." He cleared his throat again and fiddled with the button on his jacket. Monica couldn't help noticing it was slightly loose already. "I just wanted to clarify things for the cooperative. I don't suppose you know anything about . . ."

"Why don't you come in?" Monica held the door wider.

"I don't want to trouble you."

"It's no trouble," Monica said, glad that she hadn't put the cake in the oven yet.

Tompkins perched on the edge of one of the chairs, his briefcase balanced on his lap, his hands folded on top of it.

Monica sat down opposite him. She thought of offering him something to drink, but she wanted to get this over with as quickly as possible.

"So *was* there a body?" Tompkins's Adam's apple bobbed up and down over the collar of his shirt, and Monica found herself staring at it, fascinated.

"Yes, there was," she admitted reluctantly. No way to keep the news under wraps now.

"What we really need to know is . . ." Tompkins hesitated. "Were those cranberries disposed of? There's no precedent for this sort of thing, you see. Plenty of insects and more than a few wild animals have found their way into the bogs as you can imagine. But a human body . . . we're quite certain this is a first."

"I understand."

"It's quite possible that the cleaning process would . . . would render the berries perfectly safe, but we don't know that for sure. I hope you can understand that."

"Absolutely," Monica said, but her mind was elsewhere— back to the conversation she'd had with Jeff about getting rid of those potentially contaminated berries. She remembered that at the time he'd sounded evasive. He had gotten rid of them, hadn't he? Of course she was hardly going to reveal her doubts to Tompkins.

Tompkins still had his hands clasped on top of his briefcase. He was twirling his thumbs around and around each other.

"So you don't know how I can reach Jeff?" He glanced at his watch quickly.

"I'm afraid not. He must be out somewhere." Monica made a vague gesture with her hands.

Tompkins nodded curtly. "I understand." He sighed. "I guess I'll continue to try the telephone number I have for him. Can you tell me if I have the right one?"

He flipped open the clasps on his briefcase and pulled out a slip of paper. He glanced at it briefly before passing it to Monica.

Monica took it and checked the number. She handed the paper back. "Yes, that's Jeff's cell phone."

Tompkins rubbed his hands together. "Great. That's great. I'll keep on trying him then." He put the paper back in his briefcase, closed the lid, snapped the locks shut and put the case beside him. He stood up and held out his hand. He was tall and thin and put Monica in mind of a loosely jointed skeleton.

She shook his hand, showed him to the door, closed it and leaned against it. Only then did she realize that she was shaking. She took a deep breath, pushed away from the door and headed back to the kitchen.

Monica was pouring the cake batter into a pan when she heard her cell phone ringing. Fortunately, she'd put it out on the counter and didn't have to dig through her purse. She wiped her hands and picked it up.

"Hello?"

"Monica?" The voice was barely more than a whisper.

"Jeff! Where are you? We've been so worried."

"I'm sorry. I never meant for you to be worried. I'm fine. Perfectly fine."

"But where are you?" Monica grabbed the sponge next to the sink and began wiping down the counter. She had to do something or she would scream.

"Like I told you before, if you don't know where I am, you can't tell the police if they ask."

"But I wouldn't—"

"Let's face it, Monica. You're lousy at lying."

Monica couldn't deny that. She wrung out the sponge and put it back in its place.

"How is Mom? Is she okay?"

"She's worried half to death, but you know Gina, she keeps on going."

"That's for sure." Monica could hear the smile in Jeff's voice. He paused for a moment. "Do you know anything about the police investigation? Are they any closer to finding out who killed Culbert?"

"No," Monica admitted. "If they are, they haven't told me anything."

Jeff sighed. "I can't stay in hiding forever. I've got to finish the harvest."

Monica was about to open her mouth to tell him about the visit from Tompkins from the cranberry cooperative, but changed her mind. Jeff already had enough on his plate. "You were out checking the temperature sensors the night Culbert was murdered. Can you think of anything, anything at all, that might tell the police something or give them some clue? Did you see any cars or sense that someone else was out and about?"

Jeff groaned. "You mean like rustling in the bushes? I wish there was something. At the time I was quite certain I was alone. I didn't hear anything, but I wasn't listening for anything, either. I was focused on what I was doing."

"If only there was something . . ."

"Wait," Jeff blurted out. "I do remember seeing a van. It was coming down the road that borders the farm. I didn't think anything of it at the time, and frankly, I'd forgotten all about it until now."

"Could you see what the van looked like?" Monica held her breath.

"It was white with some red lettering on the side."

"Could you see what it said?"

"I wish. No, it went by too fast, and anyway, I wasn't really paying attention. Like I said—I was focused on what I was doing."

Monica sighed. Well, it was something at least, although she suspected she was grasping at straws.

It wasn't until she'd hung up that she remembered Greg Harper had a van. White, with red lettering on the side. And he had every reason to hate Sam Culbert enough to kill him.

Monica's dinner got off to a bad start. She was worried and distracted when Greg arrived. She couldn't stop thinking about Jeff and on top of that, she was growing more and more suspicious of Greg. Had she invited a murderer to dinner?

When Monica opened the door at Greg's ring, he stood on her doorstep holding a paper-wrapped bundle of chrysanthemums in one hand and a bottle of wine in the other. Looking at him with his boyishly rumpled hair, blue pullover sweater that almost matched his eyes and slightly wrinkled khakis, she couldn't really believe he could commit murder. Surely it was a coincidence that someone in a white van with red lettering had been passing the farm the night Culbert was murdered?

Somehow Monica managed to overcook the steak and, although Greg protested to the contrary, she could see how he was struggling to cut the meat. Conversation was equally awkward—bouncing from topic to topic with nothing quite taking hold. The ease with which they'd conversed in Greg's shop had dissipated into thin air. Monica searched for something to say.

"I didn't realize you grew up in Cranberry Cove," she said finally. "You never mentioned it."

"I guess I thought everyone knew." Greg smiled and wiped his mouth with his napkin. "I keep forgetting you're not a local. So who spilled the beans on me?"

Monica was embarrassed. "Bart from the butcher shop."

"Bart sure loves to talk. Especially to the ladies." He smiled at Monica, and his eyes twinkled. "What else has Bart been saying about me?"

Monica's embarrassment intensified. Should she tell him the truth?

"Come on, out with it." Greg laughed and pushed his plate away.

Jeff was right, Monica thought. She was no good at lying. "He told me that you and Culbert had been friends and that—"

"That Culbert had implicated me in the fire that had been set in that old abandoned barn out on Porter Road. Was that it?"

"Yes, actually, it was."

Greg's mouth set in a grim line. "I had hoped that by now I would be able to put that behind me, but I guess not. People in Cranberry Cove have good memories."

"I'm sorry. I shouldn't have said anything."

"It's not your fault." Greg reached for the wine bottle and refilled their glasses. "Unfortunately I can just imagine what people are saying. Everyone knows that I was furious with Culbert for cheating in the mayoral race. I had plans for this town. Ideas. But I couldn't compete with someone who bought votes." He took a big drink of his wine. "And then everyone in

Cranberry Cove still remembers the incident with the fire, and they're more than willing to remind anyone who doesn't." He held his wrists out in front of him. "I'm surprised they haven't come and put the cuffs on me yet." He smiled at Monica as if to show he was joking, but she could see the concern in his eyes.

"But if you have an alibi for the murder . . ." Monica hoped Greg wouldn't realize she was probing.

Greg shrugged. "I was home alone. Reading the new Dick Francis. Although they're actually written by his son Felix now."

"Did you enjoy it?"

"Yes. I've always been a fan. I'm glad his son is continuing the franchise."

Suddenly the conversation veered onto the topic of books—specifically mysteries—and the talk began to flow more smoothly and naturally. Monica was shocked to note that an hour later they were still sitting at the table, surrounded by the detritus of their dinner.

Greg left soon afterward, and Monica cleaned up the dishes. The evening had taken a decided turn for the better in the end. Greg had raved about her cranberry cake and had had two pieces. She hoped he would remember that and not the overcooked steak.

Monica filled the sink with hot, soapy water and slipped in the dirty pots. Greg certainly didn't fit the role of murderer, she thought. On the other hand, if she were writing a mystery herself, she could imagine casting him in the part—the innocent-seeming, slightly bookish character who looked as if he wouldn't hurt a fly and whose guilt would take the reader by surprise.

But this was real life and not a book. Then again, there was that old saw about truth being stranger than fiction.

# Chapter 22

Monica overslept the next morning. It had been a night of wild dreams—bodies bobbing to the surface of the bog instead of cranberries, Jeff in handcuffs silently pleading for her to save him, Gina running around in circles pulling at her hair. She woke up more exhausted than when she'd gone to bed.

She had to hurry if she was going to get all the baked goods into the oven in time. Her jeans from the day before were tossed over the small chair beside her bed. That wasn't like her, but she'd been in a hurry to change before Greg arrived and then she'd fallen into bed afterward, barely having the energy to brush her teeth. She pulled the jeans on quickly and grabbed a sweatshirt from her drawer.

She was halfway down the stairs to the kitchen when she felt as if she was going to sneeze. She stuck her hand in her pocket, where she almost always had at least one crumpled tissue—this time was no different. She pulled out the tissue and quickly pressed it to her nose. Just before she sneezed, she heard something hit the stair below her, bounce and roll down to the landing.

Monica stuffed the tissue back in her pocket and continued down the stairs. She paused on the landing and looked around. At first she didn't see anything, but she knew she'd heard the ping of something hitting the floor. Whatever it was had to be there somewhere.

She flicked on the overhead fixture, and the light glanced off something shiny in the corner by the baseboard. Monica picked it up. It was the ring she'd found on the ground yesterday—the one Darlene insisted belonged to Andrea Culbert. She had forgotten all about it.

Monica's first urge was to get rid of it—it didn't belong to her, and it looked valuable. What if someone thought she'd stolen it? She would call Detective Stevens right away and turn it over to her. If it was evidence of some sort, she would know what to do with it.

Monica mixed up the first batch of cranberry muffins and got them into the oven. By now, she could practically do it in her sleep. She was almost out of flour, and made a mental note to pick some up later that morning. As soon as that was done, she reached for her cell phone and dialed the number for the Cranberry Cove police station.

A rather tired-sounding voice on the other end assured her that her message would be given to Detective Stevens as soon as she got in.

Monica finished the batter for the day's coffee cake. The cranberries in it winked as red as the ruby ring she'd found, and Monica glanced over to the table where she'd put it for safekeeping. She hoped Stevens would return her call soon. The sooner she got if off her hands, the better.

The cranberry cake that Monica had tried out on Greg the night before was almost finished when Monica's front doorbell rang. *Stevens?* She hoped so.

Stevens was standing on the doorstep when Monica opened the door. As usual, her trench coat was open, and her protruding belly looked even bigger than the last time Monica had seen her.

"T minus one and counting," she said as she edged her way around Monica's open door. "I'd hoped to have this case wrapped up by now." She rubbed the small of her back and winced. "At least I've got the crib put together, so I have a place to put the baby when it comes, even if the Winnie-the-Pooh border isn't up yet, and the changing table is still in pieces in the box it came in." She sighed as she followed Monica out to the kitchen.

"Cup of tea?" Monica reached for the kettle.

"Decaf?"

"No problem."

Stevens sat at the kitchen table, her feet propped on one of the chairs as Monica made them each a cup of tea.

"It smells heavenly in here. What are you baking?"

"I've made muffins and a coffee cake, and a cranberry cake is now in the oven," Monica said as she put the kettle on the stove and turned on the gas.

"Everything cranberry, I gather?"

"Yes. Cranberries are our stock in trade."

"Okay," Stevens said, when Monica handed her a mug of tea. "What's all this about a ring?"

Monica reached across the table and handed Stevens the ruby ring.

Stevens held it up to the light and checked the inside of the band. "There's an inscription, but it's too faint to read. Maybe the guys in the lab will be able to make it out." She turned the ring this way and that. "Looks expensive. I suppose that's a real ruby." She took a sip of her tea. "How did you come to find this?"

Monica explained about spotting it on the ground on the path by the bog.

"So anyone could have dropped it. Although, unless it was extremely loose, I can't see it just falling off someone's finger."

"Maybe they'd taken it off for some reason and had it in their pocket?"

"And the pocket had a hole?" Stevens smiled. "What bad luck."

"But that's not all," Monica said, moving over to the kitchen counter and leaning against it, her mug of tea cradled in her hands. "Darlene—she's the girl who works in our farm store," she said when she saw Stevens raise her eyebrows. "Darlene claims it belongs to Andrea Culbert, Sam Culbert's wife."

"I know who she is. I've already spoken to her a number of times. Seems she and Culbert weren't exactly a match made in heaven. But how would this Darlene know—"

"She cleans for the Culberts once a week and remembers seeing that ring on Andrea Culbert's dressing table."

"And you found this near the bog? The one where the body was discovered?"

"Yes."

"Odd."

Monica gave Stevens a puzzled look, but Stevens didn't elaborate. Instead she heaved herself to her feet.

"Mind if I take this with me?" She held out the ring in the palm of her hand.

"Please, I don't want to have anything to do with it. Do you think you'll find out who owns it?"

"If we do, I'll let you know."

The aroma of freshly baked goods wafted around Monica as she hurried to the farm store. She passed the bog where Culbert's body had been found and shivered. She didn't know if she would ever get over the shock of finding him floating amidst the cranberries. She averted her eyes but could still see, in her mind's eye, the scene as it had been that day—the yellow-and-black police tape flapping in the breeze, the officers clustered around the bog searching the ground for any clues, their patrol cars pulled up haphazardly on the grass.

Monica was relieved when the farm store came into view. She was surprised to find Lauren behind the counter instead of Darlene. She looked as if she, too, had had a restless night. Her usually shiny hair was dull, and her eyelids had the slightly swollen look of someone who hadn't slept well.

"Where's Darlene?" Monica asked as she hoisted her baskets onto the counter.

"She called to say she was sick. She asked me if I would mind taking her place today." She smiled. "It's no problem."

"I really appreciate it," Monica said, and she meant it. Lauren was always willing to pitch in whenever and wherever necessary.

Monica arranged the cakes and muffins in the glass case and then began carrying the jars of salsa to the cooler. She realized she hadn't yet heard from Fresh Gourmet. She had her fingers crossed that the store would be willing to stock her product. The extra source of revenue would put Sassamanash Farm on considerably sturdier financial ground.

"Do you mind if I run into town?" Monica asked Lauren, who was straightening their stock of tea towels. "I need to pick up some more flour before I forget."

"Sure. Weekdays are usually pretty slow. I can handle it."

Monica grabbed her jacket and purse and headed toward the door. She turned around as she was leaving. "Thanks again, Lauren. I don't know what we'd do without you."

Lauren's face lit up and she smiled. It gave Monica a good feeling as she walked to her car.

The day had started out overcast, but the clouds were moving swiftly and sunlight was breaking through. The leaves had nearly reached their peak of color and the trees were a vivid red and yellow. Monica took a deep breath. The air had that indefinable autumn smell to it, and there was a hint of wood smoke on the breeze that blew her hair across her face.

Monica beeped open the Focus and got behind the wheel. Traffic was scarce as she made her way into town, although almost all the parking places on Beach Hollow Road were taken when she got there. Monica finally found a spot two doors down from Gina's new shop. A van was pulled up in front of it, and Monica glanced at it curiously. It was white with *Ralph's Plumbing* written on the side in red letters. The van Jeff claimed to have seen the night of Culbert's murder was white with red lettering—obviously Greg's wasn't the only one in town like it.

Monica turned into the doorway of Gina's shop. Carpenters were nailing wallboard to the studs, their electric nail guns nearly deafening in the small space. Gina was in the back of the shop talking to a man in denim overalls and a T-shirt with *Ralph's Plumbing* on the back. Obviously that was his van outside.

Gina waved her over, and Monica picked her way across a floor strewn with loose boards, various tools and abandoned fast-food containers.

"I want to hear all about your evening," Gina said when Monica reached her. "Just let me finish up with Ralph, okay? It seems there's some sort of problem with the pipes, but Ralph is going to sort it all out for me. Right, Ralph?" Gina turned to him and graced him with her most flirtatious look.

Ralph nodded and smiled at Monica.

"I take it that's your truck outside?" *Talk about stating the obvious.*

"Yup. The one with *Ralph's Plumbing* on the side."

"Have you heard about the murder out at Sassamanash Farm?" Monica asked casually.

"You bet." Ralph stuck his thumbs through the straps of his overalls. "Probably ain't nobody in town who hasn't heard of it."

"You didn't happen to be out that night, did you? In your van." Monica waved toward the street. "My brother saw a white van on the road that night near the farm. It could be that the driver saw something and didn't realize it."

Ralph puffed himself up. "Really? And, like, would they get to talk to the police and all?"

"I should imagine so." Monica shot a warning look at Gina who had opened her mouth to say something. "They might even get their name in the paper." She felt guilty leading on the obviously gullible Ralph.

"As a matter of fact, I was out in the van that night." Ralph unhooked his thumbs from his overall straps and pointed them toward his chest. "A buddy of mine hosts a weekly poker game for us guys." He patted his stomach. "His wife always puts out a nice spread for us. I took the van so I could leave the Taurus for the wife."

"Do you remember if you drove past Sassamanash Farm?"

"That the place that Sam Culbert used to run?"

Monica nodded.

"I sure did. It's right on my way. Eric, that's my friend, lives over on Evergreen Road." He pointed out the window of the shop.

"You didn't happen to see anything out of the ordinary, did you?"

Ralph stroked his chin. "I passed someone out walking. That what you mean? I I did think it was kind of odd given the hour. This was on my way back home, see."

"Do you remember if it was a man or a woman?"

"Couldn't tell," Ralph said succinctly. "Had on jeans and some kind of sweatshirt or jacket with a hood that was pulled up. Covered their face. Besides I wasn't really paying any attention."

Monica nodded.

"Do you think I should go to the police?" Ralph's eyes shone.

"Yes. They might find it helpful."

"But you're going to finish up here first, right?" Gina gave him a stern look.

"Sure, Ms. Albertson. Don't you worry."

"I've got to get going," Monica said quickly, touching Gina's arm. "Lauren is at the store all by herself. I'll tell you about my evening when you get back tonight."

Gina looked disappointed, but Monica hastily said goodbye and left the shop before Gina could detain her further.

Monica caught a glimpse of the awning over Book 'Em as she headed toward her car and blanched at how close she had come to accusing Greg of murder. Hopefully he would never know.

She almost forgot she'd come into town for some flour and nearly walked back to the Focus empty-handed, but after her purchase was duly made, Monica headed to her car to go home to the farm.

She was pretty sure that Ralph would go running to the police with his information the minute he finished his work in Gina's shop. It might have been a coincidence that someone was out walking near the farm that night, but then again, maybe not. She would let Stevens deal with the information.

Monica was about to pull out of the parking space when her cell rang. She put the car in park and fished her phone from her purse.

"Hello?"

"Detective Stevens here. I thought you'd want to know that we found Culbert's car in the driveway of an abandoned house down a dirt road not far from the farm."

"So he parked there and walked back to Sassamanash? I wonder why. Do you think he was meeting someone and didn't want to be seen?"

Monica thought back to what everyone had been saying about Culbert's marriage—was he seeing someone on the side? But why meet them at the farm? Hardly a romantic—or comfortable—destination. Unless this had been business? Funny business of some sort?

"We're quite certain he drove out to the farm in his own car. We've got the analysis back on the tire tracks that were found. They were faint—the ground was pretty hard—but there's no doubt they're consistent with Culbert's Mercedes. We think someone lured him to the farm, killed him and then drove his car away, thinking that it would be a while before the body was found. We're testing it for prints now."

"What about another car? The person he was meeting must have driven to the farm themselves."

There was a pause long enough to cause Monica's hands to begin to sweat, and the phone almost slipped from her grasp.

"There aren't any other tracks. At least not anywhere near where Culbert's car must have been parked. Of course that doesn't mean that the person, whoever they were, didn't park farther away. But it doesn't rule out the fact that the murderer could have been someone from the farm. It would have been easy enough for them to walk to the spot where Culbert was waiting for them."

"You don't think . . ." Monica tried to keep the panic out of her voice.

"I don't think anything," Stevens said wearily. "I can't draw any conclusions until I have all the facts. Otherwise, it's just guesswork. Hopefully the techs will find something useful in Culbert's car."

Monica thanked Stevens for keeping her informed, tossed her phone in her purse and put the car back in drive. If the murderer had any brains, the police wouldn't find anything incriminating in Culbert's car. Jeff was smart. Monica pushed the thought away. Jeff had had nothing to do with this. She was positive.

Monica tried to imagine how things might have happened—someone luring Culbert out to the farm, killing him and dumping his body, then driving his car out to this deserted house. Had they left their own car there? Did the person Ralph saw walking along the road have anything to do with it? She should have told Stevens about that, but Monica was certain Ralph would be heading to the police station with his information the second he was finished at Gina's shop.

Once again the scene at the cranberry bog flashed through Monica's mind—the police surrounding the area with tape and the men searching for clues. Jeff had said that afterward the techs had arrived and had taken casts of any tire tracks

A thought occurred to her so suddenly she nearly slammed on her brakes. The horn from the car behind her blared, and Monica waved to indicate she was sorry.

The pieces were falling into place—or some of them at least. That ring had to have been dropped *after* Culbert's body was found. The police had combed the area around the bog. Monica remembered how they had divided the area into a grid and were going about it in an orderly fashion hoping to find something—anything—that would lead to the murderer's identity. If that gold and ruby ring had been there that day, they would certainly have found it. If it had caught her eye as she was just walking past, surely the police would not have missed it.

And what if someone hadn't dropped the ring? What if they had planted it there on purpose, wanting it to be found? Monica chewed on her lower lip. They must have hoped to incriminate someone.

And if that ring really did belong to Culbert's wife then that someone must be Andrea Culbert.

# Chapter 23

Monica pulled into the driveway of her cottage without really knowing how she'd gotten there. So many thoughts were chasing each other around her head—Stevens's not-so-subtle insinuation that someone from the farm could be responsible for Culbert's death, the idea that the ruby ring had been planted to incriminate Andrea Culbert, her own ongoing concerns as to where Jeff was and what he was doing.

Monica dumped her purse on the kitchen table and opened the refrigerator door. She was starving. She rummaged around and found a hunk of cheese, some rather stale country bread and a few slices of deli ham. She could toast the bread and make an open-faced ham and cheese sandwich.

Monica was spreading some grainy mustard on the toasted bread when the back door was flung open, and Gina barged in.

Monica jumped.

"Sorry. Did I scare you?" Gina slung her jacket over a chair. "Look what I did." She turned her back to Monica.

Gina's pants were ripped—a large flap of material hanging down, revealing her leopard-print thong beneath.

"I caught my back pocket on a nail, and next thing I knew . . ." She shook her head, and the hair piled on top quivered like gelatin. "Someone didn't pound the nail in properly and it was sticking out of the wall. At least no one was hurt. But I had to come back and change. I could hardly spend the day going around like this." She looked over her shoulder at the hole in her jeans.

"Are you hungry?" Monica gestured toward her sandwich. "There's enough for two."

"That would be heavenly. I'll just run up and change. Be right back," Gina called as she headed toward the stairs.

Monica had noticed the label on Gina's jeans. That was an expensive rip. She knew that brand went for upwards of two hundred dollars, unlike the ones Monica bought at JCPenney.

By the time Monica had put together a second sandwich, Gina was back downstairs. She slid into the seat opposite Monica.

"Did you ever do anything about that ring you found?" Gina asked picking up her sandwich.

"Yes. I gave it to Detective Stevens."

"It was an expensive piece of jewelry. You'd think someone would be looking for it."

"Darlene said she thought it belonged to Andrea Culbert. She'd seen one just like it on Andrea's dressing table once."

"That must mean that Andrea Culbert was out at the farm the night Culbert was killed," Gina exclaimed.

Monica hated to burst Gina's bubble. "I doubt it. If the ring had been there that night, the police would have found it when they searched the grounds. No, I think someone planted it to throw suspicion on Andrea."

"Maybe Darlene did." Gina dabbed at her mouth with a napkin.

Monica stopped with her sandwich halfway to her mouth. "Darlene did say Andrea had to let her go. Maybe she was resentful—"

"Let her go, my eye! She fired her. You've seen how that girl works. Or maybe I should say *doesn't work*. I'll bet you anything she swiped that ring and left it in a place where you would find it and draw the natural conclusion. Although that would require more brains than I thought Darlene possessed."

Monica nodded. "She wanted to get back at Andrea for firing her."

"She strikes me as the sort who would stoop to something like that."

"And I gave the ring to Detective Stevens thinking it might have something to do with the case. I hate to think of the police wasting their time investigating it when it's most likely a dead end. . . ."

"Can you talk to this Darlene and get her to fess up?"

"I don't know. . . ." Monica thought about it. "I guess I could try. She's not working today, but we must have her address in the office." She pushed her chair back. "I'll do it as soon as I get these dishes cleaned up. I can see how Lauren is doing at the same time."

• • •

As Monica had expected, Lauren was doing fine when she arrived at the store. Lauren was behind the counter ringing up purchases for one of their frequent customers—a tall woman with over-permed blond hair. Lauren gave Monica a brief wave as Monica headed to the office off the processing room.

The office was little more than some seven-foot-tall partitions separating off the area and a door that didn't want to stay closed. The furnishings were equally basic—a battered metal desk and filing cabinet and a chair that was starting to lose its stuffing.

Monica pulled open the top drawer of the filing cabinet and began going through the folders. She found one marked *Employees* and pulled it out. The folder had been used before and had been turned inside out and relabeled. There was a copy of Darlene's W-4 withholding form and, paper-clipped to it, was her employment application. Her address and phone number were written on it in pencil. Monica copied both down and replaced the folder in the filing cabinet.

She waved to Lauren again on her way out. She was waiting on someone else this time—a rather sophisticated-looking woman who had a basket filled with tea towels, pot holders and napkins. Monica had better check the stock when she got back—it might be time to replenish.

She put the piece of paper with Darlene's address on it beside her on the passenger seat where she could see it. It appeared as if Darlene lived in the same mobile home park as Cora—Park View Estates.

Monica drove through the entrance and began checking

the house numbers. She passed Dawn's house, and, as usual, Dawn was out on the deck having a cigarette. Monica pulled over to the curb.

"Hi," she called out her open window.

Dawn walked over to Monica's car. "I didn't expect to see you back here again." She took another drag, her cigarette pinched between her thumb and index finger.

"I'm looking for Darlene Polk. She works for my brother."

Dawn ran a hand through her dark hair, leaving it standing upright. With the blond streak in front, she reminded Monica of a skunk. "Never heard of her, I'm afraid."

Monica consulted the piece of paper next to her on the car seat. "She's on Floral Drive."

"Keep going straight," Dawn pointed down the street where a lone boy was riding around and around in circles on his bicycle, "and make the first left. I'm pretty sure that's Floral."

"Thanks." Monica rolled her window back up and headed down the street.

She made the left turn onto Floral Drive that Dawn had indicated and began checking house numbers. Some of the houses had numbers that had fallen off or were missing altogether. Monica sighed in frustration and pulled over to the curb.

A woman was sitting on a lawn chair in front of one of the houses. Monica walked over to her. There was a second, empty chair next to her. The webbing was coming undone and the frame was rusted.

"Do you know where . . ." Monica consulted her piece of paper. "Number 2799 is? I'm looking for Darlene Polk."

"Darlene?" the woman said in a wheezy voice. She was

probably in her forties but looked much older. She had thin, nicotine-stained fingers with yellowed nails and the remains of some red polish around the edges.

"I've known Darlene since she was a baby. Sullen little thing, never a smile on her face." The woman began coughing furiously. "I quit smoking a year ago. Doctor's orders. I can't get rid of this cough though," she said when it finally stopped. "I have half a mind to take it up again."

She gestured to the chair next to her. "Have a seat."

Monica perched on the edge of the chair. "So you know Darlene?"

"Sure do. Knew her mother, too. May she rest in peace, the poor soul. She was taken way too young." She swiped at a tear in the corner of her eye.

The wind picked up sending a swirl of dried leaves across the driveway and making the woman shiver. She was wearing jeans and a thin, long-sleeved top.

"Why don't you come inside where it's warm?"

Monica hesitated. She hated to be rude. Jeff used to tease her about her inability to say no, and would try to get her to agree to do outrageous things. It usually worked, she thought ruefully.

The woman started up the stairs. "Name's Brenda, by the way," she said over her shoulder.

The inside of the trailer was neat, although the furniture was worn.

"Why don't you go have a seat on the davenport, while I rustle us up something cold to drink." She pointed to the sofa, where an orange and brown crocheted afghan was tossed across the arm.

Monica sat down. The sofa fabric was rough and itchy.

Moments later Brenda returned with two mismatched glasses of iced coffee. She handed one to Monica.

"I hope that's okay. I'm out of sugar."

Monica nodded and took a sip to be polite. "It's fine." She struggled not to grimace. The coffee was bitter and strong with that taste coffee gets when it sits on the warmer too long. She put the glass down on the coffee table and hoped Brenda wouldn't notice she wasn't drinking it.

"Yes, I've known Darlene all her life, and her mother and I were friends. Darlene's mother—her name was Heather—was smart. We all thought she'd leave Cranberry Cove and head to the big city but then she got," she leaned closer to Monica and whispered, "pregnant."

A telephone shrilled from somewhere inside the trailer.

"I'm waiting on a call from my doctor. I'll just be a moment." Brenda heaved herself out of her chair. She stopped in front of a bookcase, pulled out a volume and handed it to Monica. "Here's our yearbook. You'll find my picture in there along with Heather's."

Monica rubbed the dust off the cover where Cranberry Cove High School was imprinted along with a lion—she supposed that was the school's mascot. The spine cracked when she opened it, and the volume fell open to a page that Brenda must have looked at often.

It was the class poll page that was standard fare in almost all yearbooks—the most likely to succeed, best dressed, class clown. Monica scanned the pictures until she came to one that made her stop in her tracks.

# Chapter 24

Monica read the names under the picture several times, but there was no mistake.

Brenda came back into the room. Monica had been concentrating so hard she jumped.

"Sorry about that." Brenda pointed at the yearbook, and with a deep sigh sank into an armchair. "Did you see my picture?"

Monica shook her head. "No, I was just looking at this page here." She held up the yearbook for Brenda to see. "The class poll. I see Darlene's mother and Sam Culbert were voted cutest couple."

"That Sam Culbert." Brenda tsk-tsked under her breath. "The two of them were a couple all through junior high and high school. Then all of a sudden he takes off on a grand tour of Europe, and she disappears for nine months. Comes home with a daughter and refuses to tell anyone who the father is."

Brenda took a sip of her iced coffee. That caused a fit of

coughing, and Monica waited impatiently for her to begin again.

"But of course being as how I was her best friend, she did tell me a little something about it. Seems Sam Culbert's parents didn't approve of Heather. They had plans for their son that didn't include settling down at eighteen with a wife and baby." Brenda gave a loud sniff. "Scraped together every penny they had and then some and sent Sam off to Europe to take his mind off his girlfriend of six years. Gave Heather a lump sum of money and made her promise never to tell anyone who Darlene's father was."

"And Heather went along with it?"

"Apparently. There was plenty of talk, believe me, but we assumed she and Sam had broken up. Besides, everyone thought Heather had taken up with someone else and gotten herself knocked up."

"So Sam never acknowledged Darlene as his daughter?"

Brenda shook her head. "No, never. Not even after he made it big. He saw how they were living. He could have spared a couple of bucks to help them out, but no. It was as if Sam had never even known Heather."

"Do you think Darlene knew Sam Culbert was her father?"

Brenda shook her head vigorously. "No. I'm pretty sure she didn't. Heather was determined she wouldn't find out. Heather kept her word, I'll say that for her. It was hard on Darlene. People made comments. She couldn't help but hear. I suppose that's why she never smiled." Brenda took a big gulp of her iced coffee, which set off another round of coughing.

"I'd better be going." Monica stood up. "Thank you for the coffee."

"It's been a lovely visit. You're welcome to come back anytime. Nothing like a good chat to take your mind off things. Heather and I used to spend almost every evening together sitting outside on the deck with a cold drink in nice weather, or around the kitchen table when it was too cold or nasty to be outside. But now that's she gone . . ."

Brenda followed Monica to the door, where she pointed to a house catty-corner from hers. "That's Heather's place over there. Well, I suppose it's Darlene's now that her mother's gone. Looks like her car is in the drive, so you should find her at home."

Monica decided to leave her own car where it was for the moment. Darlene's place was only a short walk away—no point in moving it. She started to step off the curb when the blare of a car horn sent her jumping backwards. She wasn't paying attention—she was still reeling from the discovery that Sam Culbert was Darlene's father. Did Darlene really not know?

Even before Monica could raise her hand to knock, Darlene yanked open her door. She must have been watching from the window and waiting. For some reason the thought gave Monica a prickle of unease.

"I suppose you want to come in." Darlene held the door wider but didn't move, so Monica had to sidle past her, crab-like.

A large television—not a flat screen but the old-fashioned kind that was almost as deep as it was wide—dominated the room. There was a dark green leather recliner with cracks that had been mended with black electrical tape, a stack of *Star* magazines on the coffee table and a large bookshelf stuffed with books. Judging by the lurid colors of the spines and the flowery fonts used for the authors' names, most of them were romance novels.

Darlene was wearing a sweatshirt and flannel pajama bottoms with cats on them. She didn't invite Monica to sit down.

Monica was about to say that she'd come to check on Darlene—to see how she was feeling—but she could tell by the look on Darlene's face that Darlene wouldn't believe that.

Monica shifted from one foot to the other uncertainly. Darlene still hadn't asked her to sit down, but Monica perched on the edge of the couch anyway. Darlene continued to stand for several moments then finally collapsed onto the recliner, pushing the lever so that the chair tilted back. Her feet popped up, and Monica could see that the soles of her slippers were black with dirt. A tray table was open next to the recliner with some wadded up tissues, an empty glass and an open magazine on top.

"I wanted to talk to you about the ring you found at the farm."

If Darlene was surprised, she didn't show it.

"I've given it to the police, since it might be evidence," Monica said.

Darlene was silent. She plucked at her lower lip.

"I'd hate for the police to waste their time on something that wasn't . . . relevant to the case."

Darlene blinked, her lids lowering and lifting in slow motion.

"What I'm trying to say is . . ." Monica could feel sweat breaking out on the back of her neck, and it wasn't just because the trailer was terribly overheated—hot air bellowed out of a vent in the floor and swirled around Monica's legs.

Finally she decided on a frank approach. "Did you take

the ring from Andrea Culbert's dressing table and then put it near the bog where someone would find it in an attempt to incriminate her?

Darlene looked baffled.

"In order to make it look as if Andrea Culbert had been to the farm and might be a suspect in her husband's murder," Monica explained.

"I was mad at her for firing me. It wasn't fair. She said I didn't clean good, but I know I did." Darlene's lower lip trembled.

"I can imagine that made you mad," Monica said soothingly. "But I need you to tell the police what you did. Otherwise, this will throw them off the track of the real murderer and waste time and effort, don't you see?"

Even as the words came out of her mouth, Monica was struck by the truth. Darlene had left the ring on the ground by the bog on purpose to mislead the investigation. Her intention hadn't been to get back at Andrea Culbert but to distract the police.

An icy coldness swept over Monica as the pieces fell into place like tumblers in a combination lock. She heard the thunk of the chair as Darlene levered the recliner back into place.

"It wasn't fair." She brushed her bangs out of her eyes. "Him having all that money, and us nothing. And here he was my father."

"Did your mother tell you that?"

Darlene shook her head slowly. "No. She made some kind of promise not to. But after she died, when I was going through the file where she kept important papers—Pastor Ken told me I should see if there was a will—I found my birth certificate. I'd never seen it before. It had my name on it, the place where I was born and my mother's name—Heather

Polk. And right where it said *father*, Sam Culbert's name was filled in on the line, plain as day."

"So you lured him to the farm to ask him for money?"

Darlene shook her head and her ponytail swished back and forth. "The next day, the day after I found out about Mr. Culbert being my father, I was supposed to clean for them. When I got there, he was in his office working on some papers. I waited until Mrs. Culbert had left to get her nails done, then I went in and talked to him. He tried to tell me he was too busy to listen, but I insisted. I told him I knew everything about him being my father." Her eyes were glazed over, as if she was reliving the scene. "He asked me what I wanted, and I told him it was only fair that I share in some of the money he'd made all these years. Seeing as how he cheated me out of a daddy and my mother out of a good life."

"What did he say?"

Darlene shifted in her chair. "At first he was angry, but then he asked me how much I wanted."

Did Culbert really think this was going to be a onetime payout—that Darlene was too naïve to go after more money later?

Monica raised her eyebrows. "What did you tell him?"

Darlene raised her chin. "I told him I wanted ten thousand dollars. I mean, he owed us . . . me. My poor mama worked hard all her life, and here he was living in a big house with a fancy car. He could have helped us out all along."

And how long would it have been before Darlene went through the ten thousand dollars and was back demanding more? Monica wondered.

"What happened then? Did you ask him to meet you at Sassamanash Farm?"

"No." The word burst from Darlene. "He agreed to give me the money. A couple of days later, he called me and told me he had the cash. But he didn't want anyone to see us so could I meet him out at the farm. I didn't care one way or the other, just so I got my money. He told me to leave my car a short distance away and walk to the farm. I didn't want to do that, but he said if I didn't, he wouldn't give me the money." Darlene frowned. "I don't like to walk much."

"What happened then? Did he give you the cash?"

Monica couldn't imagine that Culbert had. Darlene struck her as the type who would have immediately gone over to Walmart to replace that old television set with one of the new flat screens.

Darlene plucked at her lower lip again. "No, I didn't get the money. He stood there in the shadows smiling at me. We were in that old shed—you know, where Jeff keeps some of the smaller equipment. He held out his arms to me and said, 'Looks like I have a daughter now.'" She gave a loud sniff. "Then he tried to get his hands around my neck." Darlene's own hands went to her neck as if to demonstrate. "He tried to kill me." The sniff became a wail.

It wasn't at all what Monica had expected. "What did you do then?"

"I didn't know what to do. I couldn't hardly breathe, and I was real scared. I reached around in back of me and found a rough piece of wood leaning against the wall. I grabbed it and hit him over the head with it real hard. I didn't mean to hurt him, I really didn't, but I couldn't breathe." She stared at Monica, her eyes welling with fresh tears.

"What happened then?"

"He fell over backwards and hit his head again—this

time against the wall. I don't think he was breathing anymore. Anyway, I had to get rid of him somehow or else someone might find out. I managed to get his body in that old wheelbarrow Jeff keeps in there. I wheeled him down to the bog and dumped him in."

"But he might have been alive."

Darlene shrugged and a hard look came over her face. "I didn't care. I just didn't want nobody to find out what I'd done."

"But if you had called the police . . . it was self-defense, after all."

Darlene sneered at Monica. She pointed to her chest. "Me against Sam Culbert? Do you think anyone would have believed me?"

Monica realized Darlene had a point. "But what about Cora? Did you kill her, too?"

"She would have told," Darlene blurted out. "She and Mama had become good friends. I'm pretty sure Mama told her about Sam Culbert being my father. They were always whispering together with that Brenda over a cold beer after work. I was at the diner getting my lunch when she told you to come by later that afternoon—I heard the two of you talking. I couldn't take the chance that she would tell you the truth. You're smart. You would have figured it out."

"Sugar," Monica said suddenly. "Hennie VanVelsen said your mother had the sugar—diabetes." She looked Darlene in the face. "She took insulin, didn't she?"

Darlene nodded very slowly.

"You injected Cora with an overdose of insulin and left her to die."

"Cora would have told," Darlene said plaintively. "It

wasn't my fault. Mr. Culbert should never have done what he did."

"Did you take his car?"

Darlene's face resumed its sulky expression. "I wasn't going to walk all the way back to my car. I told you. I don't like walking much. It makes the inside of my legs rub together and that hurts." She rubbed her thigh.

Monica reached for her purse. "I'm going to call the police, and you need to tell them everything." She stuck her hand in her bag and began to rummage for her cell.

"I'm not telling the police anything."

"You have to, Darlene. We'll get a lawyer, and he'll handle things. I'm sure the court will go easy on you."

"I'm not going to jail," Darlene said, her voice rising belligerently.

Monica had her cell phone in her hand and had punched in the number nine when she noticed Darlene reaching for something on the tray table underneath the splayed magazine.

Before she could tap the next number on her keypad, Darlene lunged forward, and Monica felt a sharp prick in her thigh. She looked down and watched as Darlene injected the contents of a large syringe into her leg.

# Chapter 25

Monica scanned her body for any unusual sensations. At first she didn't notice any, but then she realized she was becoming light-headed and slightly shaky. Sweat broke out all over, making her skin feel clammy, and her heart was like a jackhammer in her chest. She tried to get up from the chair but her muscles refused to cooperate. Her body felt liquid, as if she would slip from the chair and end up as a puddle on the floor. She forced herself to concentrate. She had to do something, but her thoughts were jumbled like pieces of a jigsaw puzzle dumped out of the box.

Darlene had disappeared into another room and came back wearing jeans, sneakers and a hooded sweatshirt. She was carrying a stack of newspapers. She tossed them onto the sofa and pulled something out of her pocket. Monica tried to see what it was, but her vision was blurred, and it was hard to focus.

She heard the flare of a match and smelled the acrid scent of sulfur. She struggled to see what Darlene was doing.

"What are you doing?"

Darlene stopped with the lit match in her hand. "These trailers will burn to the ground in eleven minutes. Mama always worried about fire—she was always fussing over the smoke alarms."

"Why are you—"

"It'll take the fire department six minutes to get here. Assuming someone notices the flames and bothers to call them. I doubt they'll find much left of you by the time they get the fire put out."

The match in Darlene's fingers had burned down, flickered and gone out. She scraped another match along the striking strip, and it burst into flame.

Darlene held the match toward Monica. "You know they dye the tip of the match red. I learned that on some show on the Discovery Channel. Mama always liked watching those shows. She was smart. She should have gone to college."

Darlene leaned forward and held the match to the edge of one of the newspapers. It caught, and the flame quickly intensified.

Monica sagged against the chair. Concentrating was so hard. She wanted to close her eyes and rest . . . only for a minute. The first whiff of smoke had her sitting bolt upright.

"Help me," she called to Darlene, but Darlene spun on her heel and made for the front door, slamming it hard in back of her.

Monica struggled to her feet, swaying wildly.

The whole pile of newspapers had now caught and was turning to black ash as the flames licked at the curtains over the front window. The fabric exploded in fire, and acrid smoke filled the room. It burned Monica's eyes and made them tear.

Flames had now crept along the worn carpet, blocking the path to the front door.

Monica staggered toward the kitchen. If she could get some sugar in her system, it might counter some of the effects of the insulin. Maybe then she could think more clearly.

Walking the few feet between the living room and kitchen felt like running a marathon, but Monica made it and, with a sigh of relief, closed the kitchen door behind her. Hopefully that would keep out some of the smoke and buy her some time.

She ripped open the cupboards until she found a half-full bag of sugar. She yanked it off the shelf, her hands shaking and clumsy, and it fell onto the counter, spewing its contents all over. Monica had a momentary thought about the mess attracting ants before she realized she was being ridiculous—in a few minutes there would be nothing left of Darlene's trailer. She scooped up a handful of sugar and put it in her mouth.

It was grainy and sickly sweet. It stuck to her tongue and the roof of her mouth. For a moment Monica thought she would choke, but she finally got the first handful down and scooped up another.

The sugar hit her bloodstream, and she began to feel a little less wobbly, although she was still sweating and her hands continued to shake. Maybe the dose of insulin hadn't been as strong as Darlene thought. Of course she had managed to kill Cora, but perhaps Cora had had a weak heart? Monica didn't want to think about that right now. She had to concentrate on getting out of the trailer. If only she hadn't left her purse and cell phone in the living room. The low blood sugar had made her too groggy to have the presence of mind to grab them.

Smoke was curling under the closed kitchen door—she didn't have much time. She ate another handful of sugar for good measure, and made her way to the back door.

Monica reached for the handle to the door to the outside, but it was loose and jiggled in her hand. She pushed against the door, but it didn't move. She pushed again. Nothing. She stepped back to examine the door and noticed that it didn't fit properly. There was a small chink between the door and the jamb through which she could see daylight. Then she noticed the nails—the door had been nailed shut, probably because it didn't stay closed properly, and it was easier to nail it closed than have it fixed. Unfortunately the only other door to the trailer was in the living room, which was now filled with smoke and flames.

For a second, Monica felt like sinking to the floor and weeping, but she forced herself to take a breath and think. Why hadn't she realized sooner that Darlene was the killer? She never would have come to the trailer alone.

She wasn't going to become another one of Darlene's victims. She was still shaky—she held her hands out in front of her, and they weren't quite steady—but the sugar was beginning to take effect. She felt a surge of energy, and her mind started to clear. She had to get that door open. She jerked out one of the kitchen drawers and rummaged around. Maybe a knife would do? She grabbed one, ran back to the door and carefully slipped the knife blade under the head of one of the nails. The nail didn't budge, and the knife snapped in two.

Monica threw it on the floor and went back to the cupboard. She opened another drawer and frantically pawed through the contents. Nothing useful, just a mishmash of cooking utensils—a nutcracker, lemon juicer and vegetable peeler along with a mismatched set of silverware.

A thin broom closet ran alongside the end of the counter. Monica yanked open the door and a mop fell out, hitting her on the forehead. She uttered an unaccustomed swear word and pushed it aside. There was a tangle of items on the floor of the closet. Monica knelt down and began to paw through them—dust rags, a feather duster with half the feathers missing, a can of furniture polish—and then her hand closed on something cool and metal. Monica held her breath—it was a screwdriver.

Flames were now licking around the edges of the kitchen door. She didn't have much time. Monica staggered back to the door with the screwdriver.

She slid the blade under the head of the first of the three nails someone had used to keep the door from swinging open and pushed down on the handle of the screwdriver. The nail slid out about an eighth of an inch. Monica moved the screwdriver slightly and tried again. Now the nail was half out.

She was able to pull it out the rest of the way, but by now the kitchen was filling with smoke. Her eyes watered, and it was hard to breathe without coughing. Two more nails to go. The second one came out easily, but the third one was stubborn. Time and time again, the blade of the screwdriver slipped, gouging the doorframe.

Monica could barely see, and her lungs burned from the smoke. She could feel the heat of the fire against her back. Flames licked along the kitchen floor and climbed the wood counters. She had minutes left, if that, before the whole room was engulfed in flames.

She couldn't restrain a sob as she tried pushing against the door, hoping the last nail would give way, but no luck. She slid the head of the screwdriver under the nail head and tried again. This time it began to budge. Monica hit the screwdriver handle so hard, her palm stung, but the nail slid out of the wood, and the door swung free with a loud creak.

Monica stumbled out of the smoke-filled trailer and collapsed on the ground. The sky above her was blue with fast-moving white clouds. She watched them, fascinated, as she tried to catch her breath.

Moments later she heard the wail of sirens, and a fire truck, quickly followed by another one, pulled up in front of the trailer. Right behind them was an ambulance.

People were pouring out of their homes now. Monica recognized Brenda and Cora's neighbor, Dawn. Someone held her head up and put a glass of water to her lips, then a paramedic was suddenly bending over her.

Another face popped into Monica's view. It was Detective Stevens.

"You're still—"

"Here? Not quite." Stevens rubbed her belly. "I was on my way to the hospital when I heard the squawk over the radio." She grimaced and rubbed her belly. "I took a bit of a detour to check things out. Someone will be around to talk to you shortly," she said over her shoulder as she began to walk away.

# Chapter 26

Monica was surprised when she woke the next morning in an unfamiliar bed in unfamiliar surroundings. She put a hand to her throat—it felt raspy and raw, as if she were coming down with a very bad cold, and her eyes stung. She rubbed them and looked around her as everything that had happened the day before flooded her mind all at once. She was in the hospital. She had protested vehemently, but the doctor had insisted on keeping her overnight for observation. Monica had inhaled a fair amount of smoke, the doctor had said, and she wanted to be sure there wouldn't be any complications.

Monica slipped into the tiny adjacent bathroom and washed her face, brushed her teeth and combed her hair. She still smelled like smoke and was contemplating a shower when there was a knock on her door.

"Yoo-hoo," a voice called from the hallway.

Monica opened the door to find Gina nearly hidden behind the most enormous bouquet of flowers Monica had ever seen.

"I brought you a little something to freshen up your room."

"That's so sweet," Monica said as she accepted the bouquet. "But I'm sure the doctor will be around to discharge me shortly. She said they only needed to keep an eye on me overnight."

Gina put the flowers down on the bedside tray. She opened her purse, dug around and pulled out a cell phone. "Here." She handed it to Monica. "I got you a new phone. I was able to get you the same number, but I'm afraid all of your other data is lost. You'll have to enter all your contacts again."

"Thanks." Monica looked at the phone and smiled. "It's so nice and shiny and new."

She heard someone clear their throat and looked up to see Jeff standing in the doorway with a huge grin on his face.

"Jeff!" Monica held out her free arm and gave him a huge hug. She let go of him and took a step back. "Where have you been? You had us all worried to death."

Jeff ducked his head. "I was sleeping rough in this old barn just outside of town. Mauricio turned me onto it. With the heat off him, he was able to move back into Primrose Cottage where he'd been living with Charlie."

"What's going to happen to him now? The authorities know he doesn't have any papers."

Jeff shrugged. "I think they have bigger fish to fry. Mauricio's managed to dodge them for over five years now. He'll manage."

Gina plumped the pillows on Monica's bed and straightened the covers. "I'll ring for the nurse to bring a vase for those." She pointed at the flowers. "And you'd better get back in bed." She patted the mattress. "You're still awfully pale."

"I'm fine," Monica said, even as a wave of tiredness swept over her. She didn't protest any further but slipped between the covers gratefully and rested her head against the pillows.

Jeff and Gina took the two chairs reserved for visitors—uncomfortable-looking molded plastic, as if the hospital wanted to discourage anyone from staying too long.

"How is the harvest going?" Monica turned her head so she could see Jeff where he sat with his long legs outstretched.

"All done. We got the last bog cleared real early this morning, and everything is ready for delivery. You'll have your work cut out for you writing checks to pay all the bills as soon as the cooperative deposits that nice chunk of change in the farm's account."

"It's a task I'm looking forward to," Monica said, reaching out a hand to grasp Jeff's. "But did you talk to that inspector from the cooperative?"

Jeff nodded. "I found two voicemails from him on my cell so I gave him a ring back first thing. I've satisfied him that we disposed of the berries harvested from the bog Culbert's body was found in. They're going to make fantastic mulch for next year's planting." Jeff grimaced. "I hated losing the money that those berries represented. I was awfully tempted to include them with the rest, but I guess my conscience got the best of me."

Gina grinned. "I might not be the best mother in the world, but I still think I raised you right." She turned back to Monica. "I can't believe it was that wretched girl from the farm shop all along."

"Darlene? I should have suspected her sooner. She knew enough about the farm to take an educated guess that I would be out helping Jeff that night with the sprinklers. She took a

thing I didn't bring more flowers. Looks like you've got all of Birnam Wood here."

Monica smiled at the reference to Shakespeare and peeked inside the bag.

"I thought you said you liked Peter Robinson."

"I do. Thanks so much." Monica ran a hand over the cover of the book. "I've been looking forward to reading this." She thought about how she'd originally suspected Greg of murder, and she could feel her face getting warm. Maybe she should confess now so it wouldn't be standing between them?

She cleared her throat. "I have something to tell you."

Greg raised an eyebrow.

"At one point I . . . I . . . thought you might have murdered Sam Culbert," she finally blurted out.

Greg threw back his head and laughed. It wasn't exactly the reaction Monica had anticipated.

"I had the feeling that something like that was going on. But I can assure you I'm innocent of Culbert's murder. Although I am planning a very different murder. . . ."

Monica straightened up. "You are?"

Greg nodded. "Promise not to laugh?"

Monica shook her head. "Promise."

"I've started writing a mystery of my own. It's not very good, I'm sure, but it's a start. It's something I've always wanted to do."

"That's wonderful."

"You think so? You don't think it's foolish of me?"

"Not at all."

"I really am enjoying it." Greg rubbed his hands together. "There's a certain vicarious thrill in creating a bad guy and then killing him off."

"I think that's why we enjoy reading mysteries."

"Probably. They're a modern day morality tale." Greg looked down at his hands. "I hope you'll give it a read when I'm done. I would value your opinion."

"You can count on it."

"When do you get out of here?" Greg waved his hand around the hospital room.

"Hopefully later today. I'm waiting to hear from the doctor."

"When you do, I hope you'll let me take you to dinner."

"I look forward to it."

ter Greg left, Monica lay back against the pillows, her m drifting. Things were working out after all. Culbert's rder was solved, the police had picked up Darlene, Gina a new lease on life, Jeff and Lauren were patching things and the cranberry harvest had been successfully completed despite all the odds.

And she had the promise of a date with Greg.

When she arrived in Cranberry Cove several weeks ago, she'd had the feeling that it was going to be both an adventure and a new start.

It was certainly turning out to be that.

# Recipes

## Sassamanash Farm
## Cranberry Coffee Cake

*¼ pound butter, softened*
*1 cup sugar*
*2 eggs, lightly beaten*
*1 teaspoon vanilla extract*
*½ pint sour cream*
*2 cups sifted flour*
*1 teaspoon baking powder*
*1 teaspoon baking soda*
*½ teaspoon salt*
*1 ½ cups fresh cranberries roughly chopped*

TOPPING:
*½ cup chopped nuts (pecans or walnuts)*
*½ cup shredded coconut*
*½ cup sugar*
*1 teaspoon cinnamon*

Mix topping ingredients in a bowl and reserve.

Cream butter and sugar together until light. Beat in eggs, vanilla and sour cream one at a time. Sift together dry ingredients in a separate bowl and add to wet mixture one third at a time. Fold in chopped cranberries.

Spread half the batter in a greased and floured tube pan. Sprinkle with half the topping. Spread remaining batter on top and sprinkle with remaining topping.

Bake in a 350 degree oven for 35 to 40 minutes. Let cool in the pan before removing.

# Cranberry Butterscotch Bars

*¼ pound butter*
*1 cup graham cracker crumbs*
*1 6-ounce package butterscotch bits*
*1 cup coconut*
*2 cups chopped fresh cranberries*
*1 6-ounce package chocolate chips*
*1 can sweetened, condensed milk*
*½ cup chopped pecans*

Melt butter and add to graham cracker crumbs in a large bowl. Press mixture into bottom of an 8" x 8" pan sprayed with cooking spray.

Sprinkle butterscotch bits over graham cracker mixture. Top with coconut, a layer of cranberries and a layer of chocolate chips.

Spread the can of condensed milk over the top and sprinkle with chopped pecans.

Bake approximately 35 minutes at 350 degrees.

# Cranberry Banana Bread with Streusel Topping

*¾ cup sugar*
*¼ cup butter*
*2 eggs, lightly beaten*
*3 mashed, ripe bananas*
*1 ½ cups chopped cranberries*
*2 cups sifted flour*
*2 teaspoons baking powder*
*½ teaspoon salt*
*¼ teaspoon baking soda*
*1 cup chopped walnuts*

STREUSEL TOPPING:
*½ cup all purpose flour*
*¼ cup packed brown sugar*

*4 tablespoons unsalted butter*
*½ teaspoon cinnamon*

Beat the sugar, butter and eggs until light. Stir in mashed bananas and cranberries.

In a separate bowl, sift together the flour, baking powder, salt and baking soda. Stir into the banana cranberry mixture until smooth. Stir in the chopped walnuts.

For the topping, combine flour, sugar, butter and cinnamon in a food processor and pulse until mixture is crumbly. Alternatively, use hands to crumble mixture.

Spread streusel topping evenly over top.

Pour into one large, greased loaf pan or four small ones. Bake approximately an hour for the large loaf pan and approximately 45 to 50 minutes for the smaller ones.